Leonard P Valentine

A House Divided Cannot Stand

Paul G Buckner

Leonard P Valentine

This is a work of fiction. All names, characters, institutions, places, and events portrayed in this novel are either products of the author's imagination or are used fictitiously. Any resemblance to actual persons, living or dead, business establishments, or events is entirely coincidental. All rights reserved, including the right to reproduce this book, or portions thereof, in any form or by any means.

Copyright © 2016 Paul G Buckner
All rights reserved.

ISBN-13:
978-1547116195
ISBN-10:
1547116196

Leonard P Valentine

To my supportive wife, Jody, and inquisitive son, Chase

Leonard P Valentine

Table of Contents

1 1
2 12
3 22
4 30
5 38
6 48
7 56
8 58
9 64
10 66
11 71
12 77
13 83
14 86
15 93
16 97
17 99
18 105
19 113
20 120
21 128
22 132

23	139
24	142
25	150
26	153
27	154
28	163
29	166
30	169
31	173
32	177
33	192
34	196
35	202
36	205
37	207
38	210
39	214
40	220
41	222
42	233
43	237
A note from the author	240
About the Author	241

Leonard P Valentine

1

"Where's that to-go order, Leonard?" Greely snapped. "Ticket's still lying on the counter!"

"Coming up now, boss," I answered, trying not to sound rattled, but he knew he could make me nervous when he yelled at me. I think he enjoyed it, sadistic bastard. I don't need the ticket anyway. I glanced at it when he laid it down. I have what you might call a photographic memory for things like that. I can see something once, and I can just pull it up in my mind again later. It helped me to get good grades in school though, so I'm not complaining mind you, but just because I can remember something doesn't mean I can understand it.

"Well, hurry it up, we've got customers waiting."

A short order cook, yup that's me. That's what I do. I took this job not long ago when I moved here from upstate. The hours are good even though the pay could be better. I'm sure most people could say that about their jobs too, no surprises there. Sure, there were other things that I could've done with my life I suppose, like a brain surgeon, astronaut, professional hockey player, but nothing appealed to me more than this. I say that with just a tiny hint of sarcasm, as I'm sure you can tell. Seriously, call me crazy, but I like it.

I'm what you might call an introvert, but I like being around people – lots of people, the more, the merrier. I'm complicated like that. Hear me out though, and I'll try to explain. I'm a people watcher. People interest me. I like to watch them much the same way as some folks would go to the zoo and look at the animals. They're different, and that makes them interesting. While it's true that I'm not much of a conversationalist, I still need to be in the middle of the action. Hopefully, no one notices me standing in the corner watching like the proverbial fly on the wall. That's the way I like it; being invisible. And I usually am – until right at this moment.

In case you couldn't tell, the rotund one at the counter window growling at me like an old sourpuss bear is my boss, Mr. Greely, Mr. Horace Greely, business owner, entrepreneur extraordinaire, tyrannical ass-clown of a boss. He's usually in a bad mood. Great big heart though. It would have to be to pump enough blood through the miles of grease-saturated veins of his to keep his big ass alive. The damn thing must be made of titanium because this lard ass has gotta weigh four-hundred pounds, and the smell? Oh, my God, I thought my old gym socks had dibs on stench, but this guy smells like a city sewer because of all the nasty, cheap cigars he smokes which he always seems to have one hanging out of his plumped up oversized lips. Greely is a large man with greasy black hair and eyes just as dark. His left eye remains in a permanent, oddly lopsided squint that seems to be the result of cigar smoke constantly drifting into it, but my guess is the other side of his cheeks is so heavy that it pulls down on that side and up on the other causing his eye to disappear slowly. When I say he's a large man, I don't mean tall; I mean fat, very round, colossally rotund. The constant bags under his bloodshot eyes have a remarkable resemblance to a bloodhound, and he can always be found wearing a white t-shirt with an apron tied around him and a short, white chef's hat on when he's in the kitchen. He insists we all wear those damn silly hats when we're working back here. His hat is usually the only thing halfway clean. He's enough to make a garbage man cry, and today he was on a roll. Lovely fella, my boss is. I have to wonder how the hell this place even has customers.

The diner where I labor most of my time away is called Greely's Po Boy's or as the locals call it, Greely's Slop Shop. It's a small place with three large plate windows in the front and a heavy wood framed, glass inset door at the end, all framed in bright fire-engine red. There must've been on sale on red paint somewhere because it's everywhere. Bright red letters on the windows, the door, and the trim inside, you name it, and it's got red on it. The entrance to this fine dining establishment is decked out not only with the posted hours but with what seems to be a permanent promiscuous plethora of posters hawking everything from the latest yoga class to last year's yard sales.

A long counter with bar stools separates the dining room from the kitchen in the back. A long, narrow window serves as the order station for the wait staff and an observatory for me to peer out whenever I get bored and curious, and not too busy slinging hash, of course. There is a double-sided breezeway door that opens both ways made of gray metal with small windows near the top which serves no valuable purpose as far as I could tell. They're too high for any of us to see out of being everyone here makes the seven dwarves look like the Knicks. Orders are taken at the counter, relayed through the window and when ready, placed in the window. The wait staff grabs them from there and delivers 'em, mostly to the people who actually ordered it.

I finished putting the food together and carried it out to the customer myself. He sat at the table in the back with another guy, both wearing suits, maybe a late business meeting or something. They talked quietly, and one of them wrote something down, but when I walked up to 'em, they clammed up. They were the only two in the place, so it wasn't hard to figure out who had ordered it.

I had a fifty-fifty shot at getting it right, and they both happened to be at the same table. Soon as I put the order down on the table, the guy with his back to me reached for his wallet inside his jacket. When he pulled it out, he didn't have enough cash, so he handed me his credit card.

"I'm in a hurry."

"Yes, sir."

I went over to the register, scanned it and took it back to him along with the receipt. After he signed it, he got up and bolted without saying a single word. Not even a thank you. When I looked at the receipt, I saw the cheapskate didn't leave a tip. Grumpy bastard! His pal barely even glanced up. These two ass clowns ain't gonna win a congeniality contest anytime soon, but that's no sweat off my nose. I had business in the kitchen, so I left them after delivering the heart attack in a sack and sauntered back to my domain. I had no idea what they were fussing about, but it didn't take a genius to figure out they weren't happy with each other.

I walked back into the kitchen and punched the receipt onto the table spike by the register. I heard Greely mutter something under his breath, which I'm sure was how awesome of a cook I am, and he wished he could give me a raise, but can't right now because he's feeding the homeless in the park and taking care of his sick mother. Swell guy, Greely is. I think highly of him. I pushed on with a wave over my shoulder as I turned away. In my mind, I'm telling him how he can take those burgers and shove them straight into the nether regions, but then I remembered I'm a coward at heart and kept a lid on it. The story of my life – don't judge.

The boss wobbled out the back door pushing past me on his way to one of his many smoke breaks leaving me alone with any customers who may or may not come in. Not that anyone else is here tonight; except the one fella still sitting alone at the table now. We usually don't need a waitress on Monday nights because we're always slow so Greely and I can handle it, lucky me.

"Com'on kid, let's get a minute of air."

I knew his minute of air was puffing on the cigar he always seems to have clenched in his teeth even when it wasn't lit and moaning on about paying all those taxes or how this city's gotten too expensive, and everyone is still trying to be cheap. I once tried to tell him he's not the one who pays the sales taxes, but he just looked at me like I'm crazy and growled like a starving dog over a freshly discovered biscuit. I never said another word about it. You can't fight city hall, and you can't argue with your boss. Besides, it's just not something I cared to participate in.

"I still got a customer out front. I better stick around in case he needs something."

"His cup is full, just topped it off and he's not eating anyway. He'll be fine."

He used a more arduous tone this time. I can't very well tell him no at this point.

"Sure thing, give me a second, I'll be right out."

The back door slammed shut just as I heard the bells ringing from the front door opening. A pretty lady with dark hair and dark eyes walked in, glanced around and saw my other customer. She walked over to him and sat down. I grabbed a menu and the coffee pot to take to her, but by the time I gathered it up, she had stood up and was walking right back out. I thought it odd at first, but after thinking about it, I can see why no one would want to stick around this joint. It's not that the place is bad; it's just not the fine dining establishment a lady like her would want to be in, especially alone at night. It struck me a little funny because she was way out of her element here at Greely's. She looked like money and a lot of it. I've no idea what she said to the guy, but whatever it was, he didn't seem to care. He smirked as she walked away. When the door closed, he turned back to his cell phone.

I put the menu back down and took the coffee pot to fill the fella's cup at the table. He drank the stuff like it was the nectar of the Gods. He was quiet, intent on whatever it was he was reading on his cell phone and never looked up or said thank you. I straightened the napkin holder on the table before returning to the kitchen. When I sat the coffee pot back on the warmer, Greely stuck his head in the back door.

"You coming?"

"Sure thing, Mr. Greely, I'm coming," I replied, trying to tidy up a bit and close the lid on the pickle jar to put it away.

His meaty jowls disappeared, and the back door slammed shut again just as the bells from the front door rang again. For a Monday night, this place was beginning to be a lot like Grand Central Station or something. At first, I thought it might be the lady from earlier coming back in because she had changed her mind, but after a quick glance, I knew better. Usually, I would have averted my eyes and pretended not to notice until they took a seat, but it wasn't hard to figure why I froze in my tracks this time. Maybe it was the scent of her perfume or the click of her heels on the peel and stick tile. Whatever it was, she was one of the most beautiful gingers I had ever seen. I was glad for the high counter top between the kitchen and the dining area on account of she couldn't see me staring at her and see the drool running down my chin.

She was an older lady, maybe in her late thirties or early forties, dressed in a short black skirt wrapped tight around her hips and a white blouse underneath a small black jacket. Her long, red hair had big curls flowing out over her shoulders from under a black fedora. The kind of hat you would see a man wear with a pin-striped suit, only she wore it cocked off to one side and looked a hell of a lot better than any fella could've pulled off. She had a two-strand pearl choker around her neck with a black and white broach in the center of it. The high heels she had on were shiny black and must've had taps on them because I've never heard anything on this floor before, except for the squishing sound of shoes being peeled off the sticky surface when you tried to walk on it.

I didn't dare move because I didn't want her to see me staring like a puppy ready to play fetch. I froze in place. I must've looked like a pervert; I'm sure because I felt like one at the moment. She looked around but didn't see me leering like a jackass from my hidey hole, my sniper's nest. It's a good thing too because I think I went slack-jawed at the same time that my pants got tighter. I'm glad I have this wonderfully hand-crafted, made-in-Pakistan, grease-stained apron on over my white t-shirt hanging down to my knees; otherwise, I would've, undoubtedly given my 'glad to see you' swagger away. And those lips… wow, was all I could think of. Ah, those plump…shiny…red…luscious lips... Sorry, I lose focus sometimes.

She walked over to the only customer in the place and sat down. I noticed the guy look up from his cell phone with a puzzled look on his face. Before I knew it, the lady pulled out a gun. It was one of those long pistols with a thing on the end of it like a silencer or something. Without saying a word, she just pulled the trigger. Phitt! Phitt! Phitt! Not once, not twice, but three times! She dropped the gun back in her purse, stood up and strolled to the door just as cool as she came in.

I must've moved, or maybe I just whimpered a little because she suddenly noticed me noticing her. I was shaking like a cat that just got dropped in the middle of a pack of wild dogs. I knew I was next. At first, she looked angry, but then, she smiled ever so slightly, winked at me and walked right out the door. Did she just wink at me?

The giant jar of pickles I held suddenly slipped from my hands and fell crashing to the floor with a loud bang like a small hand grenade had just been thrown into the kitchen. I jumped back out of sheer reflex, but it didn't save me from getting soaked by the half-sours. One of the little green gremlins launched across the slick kitchen floor banged against the freezer and ricocheted like a boomerang back in my direction. On impulse, I jumped out of the way, and it shot through my feet to come to rest underneath my prep table. When I landed, my feet slipped on the wet surface, and I fell forward. Fearing the glass shards on the floor, I made a desperate grab for the table to catch my fall and found the edge with my fingertips at the last moment. Afraid to move from fear I'd lose my grip, I hung off the side of the table with my feet stretched back behind me like a roller skater trying to pick himself back up, but my wheels kept spinning, not allowing me to get any traction. I was just glad the stainless-steel table was so big and heavy that I didn't worry about it tipping over under my weight. It took me a moment to realize my predicament wasn't going to fix itself. I reached up for a better handhold to hoist myself up without stepping on another slippery pickle only to find the next handhold wasn't as good as the edge of the table. An entire stack of pots and pans came crashing down on top of me.

I laid there panting for breath and hoping she didn't walk into the kitchen and put holes in me. When I didn't hear anything else, I picked myself up slow and easy, and looked around. The ginger had crossed the street to a waiting limo. I watched as a big guy in a dark suit held the door open for her as she climbed in. He shut the door and got behind the wheel. I turned my attention back to her where she lowered the window. She looked straight at me as the car pulled away from the curb before raising the window and disappearing into the New York night.

***

I knew the guy was dead. No one could live after having your brain splattered all over the wall, but I stared at the carnage anyway; human nature I suppose. It wasn't pretty. I must've been in shock or something because afterward, I knelt to inspect the damaged pickle jar and my soggy shoes. I realized that more than my shoes were soaked at this point. I patted my jeans down thinking I may have pissed myself. Much to my relief, I realized I hadn't wet myself after all, not exactly anyway. It was only pickle juice. When the jar exploded on the concrete floor of the kitchen, it all splashed out and soaked me from my feet up to my waist in the briny, foul smelling stuff. That's the story I'm telling anyways, and I'm sticking to it. Doesn't matter I suppose because either way, I was more than a smidge on the soggy side.

The back door suddenly opened, and I nearly jumped out of my skin. Heavy footsteps were coming in my direction. The bells were silent by the time Greely decided to trundle his big ass back in.

That's when my whole life changed...

"What the hell was all that?" he growled, as he gasped and wheezed his way back in with his cigar still stuck in his puffed up, oversized lips.

The long stem of gray ashes fell from it where he had just sucked in more nicotine and tar than could've choked a horse. Not that horses smoke. They aren't as dumb as this guy. Greely never smoked inside, so he must've been freaked smooth out when he heard the pickle jar explosion.

I stood there with a dumb look on my face pretending I didn't hear him, which seemed to piss the guy off. I'm sure the scene wasn't something he expected. I'm just shy of six feet tall, thin, lanky frame and brown hair. I'm wearing wet jeans with my pant legs rolled up and red Chucks with pickle juice all over them. He looked me up and down, bent over and picked a pickle out of my jeans cuff and held it in front of my face.

"I just heard an explosion! What the hell are you doing in here?" he barked.

"Noth...nothin' Mr. Greely, I didn't do nothin'!" I managed to stammer. I'm sure I was convincing too. It was the only voice I could muster at the moment anyway. I was shaking so hard I swear I was chipping my own teeth.

"What do you mean nothing, you imbecile?" he growled with a bit of slobber falling out of his fatty jowls. He took another drag off of his smelly, cheap cigar and held it between his big, sausage-fat fingers.

"Please tell me when I hired an idiot I didn't also hire a bold-faced liar too!" He pointed at the pickles on the floor.

I wanted to disappear; to pretend what I had just witnessed wasn't real. Maybe none of it was real. Perhaps she wasn't real, just a figment of a vivid imagination. Maybe it was all a delusion because I haven't been sleeping well. I mean, why would a woman like her come into this diner, to begin with? And for that matter, why would any of these people come into this diner at this time of night? Why would anyone want to kill a guy in this diner?

"I'm sorry... I dropped the pickles, and it exploded on the floor. I was just about to clean it up."

I'm not sure why I was worried about those damn pickles. In my mind, I contemplated running for the door, but my legs were so wobbly I didn't think I could walk much less run. Besides, I'm not coordinated enough. I've been called a klutz many times, but I'm coming into my own, so I'm not worried about it. I'll man up – someday. But at this very moment, I was scared out of my wits. I had never seen anything like it. One minute I had a customer drinking coffee and the next, I have a dead customer and blood all over the floor. I dropped down on my hands and knees in the puddle of pickle juice and glass and began gathering up the slippery little green half-sours. I guess I thought that if I avert my attention elsewhere, I wouldn't have to deal with it.

"Well, see you get it all cleaned up. Those things smell up the place something awful anyway..." Greely was saying before his voice trailed off into silence.

He noticed something was off.

"Oh my God, Leonard, what have you done? Oh my God!" he yelled. "I told you to come outside with me. Why didn't you listen to me?" His hands were holding the sides of his head like it was about to explode.

I'm guessing he had just seen the dead guy sitting out front in one of his plush, ritzy dinettes because even Greely wouldn't flip out over pickles. He didn't hesitate long before he reached down and grabbed me by the back of my shirt collar and hauled me up to my feet. The poor guy was slumped back in his chair staring at the ceiling with a perfect circle in the middle of his forehead. At first, it didn't register with me, but a moment later I saw the blood splatter on the wall behind him and the circle on his forehead that dripped dark crimson.

"Is…is…is he dead?" he asked, pointing at the poor bastard.

I looked, but I had already seen it. I saw it just minutes ago, seconds even, and I saw the killer, but I'll never say nothin'. No sir, not me. I'm no rat, and besides, if I talked, I'd end up like that guy. Of all the places for a fella to get murdered, it had to be at Greely's Po Boy's. Or what I referred to as Greely's Slop Shop. Not that I'm a lousy cook, on the contrary. I'm a good cook, but the crap I'm given to cook with is just that, crap! Greely makes us use meat that should be thrown out. Not only did it smell bad, but it no longer resembled an edible product. Oh well, who am I to complain? But, I digress. I tend to babble when I'm scared or worried. My apologies, I do what I'm told, and I keep my mouth shut. What can I say? I need the job. I'm just the short-order cook around here … *And* chief bottle washer.

2

"Huh? What guy?" I tried pretending I had no idea what he was talking about. Suddenly, I had an idea.

"Oh my God, what have you done?" I shouted with my best impression of shock and surprise when I looked out into the dining area. I was beginning to regain my wits and think straight; my head was clearing. I knew damn good and well the boss didn't do it, but he didn't know that, and I took the opportunity to mess with the maniacal man's head. I feigned ignorance.

"Mr. Greely, what did that man ever do to you? Why did you do it? Did he not pay for his burger? Surely that's no reason to kill a guy over," I said in my best awe-struck acting voice. I should be in Hollywood because I think I missed my calling.

I laid it on thick. I could see the sweat pouring out of every bare inch of the fat man's skin. It was like slow-motion, and we were stuck in some sort of time-space continuum. He stood quietly as if in a trance, just staring at the dead man with the back of his head missing, splattered across his beautiful, hand-stuck black and white plastic floor tile. Well, they used to be black and white. Not so much anymore. He snapped out of his coma.

"I didn't do it, you moron. I was out back. You know that. You know where I was. You were the only one inside with him." He gestured at the stiff while mean-mugging me.

"Honest, I was too busy to notice anything. I dropped the pickle jar when I tried to put the lid back on. It splashed pickle juice everywhere. I didn't see a thing," I lied.

"Well, how do you explain that?" He turned his head and stared at the dead guy. His grip never lets go of my shirt collar. I stood there on my tip-toes, choking, for what seemed like minutes. In reality, it was minutes! I was relieved when he let go of me, but my relief was fleeting.

"Go check on him," he ordered with a shove.

"Are ya fricking nuts, man? I ain't going out there!" He prodded me forward anyway, but I stopped myself at the counter. I was not going out there and getting my fingerprints and shoe prints all over the murder scene. I'm not as dumb as I look – wait, umm, well, you know what I mean.

"I don't think it's such a good idea. Besides, any fool can tell he's not getting up on his own! We'd better call the cops – unless, of course, you're trying to hide something." I added that last part just to keep him on his toes.

"No, no, I'm not trying to hide anything. Not me! Somebody waltzed right in here off the street and murdered the guy. Right here in *my* diner. Are you sure you didn't see anything?"

"No, nothing," I lied again. Apparently, I'm a good liar.

He turned and stared me down.

"I gotta call the cops. Don't go anywhere, don't you move a muscle. You're gonna tell 'em I was outside and nowhere near him when this happened. Got it? The cops are gonna wanna talk to you, so you be sure to tell 'em, kid," he muttered in a low, gravel-laden voice while he picked up the phone and dialed.

I went back to gathering up the pickles off the floor. Greely sat down on the rickety bar stool near the kitchen prep counter where he usually perched like a whale stuck on a small pier so he could oversee the kitchen in the back and see into the dining area. I had no idea how that barstool held the behemoth up. He hung up the phone, and I glanced up from my embattled state wallowing in the pickle juice. I saw him lean down with his elbows resting on the counter and his fat jowls resting in his hands 'just staring at the dead guy. I wasn't worried about any other customers coming in. Not tonight anyway. It was Monday night, and we never had any business. I didn't understand why we even opened on Monday nights. But hey, I got paid for it and what else was I going to do, eh?

It didn't take long before the cops showed up. I heard the siren long before I ever saw the blue lights flashing outside. It was like our own cops didn't know their way around town. I could hear them racing up on Parsons, in the wrong direction mind you, and then coming back on what sounded like Holly. They finally found the place though. Greely's Slop Shop isn't hard to find, but they seemed to have had issues. Maybe they can't read the Chinese street signs, I don't know. Queens isn't the easiest place to find your way around, I suppose.

A couple of flatfoots came rushing into the place like they owned it. They looked pissed they were disturbed by a call apparently, or maybe there wasn't any donuts and coffee waiting for 'em. They wore black uniforms and the little ass-clown hats with the shiny black brim. They reminded me of the two comedians from back in the day because one of 'em was skinny and the other one was a chubster. They pulled up short when they spotted the stiff.

"You Greely?" the fat one asked from the doorway.

"Yeah, this is my place," the boss said. He walked around the kitchen counter, through the breezeway door, and to the outside dining area, careful not to go anywhere near the body. I followed along right behind him like a scared little kid, which I kinda was.

The other cop, the skinny, dumb-looking one walked over to the dead guy and touched his neck. "This guy's dead as a doornail, Murph."

Boy, was I wrong? It was obvious, he's the smart one, but hey, I had a fifty-fifty chance. I'm guessing he has bad eyesight because a blind man could see half of the dead man's head was splattered all over Greely's wall. What the hell was this idiot thinking, checking for a pulse? I figured this was going to take a while.

"I'm officer Murphy, and this is my partner Dobbs. What can you tell us, who did it? How long ago did it happen?"

"I can't tell you much. I was outside when it happened. Leonard can vouch for that, huh Leonard?" he asked while munching on his unlit cigar, but he didn't wait for an answer before yammering on. "I was outside taking a smoke break. Leonard was the only one in here," Greely said, turning to look at me like I was guilty of something.

Does this moron think I'm some kind of Navy Seal commando and took the guy out clean as a whistle, even though I can't even put a lid back on a pickle jar without adult supervision? Thanks a lot, Greely. Sell me out, you bastard. I was set to play it cool, though, I didn't sweat it.

"I was working back there in the kitchen when Mr. Greely came in. I dropped a big glass jar of pickles on the floor. You know the kind, about this big…" I extended my hands to show him how big the jar was. "You know, big green half sours."

"Yeah, yeah, we get it. Go on," Officer Murphy demanded.

"Well, it exploded all over the place when it hit the floor, so I was down there cleaning it up. I didn't see a thing."

"So, nobody else has been in all night?" Dobbs asked.

Greely started to say something, but like the idiot, I can sometimes be I opened my trap and cut him off before he could.

"There was another fella with him earlier. He had ordered a burger to go, but soon as I had it ready, he left. He sat with his back to me. There were a couple of women that came in, but neither of them stuck around, and they left without ordering." I stopped and cursed myself. Too much information, but it was too late. Greely pounced like he was one of them now. I've got to learn to quit babbling when I'm rattled.

"I never saw anyone else come in; the place was empty when I went outside to smoke, except for those two men. Who are you talking about?" he asked turning to look at me again.

Murphy, who had been looking over the scene suddenly turned his attention back to the boss and me and came at me hard again.

"What was that kid? What did this other fella look like? What was he wearing? You ever saw him before? Do you know him? What about this guy?" He gestured to the stiff.

"Do either of you know him? Ever seen him before?" He asked rapid fire while his head bobbed back and forth looking at the boss then at me. "What about these women? What'd they look like?"

I took a deep breath and stumbled around for something to say when another cop car came flying up with sirens blaring and then another.

"So, what gives? Tell us what you saw kid. Don't be scared."

I'm sure in their mind I had all of the answers, and it was going to be a short night for 'em, but what they didn't count on was the fact I'm no snitch. The dead guy is dead for a reason. I don't know what that reason is and I don't care. It's none of my business. I'm not telling 'em nothin' that's gonna get me killed. I haven't seen a lot of years in my life, but I'd sure like to see a few more, that's for sure.

"I'm not scared. I dunno, as I said, I was busy in the kitchen. I just saw someone walk in out of the corner of my eye or something, and that's when I dropped the jar of pickles on the floor. I bent down to clean it up when Mr. Greely came busting in the back door, I didn't get a good look at anyone, you get to where you don't pay attention working back in the kitchen," I said.

I wasn't about to give them any more information about either of the women. No sir, not this guy!

Dobbs took his turn at me and pressed me some more, "So what did this person sitting with the dead guy look like, kid? You're not giving us anything here."

"Look, Mister, I'm telling you all I know. I didn't see but a glimpse of 'im. Maybe it was a drive-by or something; I don't know," I replied.

I could tell from the way the cops looked at me that they weren't buying it. He knew I was lying, I knew I was lying, Greely knew I was lying, but I wasn't about to rat anyone out. Anyone that could bust a cap on a guy as cool like that and never blink an eye – you know what I mean – isn't someone I want to cross. No sir, not me. I like living too much. I grew up on these streets, and buddy let me tell you something. That's the last thing a fella could ever do is to rat someone out.

Another guy sauntered in wearing a sloppy sports jacket and jeans and started snapping pictures with his cell phone. The flatfoots hollered at him.

"Hey, you, beat it. This is a crime scene!" Officer Murphy growled at to the newcomer.

The guy flashed a plastic ID hanging around his neck and said, "Press, fellas. So, what happened? Who killed the commissioner?"

"Commissioner? What's that you say? Hey, look here, we're still investigating the scene, and you're impeding our investigation. I dunno, Murph, maybe we should cuff him and put his ass in the cruiser 'til we're done?" He motioned toward the reporter with a head nod.

"Hey look, fellas, I'm just tryin' to do my job too," the new guy replied.

"That sounds like a pretty good idea to me, Dobbs."

During this back and forth dispute a couple of suits walked in and boy oh boy did they mean business. One, wearing a gray suit, barked out a few orders to the beat cops and had them escort the reporter outside before they taped the place off. The other one in a navy-blue jacket directed Greely and me to have a seat in the kitchen and not move until they were done with us. We did exactly that.

It was apparent the suits knew the guy, but they kept pretty quiet when they talked among themselves. I overheard one of them say the name William Wood, but the name meant nothing to me. At that point, gray suit ordered the flatfoots to take our statements while they investigated. Fantastic! I anticipated more brilliant conversation and eagerly awaited the arrival of whichever one drew the short straw. I noticed the cop in the gray suit put on a rubber glove and examine the victim's cell phone before placing it in a plastic bag. He looked at his partner and shook his head as if indicating, *no luck*.

Officer Dobbs walked up and said, "Let's you and me step out back, kid."

Here we go again.

I got up from my perch and walked out the back door with Officer Dobbs on my heels. I glanced back and saw Murphy sit down where I was and started grilling Greely. Typical, I suppose, separate the witnesses and see if the stories corroborate. Wait a minute, isn't that what they do to suspects?

It didn't take but a few minutes. He wrote my name and address down, and I told him exactly what I said earlier – again. After a few minutes, he let me go back to my perch and told us to wait to see if the suits needed anything else from us. The other cop had just finished with Greely and was helping himself to a cup of coffee when I walked in and sat down. The boss seemed awful chummy with the guy now, but I couldn't pay attention. I just sat and stared at the suits doing their investigation. While I was outside with the cop giving my statement, another team of people came in with all sorts of equipment and began working. I figured this was the kind of people you see on the television shows like CSI, going over every little detail and looking for fingerprints and stuff.

Finally, the meat-wagon backed up to the front door, and a small fella wearing glasses came into prepare the guy for departure.

It's pretty obvious he was the medical examiner after he did a quick examination and told the suits precisely what everyone else already knew.

"Cause of death, gunshot wound to the head." He turned to Greely, "What time did you say this occurred?"

"It was a few minutes after nine when I came back in and found him," Greely said.

"That sounds about right. Time of death, nine-o-five pm," he said with a hint of a smile in his eyes. "Where do I send the bill?"

No one said a word; we all just stared at him.

"Just kidding fellas. Geez, tough crowd tonight."

I guessed that must be some kind of morgue humor. No one laughed.

"Of course, none of that's official until I get him back and complete an autopsy," the little guy said as he unfolded a black body bag next to a gurney.

A few minutes later, with the help of the uniforms, they had the guy loaded on the gurney and in the back of the wagon. Even though this place is dead at night, no pun intended, there was quite a crowd gathered up outside.

Gray suit walked through the breezeway door and with a stern look on his face asked, "What's your name again kid?"

"Leonard. Leonard P Valentine."

"So, you didn't see nothing, didn't hear nothing and don't know nothing," he said while tapping his notepad with a pencil. "Standing right here not more than twenty feet away?"

"No sir, nothing I can remember – other than dropping a jar of pickles in the kitchen, must have been when all this happened. I was down on the floor cleaning it up."

"Yeah, I read that in the statement you gave Officer Dobbs. Tell *me* what you didn't tell *him*," he said tersely while staring a hole through me.

I gulped hard, "Honestly, I didn't see anything at all. You get accustomed to not paying attention to what's happening out there when you work back here, ya know."

I tried my best to convince him. I'm sure I sounded like a broken record, but I was sticking to my story.

The detective stood there for a moment, staring into my eyes, still tapping his pad with his pencil. He was a small man with jet black hair and dark, piercing eyes; the kind that burned away every ounce of courage a fella had. I was forced to look away before I spilled my entire life story beginning with the time I threw up in the middle of social studies class during an oral report. I think that was the fourth grade, but I digress. He's a little shorter than me when I stood up. Actually, he's a good two inches shorter; seemed to have a chip on his shoulder because of it, too. I call it short man syndrome. It seemed evident to me he was overcompensating for it by the look of the large handgun protruding from his suit coat; a veritable cannon, it was. He had the demeanor of a tough customer, sure, but at the same time, I wasn't scared of him.

They finally put their notepads away, and gray suit stuck a business card in my hand and gave one to Greely. I glanced down at it as an excuse to look away from his gaze. *Frank O'Conner, Detective.* I dropped it into the pocket of my soggy apron.

"Okay, we have all we need for now, but we'll be in touch. We may need you to come down to the station at some point to go over your statements. In the meantime, if either of you thinks of anything else, give me a call."

I looked back up at him and gulped hard. He stared straight into my eyes again, and I knew, that he knew, that I wasn't telling 'em everything. I gotta give him credit though; he didn't bust me out right there in front of Greely and try to break me down. He held his gaze a few seconds longer and before turning to leave. He seemed like a straight-up kinda fella, but I wasn't about to say anything more than what I had already.

Great! They were finally cutting me lose.

Greely piped up, "Say, um…Fellas, we can clean the place up now? I'm trying to run uh business here, ya know," he asked.

O'Conner said, "Sure," without missing a beat. "As soon as forensics gets what they need. We'll let you know when that happens."

"How long do you think that'll be?"

O'Conner suddenly spun around, "As long as it takes. A man was killed here. Murdered in cold blood. It's going to be a few days. In the meantime, I'll have to ask you to close it down. No one is to enter this area, period. Being your office is in the back, I can allow you to enter through the back door to your office. If you even crack open the kitchen door and peek out here, I'll have you in cuffs for destruction of evidence. Got it?"

"Oh, jeez fellas, you're killin' me," Greely snapped back. "How am I supposed to make a living? I have employees depending on this place too. What about them?" he asked. The hard-nosed detective seemed to soften a touch, "I understand, and I'll be sure to let the evidence recovery team know. In the meantime, that door," he turned and pointed at the breezeway door, "That's as far as you go. Got it?"

"Yeah, yeah I got it." Greely wasn't happy about it, but he wasn't about to argue with the detective anymore.

"I'll have someone posted here to keep a watch."

After the detectives left, the boss told me to finish cleaning the kitchen before I went home and to be sure to check in every day. As soon as he was given the green light to open back up, he would let me know. With slumping shoulders, he slogged his way back to his office to call the other employees to give them the bad news. I grabbed a mop and got back to work.

Greely made his phone calls to the other employees and walked out of his office fifteen minutes later.

"Lock up when you're finished, and remember to use the back door, might get tackled by one of those forensic people in there if you try to go out the front," he sighed and glanced back at the yellow tape across the kitchen door and the people in the dining room, "It's been a long night. I'm tired, and I'm going home."

"Sure thing, Boss."

3

The erratic strobe of the red and blue emergency lights flashed their brilliant warnings in near silence. Only the steady rotation of the small motors inside, whirling about in a slow cautionary cadence and the occasional crackle of a distant voice coming over the radios in the police cruisers could be heard. Some of the lights on the vehicles blinked fast while others performed slow cascading patterns which reflected off the nearest hard surface of the tightly huddled row of businesses, mostly small diners and specialty food stores in the old neighborhood market street.

The hour was late, and only a few bystanders were out, but the police caution tape had been strung around the perimeter of the scene to keep any curious onlookers out while the officers inside investigated. Uniformed police officers standing guard could be seen in small groups at each end of the street talking among themselves in hushed tones.

The two detectives exited the greasy spoon diner and made their way through the maze of police cars and emergency vehicles to a black Dodge Charger parked across the street. Detective Frank O'Conner climbed in behind the wheel as his junior partner, Mike

Freeman, slid his tall and lanky frame of six feet three inches into the passenger seat.

"Jeez, Frank, Commissioner Wood killed right here on our beat! This can't be good, had to be a mob hit straight up!" Mike declared.

"I can't argue with that. I'm hoping we can get to the bottom of it before this turns into some kind of war between cartels or something. Nobody murders a public figure like that randomly," Frank stated. "We'd better let the captain know right away, but first things first, we need to head over to the commissioner's house and give his wife the bad news."

"This is the part of this job I hate."

O'Conner shifted the car into drive and pulled away from the curb leaving the evidence collection team behind to do their jobs. He knew the forensics people were professionals and quick but thorough. After taking all the statements and gathering what little evidence they could, the detectives left the crime scene in the hands of their teammates to deliver the news of the murder of County Commissioner William Wood to his widow.

Frank O'Conner had begun his career much the same way as most did once graduating the Academy, as a patrol officer working odd shifts. As he made rank and gained seniority, he applied for the position of detective and was promoted on his first attempt. For the next twenty-two years, he solved many crimes including several high-profile cases such as the one he had been dealt earlier this evening. He was no stranger to the politics involved in these types of cases, but he held the same standards for all criminals regardless of social class.

Standing two inches short of six feet tall, Frank made up for his lack of physical height with quiet confidence. Though he was in his early fifties, he stayed in good physical shape by means of a regimented workout. His jet-black hair was cut short, and his dark, piercing eyes were the kind that could burn away every ounce of courage in a suspect unlucky enough to be seated across from him at an interrogation table. A small scar obtained in a scuffle during an arrest gone wrong extended from the left corner of his bottom lip to the middle of his sharp, powerful chin. Usually clean shaven, tonight his five o'clock shadow enhanced the lines etched into his face given to him by age and stress.

Frank had received the call from dispatch only an hour earlier, picked up his partner and raced to the scene to begin the investigation of a county commissioner murdered at the Po Boy's diner. Unfortunately, because it was early in the week and late in the evening, there were no witnesses to the actual shooting. The owner of the diner and the cook were both in the back when the crime purportedly happened, and neither saw nor heard the shooting take place.

"The kid said our victim was on his cell phone the last he noticed, but the damn thing has a lock on it and without knowing the password, we may never know what was on it. At the very least though, we can get a list of the names and numbers he's talked to, but we'll have to get a warrant for the phone company in the morning. Maybe that will turn up something, give us some kind of clue, something to go on," Mike said.

"Maybe his wife will know the password," Frank mused.

"We could only get so lucky, but it's a starting place anyway."

The commissioner lived in an affluent neighborhood on a hillside overlooking the city. The drive took twenty minutes in the light traffic of the late evening though it felt much quicker. When they arrived at the front gate, Frank reached out and punched the button on the intercom system. They waited in silence for a couple of minutes as the headlights shined brightly on the closed gate impeding their way. When no answer came, Frank reached out to hit the button again. Just as he did, a woman answered in an agitated voice.

"Who's there? May I help you?"

"Mrs. Wood, my name is Detective Frank O'Conner with the 109th precinct. I'm with my partner, Mike Freeman. I'm sorry to bother you at such an hour ma'am, but I'm afraid we need a moment of your time," he stated, holding his badge up to the gate camera for her to see.

"I'm sorry but my husband isn't home at the moment, Detective, and I'm not sure how I can be of any assistance to you," she stated.

"We need to speak with you, ma'am. It's about your husband," Frank said.

"What is this about? It's awfully late at night."

"Yes ma'am, I understand, but it is imperative, and I'm afraid we must insist."

Another moment of silence ensued before she responded. "Of course, detective, please come on through," Mrs. Wood replied. Her brash voice now tinged with nervousness.

The massive entrance gate was made of thick oak timber, framed in iron and adorned with large, intricately forged hinges giving it the appearance of a medieval castle door. The gate separated in the middle swinging outward, allowing the detectives a view up the cobblestone drive. The ivy-covered mansion loomed stately and proud behind the baroque gate, surrounded by squaddies of Thuja Green Giants. The tall evergreens gave the appearance of sentries guarding against intruders. During the day, the home must have been magnificent with its marble statuary and fountains resonating with the sound of water chattering into concrete pools. The crystal-clear ponds were lined with flora, and bright colors emblazoned the gardens throughout. During the night, especially this night, it seemed dark and foreboding; unwelcoming even. Frank considered the reason to be due more to the entitled exclusiveness that pervaded the structure, the haughty, arrogant nature of society's manufacture that created for him the feeling they were intruding. He shook it off.

Perhaps it was the news to be delivered that made the night seem so drab and lifeless. It was never easy, and no matter how many times he performed the task, Frank was never comfortable with the misfortune of others. He shuddered at the thought. Maybe that's why he never married. It wasn't that he was void of feelings, it was quite the opposite. His first love was police work, and he never wanted to put someone through the countless lonely nights when he was out on a case and the thoughts he may not come home after a shift.

He shifted the car into drive and eased through the gate, making their way up the winding stone path to the house. He parked in the middle of the drive and stepped out into the brisk evening air. Together, the men walked up the broad, stone steps. Before they could ring the bell, a woman appeared at the door.

"Mrs. Wood?" Frank inquired.

"Yes, won't you tell me what this is all about, Detective? What has William gotten into now?" she asked with measured patience.

"Ma'am, do you mind if we go inside to talk please?" Frank requested, once again showing her his badge.

She seemed a proud, dignified woman with practiced restraint, Frank mused. He noticed a look of consternation come over her face, particularly her eyes. Though fleeting, he did notice.

"Certainly, please come in," she said as she stepped back and held the door for the two men to enter.

The door closed with an audible click reverberating off the polished wood floors of the grand vestibule when Mrs. Wood closed it behind them. She turned and led the men into the foyer and invited them to sit.

What appeared to be a coat closet was tucked away in a corner, and a hat rack with accompanying umbrella stand was placed strategically near the front door as the men entered. Curved, graceful banisters of twin staircases on either side met at the center of a common landing area on the next floor surrounding the opening into the grand entry of the main room directly below. Heavy mahogany double doors with polished brass handles stood closed and imposing on each side of the room. An elegant Tiffany lamp sat alone on a table placed against a wall with two high-back chairs standing guard where the two detectives were directed to sit. Mrs. Wood sat directly across from the detectives on a matching Victorian-style settee.

Dressed in casual, dark blue pants, white top, and tennis shoes, she had auburn hair with slight graying at the temples pulled up in a tight bun. Her face wore the wrinkles of many years of love, laughter, and heartache as well as prolonged exposure to the sun's harsh rays. Frank guessed her age to be in the late fifties and beautiful by any standard of measure.

When they were seated, Frank began in a soft but stern tone, "Ma'am I'm afraid there's no easy way to say this. I'm terribly sorry, but about your husband…" Frank paused expecting an emotional outburst at this moment in his practiced speech, but the lady sat stoic and silent waiting for him to complete his sentence.

"Please go on, Detective. What about my husband? I've no time for suspense and drama, get on with it," she demanded.

"He's dead ma'am. He was killed tonight, gunned down at a small diner over on Kissena," Frank blurted.

The detectives watched as the sudden shock of what was said come in a rush of emotion over Mrs. Wood. Her shoulders visibly slumped, and her entire body seemed to tremble at the news. She turned her head away from the detectives without uttering a single word, only a sudden intake of breath and the struggle to hold back the horror of hearing of her husband's fate. With her face buried in her hands, Frank watched in silence as she began sobbing. The once strong, proud and rigid woman was reduced to an inconsolable muddle with a single phrase.

The men offered condolences and allowed her the time she needed to collect her thoughts before pressing further.

"Ma'am I know this must be hard for you, but if we could just ask you a couple of questions, maybe it will help us catch the person responsible. Time is always critical in these situations. Do you feel up to it?

"Situations?" she asked. "Is that what this is to you, a situation? You give me news my husband of twenty-seven years has been killed, and it's nothing more than a situation to you?"

"I'm sorry ma'am, I am. I don't mean to sound insensitive if you'll forgive me. We just want to catch the scum that did this," Frank said.

After another moment, she was able to control her sobbing long enough to ask the detective, "How can I help?"

"He was at a small diner in Flushing when this happened. We think maybe he was meeting with someone. Do you know who that meeting was with?" Franked asked.

"No, I'm sorry, I don't," she replied. "He's a very private man, especially where business is concerned. We have a rule we don't discuss business unless it directly impacts us. It's much less stressful."

"We know he was on his cell phone when this happened, but it's locked now. Do you happen to know his password? Maybe it will give us a clue if he was talking with anyone when it happened?"

"No, I'm sorry. Can't you trace the calls?"

"Yes ma'am, but what we can't see is any texts," Frank said.

"I'm sorry, I don't seem to be able to help in any way," she said, again visibly upset.

"That's okay ma'am; I know this is hard for you. Do you know if he had been having any issues with anyone? Did he have any enemies you know of?"

"He was a commissioner; he had lots of enemies. Always someone angry over a decision," she paused and reflected a moment. "Come to think of it, there was someone he mentioned he was having issues with. He never said anything to me, but I overheard him talking once. I never got a name, but I understood there were problems with a recent land purchase agreement. I'm afraid that's all I know, though."

"Thank you, ma'am, we truly appreciate your help," Frank reached into his pocket and gave her one of his cards. "We will do everything we can to catch the person responsible, Mrs. Wood."

"I hope you do Detective."

"If you're up to it, we'd like for you to go down to the coroner's office and ID your husband, but I'm sure it can wait until morning."

"No, detective, I'll get dressed and go tonight. I'll be fine."

When the detectives returned to their vehicle, Mike mentioned the obvious.

"She seemed pretty tore up about her husband being killed."

"Yeah, she did," Frank said. "You can't fake that kind of emotion. Let's get home and get some sleep. Pick back up in the morning."

4

I turned back to my cleaning as soon as the boss left. I made sure all the glass from the pickle jar was swept up, and I mopped the floor with a heavy dose of bleach and water. When I rang out my mop, I noticed the back door slowly creeping open. My heart skipped a beat, and I thought I was going to have a heart attack at that very moment – until I saw the reporter from earlier stepping inside.

"Hey kid," the guy called out in a hushed tone.

"Jeez, Mister, you're not supposed to be in here. We're closed, and as you can see, I got work to do." *What a jackass*, I thought.

"Com' on kid, gimme me a break here. I'm just doing my job. What'd ya see? Did you know the Commissioner? Does he come here often?" he whispered.

"I didn't see nothin'. I was here in the kitchen when it happened, and I don't know nobody," I replied.

"Can I quote you on that?" he persisted.

"Quote this, Bub. You're out of here!"

I grabbed the guy by his arm, led him to the door, pushed his butt out into the alley and locked it behind him. That was about all the confrontation I could handle for one night. My nerves were shot.

The breeze-way door opened and one of the forensics guys stood there looking at me. "Everything okay in here?" he asked.

"Yeah, sorry, I was just finishing up," I said as nonchalantly as I could. I turned back to my mopping.

He looked around the kitchen before he closed the door to the dining area and went back to work. Those doors don't have a knob on them or anything to keep them shut, but I heard him doing something to them. A moment later he stuck his head in the order window which is about five feet long and rectangular and said he had put a lock on the handles and those were official.

I turned back to my mop and carried on. I kept thinking about everything that went down; the hot redhead, the sexy brunette, the stiff and his friend, the detective, which I'm sure I haven't seen the last of. Jeez, that guy reminded me of a Pitbull. He's a little guy, sure, maybe weighing in at a buck sixty, but I get the impression he's tough as nails and smart too. When he looked me in the eyes, I swear he could read my mind.

I finished cleaning up, turned off all the lights in the kitchen and made sure the door was locked. It gave me the creeps being there alone in the middle of the night. Sure, the evidence people were still in the dining room, but they didn't pay any attention to me at all. I might as well go home and get some sleep; I seem to be on vacation now. Oh well, a little break from the morning rush. I say that with sarcasm, there was never a rush. What there was, however, was a steady stream of customers throughout the mornings.

It occurred to me, the bus stops running at midnight, and I didn't have enough cash on me for cab fare so, lucky me, I get to walk home. Could this night get any worse? I put my backpack on both shoulders, put my head down and hoofed it double time.

***

My shift is what I call a split shift. I work mornings from six-thirty to about eleven or so before leaving. I come back in the evenings and work 'til close. I take care of the books during the slow times. I'm no accountant by trade, but when you grow up on the streets and run book to make a living, you learn things. Greely trusted me with the numbers.

Marvin comes in and works the lunch crowd from eleven to five when I take over again. That's his regular shift anyway. He's a cool dude, and I like him a lot. He makes me laugh. Marvin should have retired long ago, but I'm sure he needs the cash same as anyone. I lock up between ten and eleven depending on how many customers we have. We have two waitresses that seem to come and go when they please. They show up in the mornings and disappear after the lunch crowd during the first of the week. I can handle those evenings alone, but the rest of the week it gets busy enough for at least one of them to work the front. I think they work out which one between themselves. I don't have a typical shift every week as Greely makes the schedule up every Friday. He asks me to work doubles from time to time or even to come in on my days off, but I don't mind, I have nothing better to do. I always get at least forty hours a week, but most times it's closer to fifty-five or sixty.

Greely will show up about nine every morning. I'll give the tyrant credit though, and that's not something I like to dole out on the guy, but he does work when he's here. That, however, is not always the case. Tonight, was the exception. I rarely see him on Monday nights. After the lunch crowd is all but gone, he leaves for the day. He takes the cash we've made over the weekend from the safe and always, without fail, drops it at the bank on Monday afternoons by two-thirty. I may not see him again until Wednesday morning. I think it's because we don't have much business on Mondays and Tuesdays, so he feels what little money we make in those few days is safe enough in the floor safe in the office.

Leonard P Valentine

***

It was a nice evening, and the air wasn't as repulsive as usual. There was a slight breeze, and the oil, diesel and urine mix was pleasantly held at bay by a delightful layer of ozone. City streets have to be the dirtiest places ever. There weren't many cars around, but I could hear the city taxi drivers honking their horns off in the distance. I turned to watch a sleek new Mercedes slow-roll by. At first, I thought, great, I'm gonna be taken out by gangbangers, and all I was doing was walking home. But I noticed the car didn't have any street mods. It was straight up off the showroom floor. Nah, this was some businessman that just took a wrong turn because he stayed too long at the office. He was probably having a late-night rendezvous with his secretary or out trolling for hookers, to keep it real. Who else would be out at this hour? As it turned the corner, I could see the license plate read *CAMGRP7*. No idea what that was supposed to mean.

Some people may accuse me of having a sour outlook on life, but that's not the case at all. I just like to keep things in perspective, that's all. You see, I grew up in what I like to call the system, being a ward of the state and all. Basically, several foster homes in upstate New York when not in a group home. My mother died before I could remember anything about her and I became a ward of the state. I never knew who my father was. He wasn't listed on my birth certificate. I'm not complaining though. I wasn't beaten or anything of that sort, and I'm certainly no Oliver Twist, so I guess I had it better than some. I came to accept my lot in life early on. This is a great big world, and we're all players of the same game. It's just there are different levels in the game, and some of us aren't exactly welcome at the table. I don't mind. I know my station in life, and I'm good with it.

In case you're wondering, my name is Leonard P Valentine. I know, believe me. I've heard it all before. I don't much care what anyone else thinks. I like it, and that's all that matters. That's what it shows on my legal documents now; birth certificate, social security card, my state-issued identification etcetera, and that's how I sign my name. I had it legally changed when I turned eighteen and was sprung from state care. Why? Because I could. To be honest, bouncing around in a throng of foster homes or state homes every few months wasn't the best set of circumstances to flourish in, not that I was ever mistreated or anything like that because I wasn't. I just wanted a new start; a fresh outlook on life where no one knows me, a blank slate if you will. So, I changed my name as soon as I could to Leonard P Valentine. It's interesting don't you think? Smith or Jones is boring, and I didn't want boring. Sure, it was a lot of trouble to go about changing it, but I didn't care. I didn't want to drag that baggage around with me for the rest of my life. And before you ask, no the *P* doesn't stand for anything. When people ask me about it, I have fun making up different names. When I went down to the courthouse to change it, I filled out the paperwork as Leonard Valentine. When I handed my papers over to the lady at the desk, she said I needed a middle name. I couldn't think of one at the time. It hadn't occurred to me. She said I could just put down an initial, so I wrote down the letter P. The Valentine part came from the day I was told my last foster home needed to make room. In other words, it was time for me to move on. So, I hit the happy trail on Saint Valentine's Day.

A city garbage truck drove past me. I stopped and watched it roll by as trash floated out of the back and went flying in the wind. Some of it drifted back onto the sidewalk, but most of it fell into the street. I thought it was somewhat poetic. One piece, in particular, a playbill for a Broadway show, caught my eye. It was one of those glossy white ones with colorful photos on the front with the name of the play and the stars' names. I didn't take the time to look at it too close, but I caught it up neatly and tucked it away in my pocket. I'll check it out later. Not that I'd ever go to a Broadway show, way too expensive, but what the hell. That's what this town is famous for. I should keep up. You know, just in case I need casual dinner conversation over caviar at the Ritz.

A few minutes later, a taxi rolled by with his light on top indicating he was off-duty. As I watched it roll by I happened to catch a peek of the black Mercedes from earlier. The driver had pulled over and stopped in a parking lot. Yup, must be trying to score drugs or a hooker down here. Either that or the poor guy must be lost and now has a real problem. Not *my* problem. I turned back to my own business and kept walking.

The night was quiet where I was so when I neared a bus stop; I sat down on the bench a moment to readjust my bag. It's an old canvas backpack I carry everywhere. It doesn't have much in it because quite frankly, I don't have much. I have an mp3 player in it which I reached in and hauled it out. I unraveled the earbuds and stuck the right side in my ear. By accident, I dropped the left one down my shirt collar and had to rescue it. I felt the playbill from earlier crinkle in my pocket, so I pulled it out and stuffed it in my pack, found my earbud and stuck it in. I stood up, slung my bag over my shoulder, cranked up the tunes, and walked home.

It took another twenty minutes to get to my building, but soon I arrived on the street where it sat back off the main road. I took out my earbuds, wrapped them back up around the mp3 player, and swiftly stuffed it back down into my backpack. When I looked at the front entrance, I saw the red-hot cherry of someone's cigarette burning in the dark though I couldn't make out who it was. As I got closer, I could see it was a tall man in a suit and tie, but I still couldn't make out his face. I'd never seen anyone around here before in a suit so you can imagine my apprehensiveness about walking up those steps. I guess he thought that too.

"How's it going, little man? It's okay, I don't bite," he said with a chuckle.

"I'm not worried. You just surprised me is all," I stammered.

"Where you headed in such a hurry?" he probed.

"Been a long day, just wanna get some rest," I said, as I hurried on in the building. I didn't want to stand around and chit-chat with this guy in the middle of the night. It was clear he wasn't from around here, so I'm sure he was up to no good. Besides, I didn't want to see his face. I don't want to be able to identify him if I ever get called on as a witness. The long hallway was lit; though the lights were dim, I could make out the stairs just fine. When the door slammed shut behind me, I practically ran up the stairs to my condo. Jeez! I was a nervous wreck. I fumbled for my key, unlocked the door and slid in.

Okay, so the place isn't a condo. It's more like a…well there's just no other way to describe it other than a pit. It ain't much, but I don't mind. It's cheap and as long as I have a roof over my head, a bed to sleep in and a microwave, I'm good. I'm lucky; there is one each of those in my somewhat 'fully furnished' economy apartment. There's not even a separate bedroom. It's a basic kitchen, bedroom and living room in one open room with a partial wall. The bathroom is the only other room, besides a small closet, which has a door. My ratty old bed sits back in a corner like a neglected and beaten dog scared of a cruel master. I have a small green sofa and an old brown chair across from it with a small coffee table I found at a nearby dumpster sitting in front of 'em. Oh, I almost forgot, there's also a lamp beside the chair. It's a real beauty too! It has a short in it because I have to replace the bulb in the friggin' thing at least once a week.

I walked over to the sofa like I always do, but I got a weird feeling and turned back to the door, locked the deadbolt and slid the chain in place for good measure. I walked to the sofa, switched on the lamp and collapsed. I was exhausted. I turned on the television, but there was nothing on that looked interesting. I turned it off. I don't have cable or nothin', just use the little antenna. It picks up quite a few channels, enough for me anyway. It was here when I moved in. I threw the remote down and ducked into the bathroom for a quick shower. I had to get rid of the stench of pickle juice. I may never wear those jeans again.

I still felt a bit antsy and wired up, so I walked over to the dirt and grime crusted window, opened it, and stepped over the seal onto the fire escape. I kept a lawn chair and a small grill out here. I come out sometimes if I have trouble sleeping or if I just want to sit and look at the sky. Nobody ever uses the fire escape, so I've made it into my little patio. Even have a picture of a palm tree chalked on the wall. It fades away when it rains, but I just draw it back. It makes me laugh.

I guess I must have drifted off not long after. When I woke up I looked through the window at the clock inside on the microwave; Five-thirty-two. I had a bad crick in my neck and stood up while I stretched and rubbed it. With a huge yawn, I climbed back inside. My knee knocked my backpack off onto the floor when I walked by my couch. I reached down and picked it up and promptly sat down. I sat under the light of the lamp for a minute or so when I suddenly remembered the playbill and pulled it out. My jaw hit the floor when I did. There, on the front of my Broadway show playbill in huge letters, 'Starring Briana Fitzgerald' was none other than the redheaded assassin!

5

On a typical day, I wake-up at 5 a.m. on the mornings that I open the diner, but today was not one of those days. I had plenty of time for a shower and to grab a bite to eat, but I soon found myself sitting on the bus headed back to the diner anyway. Having slept for only a few hours, I was in a wonderfully pleasant mood. More sarcasm, but you'll get used to that from me. Greely asked me to check in with him each day because I don't have a phone for him to call me. I had no idea how long it would take for the cops to let us reopen, but I figured it shouldn't be too long. I hoped not, anyway, I need to be working.

When I finally stumbled in the back door, looking more or less like a street urchin, I noticed the yellow tape still strung-up across the kitchen door effectively separating the kitchen from the dining room. I walked over to the prep counter and peeked into the dining room and could see the outline of the body and the blood still on the wall and floor.

"Ehk, what a mess," I said out loud to no one in particular.

"Leonard, is that you? Come on into the office," Greely bellowed from his office in the back.

I took another quick look at the crime scene before I replied. "Yeah, Mr. Greely, it's me,"

I walked through the kitchen making my way around the big stainless-steel island and turned down the narrow hallway leading to his office where he sat behind his desk. He looked like hell and quite frankly, I couldn't blame him. I mean, after all, this was his diner where the murder took place that now stood closed. This could hurt business, but we should be able to open back up soon.

"How's it going," I managed as I slumped down in a seat in front of him.

"How the hell do you think it's going? A guy was killed here last night!" he exclaimed. "Right under our noses," he finished.

I just sat there. I didn't know what to say. I had nothing.

"The guy from the forensics team is supposed to let me know something today about when we can open back up. He said it might be as early as tomorrow. They're supposed to be back out this morning, but I haven't seen anyone yet," he said dejectedly.

"That's good Mr. Greely. Were you able to get ahold of the others to let them know?" I probed.

"Yeah, I called 'em all. Just told 'em we had to close for a few days and I'd have to let 'em know when they could come back."

Again, I just sat there. Conversation was not my strong suit. He wasn't looking at me anyway, just studying something on the computer.

"While you're here, you could go ahead and check inventory. We're supposed to have some deliveries this morning. You might as well stick around and work a few hours."

"Sure thing, I can do that," I mumbled.

The front door opened and startled us. Greely looked at me at the same time I looked at him. We got up and hurried out, but were relieved to see it was the cops coming back to finish their investigation. Greely went over to the order window when the one in charge asked to speak with him. I figured this was as good a time as ever to get started on the freezer.

A few minutes later, Greely walked back over to me.

"They said their team would be finished with everything they need by the end of the day, which means we can open back up in the morning. I thought that was incredibly fast, but what do I know? They're the experts."

I worked through the rest of the day and before I went home later that afternoon, Greely instructed me to come in extra early in the morning and have the place cleaned up before the diner opened. *Seriously?* I thought. *You sorry, no good for nothing, twelve-hundred pound, Walrus looking, Jabba the Hutt mother fu…* Oh well, who was I kiddin'? It is what it is. I guess I thought somebody else would clean this up. I shrugged my shoulders, and just muttered, "Yes sir."

***

When I left work, I decided to walk home instead of taking public transportation. I just wanted to be alone, I suppose. I get like that sometimes. Maybe it was due to growing up the way I did. Group homes, or even in the foster homes, it didn't matter there were always lots of people around and never any privacy. Alone time is my way recharging my batteries, and after the other night, I needed recharging.

It was a beautiful, sunny day and I didn't feel like hibernating in my apartment, so I took a slight detour and ended up at the park. There were always a lot of people around, but still plenty of places where I could be alone. I found an empty bench overlooking a small pond and sat down exhausted. The pond was encircled by sculpted concrete blocks about a foot high, small ornamental trees and a fountain in the center that gushed water straight up causing it to come cascading down, splashing in a melodic and relaxing rush. I didn't realize just how tired I was until that moment.

The bench I chose was a metal, skeletal frame, painted white and bolted down to a concrete slab. There was a small brass plate built into the backrest. I didn't bother to read it before sitting down. I'm sure it was one of those placards where someone donated a lot of money in the memory of a passed relative so they could dedicate it to them. Parks are full of that kind of stuff. The bench was hot from the sun, but it felt good on my back and was surprisingly comfortable.

I sat quietly soaking up the warmth and daydreaming about nothing in particular when I noticed a young boy that couldn't have been more than three years old, if I had to guess, playing with a dog. He wore a blue Transformers cartoon t-shirt, red shorts, and white tennis shoes. His jet-black hair bounced wildly as he ran after the little black and white mongrel. He laughed and giggled each time his furry friend darted just out of his grasp. A lady stood nearby with a dog's leash in one hand, a cell phone in the other and talked with another lady. I assumed her to be the boy's mother.

I sat quietly people watching and listening to my mp3 player for the afternoon, maybe longer than I should have before finally deciding I was hungry. I think the determining factor was the smells drifting across my nose coming from the park vendors. I got up from my perch and strolled down the walkway to the vendor area and determined I desperately needed a jumbo hotdog with everything on it.

The hawker of the deliciously edible street fare wore a white apron with the words, New York's Best, and a picture of a colossal hotdog on it over a yellow t-shirt underneath. The older man was very friendly and energetic with a huge smile, and curly salt and pepper hair protruding out from under a small white hat. I wasn't in the most conversational mood, and I would have preferred not to have to speak to anyone at all, but I gave him my order after a few forced pleasantries, and within a few minutes, I was munching on the dog as if I hadn't eaten in days.

Sometimes, interacting with people wears me out; my eyes will glaze over, my head will whirl about with thoughts of being trapped, and I'll start searching for a way to escape. I'm more than certain people think I'm rude, which I am I know, but I just can't help it. It's not that I'm trying to be by any means – most of the time anyway.

After I finished eating, my thoughts turned to the early morning ahead of me, and I decided to leave the park to go home and get to bed early. I dreaded the idea of having to be at the diner alone to clean up. I had hoped the cops would do it, but I seriously doubted that I'd walk into a clean diner. I was walking out of the park when I noticed a man in a light tan suit standing off to the sidewalk and under the trees nearby looking directly at me. He had blonde hair, tall and wore sunglasses. My first thought was if this is the same guy that was at my apartment building last night when I went home. I never saw his face clearly so I couldn't be sure. When he saw that I noticed him, he seemed to have flinched ever so slightly as if he were nervous. He reached into his pocket and withdrew a cell phone and put it to his ear. I found it quite odd because I never heard it ring, but he seemed to be having a very in-depth conversation now, and he turned away from me. I took that as my cue to leave, so I slipped off behind the vendor carts and tried my best to blend in with the crowd.

The walk home didn't take long, especially after catching too-tall watching me in the park. He must've followed me from the diner, but who is he and why is he watching me? I'd never seen him before. My bet was he was a cop and thought I was in on the murder or something. Maybe he worked with the redhead, and he came to take me out, you know, tie-up all the loose ends sort of thing. Oh jeez, I had a million thoughts running through my head, but what could I do?

***

Morning came quickly, but I was ready for it after a good hot shower. It didn't take me long, and I stood at the door to the diner eager to get to work. As soon as I walked in, I turned on every light in the place. I keep it sort of dim while I do all my prep work, but this morning was different. I had to clean up that…mess, out front.

It took me a good hour of bleach and water mopping, but I had the place cleaner than it had ever been. After I straightened up the tables, I pulled the yellow tape down from inside and out and carried it all out to the trash bins out back. The city was waking and I could hear the traffic out front picking up. I took a moment to get some fresh air, and when I returned to the diner, I saw Helen had already set the menus out on the tables getting ready for the day. She must have come in through the front while I was outside in the back alley.

Helen is an older lady but dresses like she's young and sexy with low cut skimpy outfits that show off forced cleavage and tattoos. Her voice is rough and gritty like sandpaper from all the cigarettes she smokes, has short dark hair, average height and smells of cheap perfume and an ashtray. She has three bratty kids and a no-account boyfriend that doesn't have a job. I think all her kids have different dads, but that's none of my business. She's always complaining about them. The dads that is. Well, the kids too for that matter. I can see why she's so pleasant. She's the head waitress because she's been here the longest of the two, and the only one that has said more than a few words to me since I began working here, so I feel like we've bonded.

"Morning," I yawned.

"What of it?" she snapped at me with a dirty look as she slid a chair back under a table with a slam. We're tight, she and I.

I grabbed my apron and wrapped it around my waist and tied it on. It reeked of pickle juice, grease, and smoke, but it seemed adequate for this fine dining establishment. It's like Greely himself had been rolling around in it. It was the other waitress's job to launder the aprons, but she hadn't been in since just before the incident.

"Hey, did you move my tables?" Helen bawled at me in her three packs a day, sandpapered, raspy voice.

"Uh, yeah. I kinda had to mop the joint up this morning. I got stuck to the floor and had to squish my way out of the muck, lost a good pair of shoes doing it too, I might add. But rest assured, it's as clean as my kitchen now," I smarted-off with a bit too much bark.

Maybe I shouldn't have said it the way I did, but all she does is wait tables, collect tips and leaves. She's supposed to clean up after her shift, but she never does. And does she ever share her tips with us cooks? That's rhetorical, of course. She's supposed to. We're all supposed to split them at the end of the night, but we all know she sand bags hers.

"What the hell's that s'posed to mean?" She stood up straight, hands on her hips and stared me down with a nasty look on her face that reminded me of a pit-bull. "I keep my side of the counter clean. You just worry about your side, precious," she bit back while pointing at the counter separating the dining room from the kitchen.

Those ridiculous jingle bells hanging from the front door rang out. Great, I thought, our first customer of the day. I noticed Helen turned to look too, so I used the distraction to make my getaway. I retreated to the safety of the kitchen and got busy. I had to get the grill heated up and ready for service.

I hate coffee. I hate the smell of it. I hate the taste of it, but here in this pit hole of a diner, our customers loved the stuff. Helen always had the coffee brewing each morning. I heard her tell the customers that just walked in, *my saviors*, to sit anywhere they'd like as she grabbed a cup for them.

Sam, the other waitress, opened the back door, walked right by me without saying a word and poured a cup for herself and sat down looking like she had the world's biggest hangover. She had her demons to fight, I suppose. I don't even pretend to care. She's not much older than me, maybe twenty-five or so. She's into Goth, and I don't understand that world. To each their own, I say. She scares me a little, to be honest. That day she wore her jet-black hair with purple tips pulled back in a ponytail. Black lipstick, black eyeliner and multiple piercings adorned her face and ears, and she wore a black Ramones t-shirt, black jeans with rips and tears scattered throughout and black combat boots. But the thing that always made me wonder was the dog collar with metal spikes she wore around her neck. Was she expecting a dogfight or vampires?

"Order up," Helen said, as she slammed the ticket down on the counter.

I reached around Sam, who never moved, grabbed the ticket off the counter and read it. *'Cluck and oink*! Seriously? Why could this woman not simply write down bacon and eggs, B & E or anything other than old style café lingo? I never understood it, but I guess it was just something people come up with to be fun; self-entertainment. There's no need for code talk around here. It's not practical, and it's not like there is some big secret customers will be ordering food. I'm more than certain that our competition knows we serve breakfast, lunch, and dinner. I suppose it's a tradition, but once again, who am I to say anything? I'm just the cook.

The morning stream of customers kept me too busy to look up so when I finally got a break; I slipped out the back to get some fresh air. Okay, so it's the city and not the most refreshing air in the world, but it's still cleaner than being inside. Lots of different smells wafted in the air. Some I recognize, but others are strictly Chinese, and I have no idea what those spices are. I would comment on never seeing any cats around here, but I bet they think even worse things about the fine cuisine I serve here at the slop shop. The back door opened and I saw Helen looking around.

"Hey, string bean, you have a customer that wants to thank the 'chef' personally. Get in here," she said, in her gratingly irritating voice.

What the hell? My mind raced to the events of the night of the murder. It must be one of the cops wanting to ask me more questions. Nobody ever asks for me, and I do mean nobody. For a moment, I thought of taking off down the alley, but only for a moment. I took a deep breath and walked back inside. Before I could walk through the breezeway by the counter, Helen stopped me.

"She asked for you by name. How's a lady like her know a no-account urchin like you?" she prodded.

I glanced over the counter into the dining area, and my heart jumped into my throat. There she sat my redheaded, glamour queen assassin. I think my knees must've locked up on me because I couldn't move. Not until Helen pushed me out the doorway anyway. *You bitch*, I almost called Helen out loud, but I refrained.

What did the lady want with me? I've no idea. I didn't rat her out for or nothing. I'm not that dumb. I walked over to her table and softly cleared my throat. She sat there with a slight smile looking up at me like nothing ever happened. Seated across from her was a man in a dark gray business suit. I briefly wondered if this could be the fella from last night, but I couldn't look at him; I just kept focused on her. I cleared my throat again and said, "Yes ma'am, you wanted to see me," I managed to squeak out.

"Hello Leonard," she purred, with a soft, sultry voice. It was like hot melted butter it was so smooth.

I nodded, but never looked away. How could anybody look away from that face? Mesmerizing as it was though, something about her struck me odd. Suddenly, I shuddered and noticed chill bumps up and down my arms.

"Leave us," she said to the guy sitting across from her.

I looked around the room after the guy made his way outside. Great! No one else around. Even Helen seemed to have disappeared, hiding in the back, but spying on me no doubt. Sam was nowhere to be seen either. What the hell?

"Sit," she stated flatly.

I sat…

"So…" she began, as she looked around the joint, "Nice place."

She turned back to look directly at me. Her eyes bore a hole into the back of my brain. I didn't know what to make of it all.

"Uh, sure. I guess."

"I was lying. This *isn't* a nice place. You didn't say anything to the cops the other night about my - presence here. That's good," she purred.

"No, ma'am! I'm no snitch," I said, with a bit of indignation. "The way I see it, it's none of my business. Besides, I didn't see nothin'."

I could see her studying my face, so I tried my best to look street tough, but it only took one stern look from her, and I was back to being the cowardly lion. I instinctively lowered my head a little and slouched down in my seat just a touch as if scolded by a parent.

"Good." She squinted her eyes ever so slightly. "Make sure it stays that way, got it?"

"Absolutely."

After another pause and dramatic glare at me, she quickly stood to leave. I took the statement for a threat but managed to respond to it as an invitation.

"Anything you need, I'm your guy."

I stood clumsily after her, knocking my chair over backward. Why I didn't just let her leave, I'll never know, but I think we've already established the fact that I can be an idiot.

She stopped in her tracks, turned back around and paused for a moment, allowing me time to pick up the chair. She smiled, "I like you, Leonard. I'll be sure to keep that in mind."

When she walked out of the diner, I could smell her perfume lingering in the air. I had no idea what it was called, but I liked it. I stared at her backside as she walked out. I couldn't help myself even if she is old enough to be my mother. Besides, if she didn't want people to look at her and appreciate her - attributes, she wouldn't be on Broadway and she darn sure wouldn't dress that way. I don't think I've ever seen a woman like her before. Not up close and personal anyway. I looked out the window and watched the suit she was with open the door of a limo and let her climb in.

That was my first conversation with Miss Briana Fitzgerald, Broadway actress, assassin at large!

6

I stood like a statue for longer than I should have apparently because Helen whacked me on the head with a rolled-up newspaper and lit into me about the diner.

"Why didn't you tell me what happened here the other night you idiot? How can you 'not' have told us the whole story just as soon as you walked in this morning? Instead, you let me work all morning, right here, in the very spot where a man was murdered! You could've said *something*, but oooooh no, not you, Mr. silent and broody. Did you see it happen? It says here in the paper you and Greely were both here," she yelled at me.

"Ouch!" I exclaimed, when she hit me over the head, "What are you blabbering about, you psycho?"

"You know darn good and well what I'm talking about!" She was at a frantic pace now.

I tried my best pick and roll move using a chair to head back to the kitchen. I wasn't about to take any abuse from this nut job. It didn't work though; Sam blocked me at the door and held me up, which gave nutjob enough time to clobber me with that damned newspaper again. She kept it in her hand, shaking it at me like a mother scolding her child; I'm sure it was designed to scare me into talking.

"You were going to go all day without telling us about this weren't you?" she fired off. "Here's your picture right here on the cover!"

"Didn't think you'd wanna know about it," I said, glancing at the photo. I look like a hyena with my tongue hanging out staring at a camera. "Besides, I figured Greely told you when he called you."

"No. He just told me the diner was closed for a few days. He mentioned something about the health department, but didn't elaborate to us *underlings*," she said emphasizing the underlings part.

"Look, it wasn't my place to tell you. He's the boss, not me. How was I to know he didn't tell you all about it," I replied.

"Honestly, Leonard, I don't wanna know about it, but how was I gonna 'not' know about it? It's on the front page! Do you know who this guy was? Huh? Well, it's obvious you have no clue, but you don't even seem to care," she snarled.

"Seriously you should've told us," Sam said, as she stood there glowering at me.

"I don't have a clue who the guy was. I just heard the name, William Wood. That's all I know," I answered Helen, as I pushed passed Sam and went about straightening up the kitchen.

"That's exactly right! William Wood, 'Commissioner' William Wood you idiot," Helen practically yelled at me, again putting her particular emphasis on the commissioner part of her unrelenting rant.

I guess that must mean he was a very important man. If he was important though, why would he be in our diner? Fine dining establishment as it is, it doesn't seem like the kind of place he would choose to spend his time. Helen stood there fuming. I knew at this point I should keep my mouth shut, but I just couldn't. It wasn't in my nature.

"Okay, so he was a commissioner. Big deal," I lipped off.

"Big deal?" Sam gasped, "Yeah it's a big deal. That's one of the most important people in the state. The commissioners control everything that goes on, don't you know that? Oh, hell no, you don't know that. You don't get it at all. You have to ask yourself, what's a big shot like him doing in a place like this at that time of night? We could be in the middle of something big, right in the line of fire!"

I heard the front doorbells ringing. Saved by the bell! We had customers, so they left me to tend to them. I was glad of that. I guess I didn't get the impact of what she said. Not right off anyway. As the morning wore on, I knew something big was happening because the diner had a lot more customers than usual and I struggled to keep up. It could get busy in there, but I'd not been that busy since I first started working there. I could overhear conversations here and there. People seemed to be curious as to where the murder took place. The back door opened and I looked up to see the boss coming in. I never thought I'd be happy to see El Tub-O-Charms.

"Where we at, kid?" he asked.

"Lots of orders Mr. Greely," I said. "I need more eggs and chops."

I gotta hand it to the big fella, he pitched right in, and we caught up in no time. By eleven-thirty, we had the breakfast club mostly taken care of. The last few customers were sauntering out the jingle bell door, and I took a moment to look around the kitchen. It was a complete mess, and yours truly would be the only one cleaning it up. Greely doesn't clean, and Helen doesn't like to come into the kitchen, even when there's nothing to do. Marvin certainly wasn't going to do it when he came in, which by the way, he was late, I noticed. And Sam...well, let's just say I'd rather do it myself than have her anywhere near me. There are knives in the kitchen ya know!

"That's it," Helen said, indicating that was the last of the customers for the time being.

Helen ran the cash register as much as possible when she was here. She seemed to relish the idea of being close to the money. I think Greely kept a real close eye on her though. His light may not shine the brightest, but he had a knack for how many orders came in and how much the cash register should be totaling up. I never went near the thing when she was there— didn't want that kind of trouble.

Sam brought the bus cart back full of dishes and dumped them in the sink. It was her job to wash them and help get the kitchen cleaned up before Marvin comes in at eleven. After she dropped them off, she headed back out and pretended to clean the dining area, but she was texting someone on her cell phone. The girl is just weird, and I try to keep my distance. The black lipstick, black hair, black eyeshadow and black everything just kinda freaks me out. Not to say that she's not hot, in a weird sort of way. Oh lord, what am I thinking? I'm sure she'd rather gut me with a butcher knife than to look at me.

Greely went out back to smoke while I tended to the dishes. When I heard the back door open and slam shut, I turned to see Marvin waltzing in.

"How's it going, my young apprentice? Break a lot of eggs this smoanin?" Marvin asked with a slight chuckle.

"Hey old man, 'bout time you rolled outta bed and got to work. You're late," I chided him.

Marvin was an older, black man, tall, lean and bald. He looked much younger than he was. He trained me when I first came to work here, but the word apprentice was a helluva an exaggeration on his part. This is a guy that can burn water. I may not be the best cook in Queens, but I'm no slouch at slinging hash. In the homes where I grew up, I always had to work, and I liked working in the kitchen because I never went to bed hungry.

"Greely knew I wasa gonuh be late," he says, "I had bidness to tend tuh."

"Well, better late than not at all I suppose."

Marvin walked over to closer to me as I put the stack of plates away, leaned over close to my ear and whispered, "I was down at Vonn's earlier, and everybody was uh tahlkin' bout it. 'Bout what happened here t'other night. Women know yet?" He nodded and gave a quick glance toward Helen and Sam.

Vonn's is a barbershop where Marvin liked to hang out. A bunch of crusty old men sitting around gossiping and telling lies to one another. I went there with him a few times.

"Yeah," I answered, "They know."

"Oooh wee!" Marvin laughed and slapped his knee in a weird contorted dance move that only he could pull off. "'Bout time something innerestin' happens 'round here! Twenty-fo years and nut'un ever happen." He stopped his cackling for a minute and looked straight at me, "Nut'un ever happen 'til you got here that is."

I stopped with the plates and just stared at the fool. "You gotta be kidding me."

"Oh com'on youngin, this dump is famous now. Ever' body been reading about what happened here t'other night," Marvin declared, with another cackle.

"Yeah, but you didn't see it happen," I responded with a resounding woefulness. Once again, I opened my mouth when it should've been closed because Marvin didn't get to be as old as he is because he's dumb. He suddenly stopped what he was doing and leaned over close to me.

"It said in the papers there weren't no witnesses," he said with a finger in my chest and staring at me intently with squinting eyes to look me over real close like. "So, you 'did' see who dun it," he affirmed more than asked. He continued looking at me in disbelief before shaking his head and saying, "No, don't tell me no mo! Listen to me youngin, you stick to your story that you didn't see nothin', you hear me?" He was emphatic about it, I could tell. I thought for a second I saw a slight trace of fear there.

I nodded and stared at him with a blank look on my face.

"Folks think you know who dun it, they'd be takin' you out, just like that," he snapped his fingers, "just to cover their tracks. You say anythin' to anybody else?" he asked.

I shook my head without taking my eyes off him.

"Good, good. Better keep it that way too." He turned away from me, found his apron, tied it on and began prepping for the lunch crowd. "I got 'dis now."

Helen popped her head around the door to the kitchen and looked at me with a sour expression on her face. "Hey Leonard, someone else here to see you."

"Be right there,"

I had no idea who this was going to be, but I had a suspicion that it may be one of the detectives from last night. I untied my apron, hung it by my cubby-hole and walked out to the dining area. Boy was I wrong. I saw a lady wearing a dark green jacket and skirt with a maroon blouse under it cut low and showing off more than most and less than some. She had platinum blond hair with soft curls and the bluest eyes I had ever seen. If I had to guess, I'd say she was about my age, and she was dangerously gorgeous; absolutely breathtaking.

The lady looked directly at me as if she expected someone. I looked around, but there was no one else in the place that looked like they were waiting for me, so I walked over to her with a bit more swagger and extended my hand.

"Leonard P Valentine, at your service ma'am," I said, using my best sophisticated, high-brow accent and even a slight bow. I smiled like a kid in a candy store, and I knew I must've looked like an idiot, but I couldn't help it. She smiled back at me in a contagious sort of way. This lady was even more mesmerizing than Briana Fitzgerald, and I didn't think that was possible. And here she was, asking to see me of all people.

Helen hovered nearby so that she could eavesdrop, I'm sure. Sam flitted about like a bumble bee, and I could see her cutting eyes at my new friend and me. Where were they when Briana was here?

"Won't you please sit down? I'd like to talk to you. I know you're very busy so I won't keep you but a minute," she said.

I looked around for Greely. He doesn't like to see us idle when there's work to be done. When I didn't see him, I sat.

"Hello Leonard, my name is Lexi Osborne, and I wanted to ask you a few questions if you don't mind?" she asked as she leaned in closer and extended her hand.

I could smell her sweet perfume. It was nice, and I liked it. Her hand was soft and warm, and she had a very firm grip.

"Are you a cop?" I asked.

She laughed at my question. So, I laughed too. I knew I looked like an idiot now, but I couldn't help myself. She's intoxicating. I wanted to be near her.

"No. No, not at all," she said. "I'm a journalist for the Daily Grind."

Red flags should have been flying all around me, but I was oblivious to them all.

"Sure, I don't mind. Fire away."

I had no idea why I said it, other than the fact I'm totally taken in by this lady. I knew exactly why she was here and why she wanted to talk to me, but I didn't care either way. I know what you're thinking. You think that I'm contrary and you're right. Did I mention how pretty she is?

"I understand that you witnessed Commissioner Woods' murder. That must've been scary, even for a brave man like you," she whispered in a low voice while looking around to make sure no one else can hear her speaking. She reached out and touched my hand now. Her hands were soft and warm and felt like velvet. It was nice.

"Yeah," I stammered, "but I wasn't scared or nothin'."

"I would've been. I don't know what I would've done had I witnessed someone walk in and shoot a guy *point blank* right in front of me. I know I would've been frightened silly," she said putting emphasis on the words point blank.

"Oh no, not me. I've seen all sorts of things in this city. Seeing a guy murdered ain't nothin' new."

"So," she says, "You did see who did it?" she asked incredulously.

Jeez, was I stupid? I walked right into that, and I even knew it was coming.

"Oh no, lady you got it all wrong," I managed to spit out, "I didn't actually see anything. Not until after. You know. Look, lady, I gotta get back to work. I'm sorry, but I can't talk anymore so… I'll see ya 'round, okay?"

"Oh, that's too bad, but I understand. Maybe we can talk another time huh?"

"Eh, yeah, I dunno, maybe… sure," I said. I stood to retreat to the kitchen.

"Okay, thanks. I'll see you later then?" She said more as a question than a statement.

She knew darn good and well I didn't wanna talk about it. I saw Helen staring at me as she pretended to clean nearby. Ms. Osborne stood to leave, and I noticed she was tall for a lady, almost as tall I am, and I'm one-inch shy of six feet. Sure, she was wearing heels, but they didn't look all that high to me. I watched her walk out the door before I turned back to the kitchen.

7

The young reporter crossed the street and hailed a passing cab. She climbed in, gave the driver the address to the newspaper office and sat back to consider her options. As they sped along in traffic, she thought about the conversation with Leonard, short as it was. The cook knew more than he was telling, she was sure of it, but she also knew he wasn't going to tell her anything at the diner. She had to get him alone somewhere. Somewhere she could get him to open up. She needed a plan, but right now her primary concern was making it to work on time. She had a deadline to meet, and she was pushing her luck by stopping by the diner.

The murder of such a prominent citizen was a story too big for her not to get involved in. Secretly involved in, that is. She knew her boss couldn't find out because she would never approve of a rookie reporter digging into something this big. Unless she thought, she could crack the case and impress her boss enough to land a front-page exclusive.

Lexi Osborne had worked at the Daily Grind since graduating less than a year earlier. Her assignments had been what she referred to as fluff pieces; small stories that found their way into the paper more often than not but buried deep within. Still, she had to admit, landing a job at such a highly regarded news organization was a big feather in her proverbial cap, no matter how she got it. She had her father to thank for it, though she didn't know it.

As fate would have it, her father, Pete Osborne, was a Fire Investigator for the city many years ago and had met Lexi's editor, Jane Moore, when she was a young reporter learning the ropes. The two had collaborated on catching a suspected arsonist. Jane wrote articles designed to draw the man out using the information he gave her. The arsonist was the only one that could understand the meaning behind the stories due to the intentional clues he left behind, and eventually, he slipped up and caught him. Jane was awarded a big promotion on her way to a successful career. She never forgot who had helped her. Lexi's father never divulged the information to his daughter and went so far as asking Ms. Moore not to as well. He wanted her to feel she had accomplished this on her own and not through the help of her overprotective daddy.

With her degree in hand, she set out to conquer the world and win the next Pulitzer Prize. Unfortunately, she was impatient. Ms. Moore would tell her often that every reporter starts at the bottom and works their way up. *Experience is irreplaceable and is the truest path to wisdom*, she often said to the young reporter. Lexi felt this case would be the one to make her career.

Lexi had met the commissioner and his popular socialite wife a couple of times at charity functions she covered as a reporter, and even though she didn't know him personally, she felt a personal connection. As soon as she heard about the murder, she took an immediate interest and began digging into the victim's background.

The reporter that first broke the story of his murder had nothing more to report and only printed what the police had released in a statement which was, *they had no leads at this time.*

She was determined to find the killer. It suddenly occurred to her. She knew what she was going to do.

8

I walked through the kitchen door smack dab into Ol' Sour Puss himself. "Uh, sorry Mr. Greely, just headin' back in to clean up."

"See that you do," Greely said, with his gruff, just smoked a cigarette in thirty seconds, voice.

I suspected Helen or Sam must've said something to him and he hurried inside to see what the rub was. I pushed past him and finished cleaning the dishes. Greely walked around, in and out of the kitchen, while I stayed busy. I tried not to make eye contact with the guy because I was desperate to get out of here for a while. I was in no mood for talking anymore, and I sure didn't want to work a double-shift. Not today. There were a few more customers that had come in, but nothing Marvin couldn't handle. I grabbed my backpack and slipped out the back door as I do every day about the same time.

Sam works the same shift that I do, but she had already flown the coop before I had my kitchen wrapped up. When I stepped out the back door, she was waiting for me. I ducked my head and pretended not to see her.

"Hey," she said, brushing up beside me and nudging me. She had to walk fast to keep up and I don't think fast is a word in her vocabulary. "Hey, can you slow down a little? You going to a fire or something?" she asked.

"I gotta be somewhere," I replied.

"Yeah, well. I wanna talk to you."

I didn't slow down; in fact, I cut across traffic and headed down Elder Street speeding up a little as I adjusted my backpack. I wasn't sure where I was going, but I was getting there as quickly as I could. There were some kids playing baseball on the ball field not far from the diner, but I kept walking toward the bus stop on 56th right past them. I'll give it to her; she was a trooper. She kept up with me, though she hadn't said another word. Finally, I stopped cold and turned to her.

"What do you want?" I asked.

"What was it like?" she asked with wide eyes.

"What was what like?"

"You know, seeing someone murdered?"

Of all the harebrained things I've ever heard. Now, this chick is starting to scare me. Total freak of nature this one is.

"Not you too? Like I've said a hundred times now, I didn't see it happen. I was in the kitchen the whole time. I didn't see nothin', and I didn't hear nothin'." I sat down to wait for the bus.

"I've seen a dead person before," she said as if I wanted to hear about it, which I didn't. I just wanted to be left alone.

"Look, Sam, I don't wanna talk about it," I stated flatly.

"Okay, okay already. Jeez, calm down Mr. freak out." She folded her arms and looked away frustrated.

I meant it too. I didn't want to talk about it to anyone. I didn't even want to think about it anymore. In my mind, it was over with, and nothin' else needed to be said. A city bus rolled by and I was reminded again to keep my mouth shut. A huge photo was on the side of it, an advertisement for the Broadway play starring Miss Briana Fitzgerald with her face staring straight at me. I looked up when a taxi drove past honking at someone on the street; the same thing was on the roof! I can't get away from her. She's everywhere!

"Look, I'm sorry. I didn't mean to come off so grumpy, but it's just not something I want to talk about."

"It's cool. I get it." She relaxed and looked around, pretending to be all casual now.

After a brief silence, I stood. "I gotta go. I'll see ya back at the diner later," I apologized and stood to leave.

She nodded and turned to look at something up the street. I walked to the next bus stop and got there just in time to jump on. It stopped near the Queens library where I got off, headed across the street and walked in. I found a comfortable chair in the back where it was quiet and sat down. I took my mp3 player out of my backpack, turned on some music and pulled out a book.

Every time someone walked by I felt the need look up to see who it was. I've never been one to be paranoid, but this whole thing had me spooked. First, I witness a Broadway star walk in off the street into a two-bit diner, put three slugs into a fella, then walk out like it was nothing. Now, I have newspaper reporters asking questions, cops asking questions and my co-workers asking questions and freaking out on me. The library used to be my go-to place for *solitudinal* thinking, but today my imagination seemed to be runnin' amuck!

***

"Sir? Sir? You've been asleep for hours. You're not allowed to sleep in here," the librarian said as she shook me awake.

"What the…" I must've fallen asleep not long after I came in. I reached up, pulled my earbuds out and stared up at the lady talking to me. "Um yeah, sorry about that, good book," I said, grabbing my bag and heading for the door.

She just stood staring at me with her hands on her hips and watched me leave.

I looked at the clock as I exited the library. "Great!" I said out loud when I saw it was almost five o'clock now. I had slept for a lot longer than I wanted to. I go to the library all the time but have never fallen asleep there. Well, not for long anyway.

By the time I got back to the diner, I could see the place was pretty full and I ended up working like a dog for the rest of the evening. My co-workers didn't mention anything further about the murder. No one had much time to talk as the dinner crowd kept us hopping. I heard customers talking about it and the dead guy, but only in hushed tones. Greely doesn't care what the hell they're talking about as long as they're ordering and paying, he's happy as a clam.

We don't have two waitresses on a Tuesday night most times, but I guess everybody heard about the murder and wanted to check out the place where it happened. I was glad Greely asked Helen and Sam to stay. He and I worked the kitchen like we'd done it together for years. It was smooth. The ladies would slam the orders down, and he and I would split the kitchen. He would work the grill, and I would put everything else together. He liked to cook, and he was the boss. He'd step out back to smoke now and then, so I'd take over 'til he decided to come back in. He was in a good mood. Isn't it funny how a murder can do that to people? Gives us something in common I suppose. Weird lot, we city people are.

Just as soon as she could, Helen washed up and bolted. As she made for the front door, she suddenly stopped, turned around and walked over to me. "I almost forgot. Here's your share of tips. Don't spend it all in one place either." She handed me a wad of cash.

I managed to mutter something like, "Thanks, appreciate it."

I stuffed the dough in my pocket without counting it. The jingle door closed and I locked up behind her. It was just Greely and me now. He was sitting on that bar stool he always kept in the kitchen and was going over the receipts for the day. He usually did that in his office, but even he was too tired tonight to make the walk back.

"Haven't had business this good on a Tuesday night in a long time," he stated.

"Yeah, it was busy," I confirmed. I wasn't in a real talkative mood, but he seemed to be.

"I guess it's like a bad car wreck, everybody slows down because they wanna see what's going on," he offered.

"I guess so," I answered. No idea what the hell that was supposed to mean.

"So, com'on kid, what gives? What'd ya see?" Greely asked me as he stopped what he was doing and peered at me over his bifocals.

"I didn't see nothin'' I swear," I professed.

"Yeah, okay kid. Okay. I'll see ya in the morning." He turned back to his accounting.

I bounced. I wasn't sticking around chit-chattin' bout the stuff that went down the other night. I headed home to my crusty little apartment. I had things to do. This was Tuesday night, and I was more than confident there were cockroaches that needed feedin'. I put in enough hours at that diner every week, no need to be there tonight any longer than necessary. *I would be a millionaire if I were paid what I thought I was worth,* I mused…*well, what I 'think' I'm worth anyway.* I crack me up sometimes.

I reached into my backpack and grabbed my mp3 player as I walked to the bus stop. After first, I didn't feel it, but then my fingers stumbled on to something new. I pulled out a piece of paper with something written on it. I couldn't quite make it out, so I stopped under a street light to check it out. It had a single line printed in black ink

"Meet me at Corona Park at noon tomorrow,"

What the hell is this, I wondered. Who could've put this in here? There wasn't a signature on it, but whoever wrote it had excellent penmanship. I knew this because I could read it without a decoder ring. My first thought was it was Sam trying to get me to meet her and talk to her clandestine like, but it was written too good to have been hers. I'd seen her chicken scratch; it could barely be called writing. Sometimes, I can't even read her orders at the diner. No, not Sam and it wasn't Marvin's thing. I wondered if it could be Helen. After all, she was extra friendly to me tonight when she left, and she gave me a wad of cash from the tips, but why would she leave the note today when she'd see me in the morning anyway? I was stumped, it seemed like everybody wanted to talk to me.

    I didn't have to wait long before the bus arrived. I climbed on and grabbed a seat near the door. No one else but the driver tonight, I had the whole place to myself. I stuffed the paper back in my backpack and turned up the tunes until we got to my stop. Twenty minutes later the driver pulled over and stopped the transit. Before I stood up, I looked around, streets were empty, so I scampered off like a good little city rodent and hit the pavement on the move. The only life I saw were a couple of younger boys hanging out, smoking cigarettes. They nodded to me but said nothing as I walked by. I got to my apartment building after a few minutes and still saw no one around, so I began feeling pretty good. Finally, I thought, I could get some rest. This had been one long day.

9

Sweat poured down Matthew Schofield's face and dripped onto the elliptical machine in the company gym. He was the only one in the building at the early morning hour other than the security guard on the first floor. A creature of habit, he ran five miles every morning as a warm-up to his intense workout at 5:30 no matter how late he stayed up working the night before. His intensity in the gym was equaled by his performance in the courtroom. He was Chief Attorney for Camden Group, Inc. and a no-nonsense, take charge type-A personality. Tall, lean and sporting a store-bought tan and a hard-set jaw he was considered a classically handsome man by the many lady admirers he had; until they got to know him well and realized what a son-of-a-bitch he truly was. He had no time for dating or romance; he didn't go on picnics or weekends away to a cozy little B & B. He wanted his women intelligent, available and ready when he beckoned. He was nothing if not upfront.

He was finishing his workout when his cell phone rang. Grabbing a towel, he wiped the sweat off his face and hands and picked up the cell phone. When he saw the caller id, he answered. "What have you got for me?"

The caller replied, "The witness was interviewed twice now and both times gave the same story. He didn't see or hear anything and gave no indication he knew anything. I tend to believe it. If he knew anything at all, O'Conner would've pulled it out of him by now, but there's nothing there Mr. Schofield."

"Okay. Let me know if there's anything further," he said, pressing the red *end-call* button on his cell phone without waiting for a reply from his informant at the police station.

Matthew Schofield III didn't get to be one of the most influential attorneys in the state by merely being superior in the courtroom. He paid for it. He paid all the right people in all the right places. He was friends with judges, senators, and even members of Congress. He kept tabs on everyone he needed or may potentially need which meant city officials, judges, attorneys, and law enforcement at every possible agency with an acronym. No one was outside of his scope of influence.

He saw the news report on the local channels and read about the murder in the paper. The police didn't seem to have any witnesses to the slaying of the commissioner, or any leads to go on.

He climbed off the machine and headed to the showers as two other employees entered the gym.

10

Not sure why I was still awake or what was so interesting on my ceiling, but there I was, staring at it in the middle of the night when I should've been sleeping. I suppose I was thinking about the wonderfully delightful little number with the open blouse sitting in front of me this morning. A girl like that could sure keep a guy awake, that's for sure.

For the most part, my apartment building is pretty quiet. The super doesn't allow any monkey business, but I got up to get a glass of water, and I could hear a couple of people out in the hallway talking, and not just at chit-chat levels either. They were carrying on pretty good. Stuff like that don't bother me any or keep me awake. Where I'm from, you get used to it. I was awake long before those two started yapping anyways. I got my water and fell back into bed exhausted.

The next thing I knew, the alarm blared like a klaxon, waking me up. I guess I had finally fallen back asleep somewhere in the night, but the first thing on my brain was the note. I took a quick shower, got dressed and grabbed a bus ride over to the diner.

"'Bout time you could join us Sunshine," Helen said in a snarky tone when I walked in.

"Okay, what gives? This is the second day in a row you're on time," I replied, in a not so humoristic manner.

"Very funny, unlike you, I have a life you know," she snapped.

I mumbled something incoherent and grabbed my apron. I was ready to get the day started. The next day was my only day off, and I had plans. I wasn't sure what those plans were, but I was going to do something. I was lost in my thoughts when I heard the jingle bells on the door. I didn't even smell the coffee on yet, and the doors don't open 'til seven anyway. What gives?

It turns out, it was only Sam coming in through the front door. She didn't even glance in my direction when she walked by me. No sweat off my nose. She carried a backpack like me instead of a purse like a normal chick would do, but there's nothing normal about the girl. She put it away in her hidey hole and tied on her apron. I watched her scurry off, so I continued getting my grill prepped for the day.

I thought about the note while working. A part of me said to go to the park and meet this mysterious person, and another part of me said to run, don't walk, as fast as possible away from the park.

The morning went by relatively quick and the next thing I knew, I was bolting for the back door passing Marvin on the way. He barely said two words to me before I was out of hearing range. I heard him cackle to himself and go inside. I was in a hurry. I'd made up my mind I was going to Corona Park to meet this note-leaving stranger, and I was going to find out what this was all about.

I didn't look up the entire time I walked to the park, but I kept an eye out anyway. It's what us city people learn to do as soon as we're ambulatory. We just don't look people in the eye when we're on the streets. Not that we're not friendly. Everyone is just in a hurry. Speaking of a hurry, I didn't have a clue where I was supposed to go once I made it to the park. I could see a park bench with nobody around, so I made my way over to it. It was the middle of the day, and there weren't too many people around. I grabbed a seat and sat down for a few minutes to watch the birds.

"Don't turn around. Pretend I'm not here," I heard a female voice whisper rather coarsely.

Of course, I turned around immediately, even though she said not to. I was face to face with none other than Lexi Osborne, the newspaper lady, standing behind me. I never heard her walk up, but I was glad she did. Her blond hair was blowing softly in the breeze as she stood silhouetted with the sun behind her. As she came into my vision, I could see her face. The rounded cheekbones, perfectly cute nose, and soft, red lips suddenly turned into a cheeky smile. She was wearing a thin white blouse that I could see spaghetti straps and just a hint of lace under and a short black skirt tight around her beautifully shaped hips. Her long legs were creamy smooth and went all the way down to her feet, which is a long way to go to get into the black and white heels she wore. I noticed she had a small, delicate necklace resting quite comfortably on her flawless chest.

"Hey, I said not to turn around. Now you've ruined it," she said with a pouting look on her face that suddenly changed to a big, playful smile. "But I'm glad you came," she purred.

"Ah jeez, miss, you scared me. What gives? What's with the secret agent stuff anyways?" I asked, trying to play it cool.

"Because we shouldn't be seen talking too often, that's all. I'm only trying to protect you," she said with a soothing, but somewhat patronizing tone.

"Protect me. How are you trying to protect me? Why do I need protection anyway?"

"Because of everything that's happened and because I'm working on a story about it. When it finally breaks, it'll be all over the news, and I wouldn't want your name being associated with it, that's how."

"Oh no, jeez lady, you mean like a big front-page expose'? I want no part of that. You can count me out."

I stood to leave, but she grabbed my arm and stopped me.

"It's too late, and I'll tell you why. I know you saw something last night. Whether you saw who it was that pulled the trigger is for you to say, but I think you know more than you're telling and maybe more than you know. I also think you're scared," Lexi said, "and that puts you in a dangerous place if you know what I mean. The guy that was murdered in your restaurant was Commissioner Wood. Certainly, you've heard of him?" she asked rhetorically.

"Of course, I've heard of 'em. Hasn't everybody?" I said, trying to sound like I haven't been living under a rock for the last twenty-two years of my life, yet knowing that before Helen told me, I didn't have a clue other than the guy's name the cops dropped on me. I sat down beside her.

She continued, "Commissioner Wood was one of the most powerful men in the county," she stated categorically, "and I think his murder was a mob execution, but I can't prove it. Not yet anyway. I want to find out why he was killed. Was it because he got in their way or did he know too much?"

"Seriously? That's crazy," I countered.

"There's a lot more to this, and I'm going to get to the bottom of it all with or without your help."

She had a determined look on her face that I didn't doubt. Okay, now she had my attention. I suppose I had thought the whole time I was in an alright position until she came along. I wasn't scared of any mob retaliation before. Well, maybe a little, but if they wanted me out of the way they could have done that already and several times too, right?

"I told ya lady, I'm not scared." I tried standing to leave again.

"Please don't go yet. Hear me out first," she pleaded, grabbing my arm with both of her hands. She pulled me close, and for a moment I thought I would do something stupid like try to kiss her. She must've read my mind because she let go of me quickly and turned away dramatically. The move caught me off guard, and I stumbled for something to say. It couldn't hurt anything to hear her out, right? And I kinda liked being near her anyway.

"Okay. I'm in. I'll help you. So, what gives?"

She turned around with a huge smile on her face and excitedly said, "That's great. I knew I could count on you. I've been working on something. I have it from an excellent source that Commissioner Wood was in the middle of a land deal with a very shady company. I think his murder had something to do with that."

"Why do you think that? It could've been some random street thug that saw an opportunity to rob a guy. This is New York City ya know. I'm just lucky it wasn't me sitting there," I replied.

"I think you know better than that Leo, may I call you Leo?" She continued without waiting for an answer, "First, he wasn't robbed. Second, because of the way he was killed. Two shots to the chest, one to the head at point blank range, right? That's the calling card of the mobs' most famous assassin; the Ghost."

11

I laughed out loud when I heard her say that. I couldn't help myself.

"The Ghost?" I repeated. I must've hurt her feelings or embarrassed her because she blushed bright red and looked down at the ground for a second before she turned her attention back to me.

"What's so funny," she demanded.

"The Ghost," I replied after I stopped laughing, "Who calls him that? You're pullin' my leg right. I've never heard of the Ghost. I may not keep up with the who's who of the high and mighty around here, but I've never heard of a mob hit man called the Ghost."

She gave me a cold, hard look. "You haven't heard of the Ghost *yet*, because, as I stated earlier, had you been listening, my editor hasn't given me the green light on my story. The Ghost is what I named this assassin because everyone knows about him, but nobody has ever seen him. He's in and out as if he hadn't ever been there. Like a ghost," she countered.

"Whoa, whoa, whoa, let's back up. What's that mean exactly? You haven't been given the green light?" I asked.

"It means just that," she stated flatly. "I'm still trying to break a big story, so my boss will know I'm a serious investigative journalist. Look, I graduated State with a degree in journalism and I'll have you know I was the top in my class."

"You went to college?" I asked perhaps a bit too incredulously.

"Yes, of course. Why? Is it so hard to believe?" She stared me down as if daring me to lip off.

I looked away for a moment not knowing exactly what to say.

"It's not that it's hard to believe. It's just I've never known anyone that went to college before, that's all," I replied somewhat apologetically.

"Oh," she paused briefly before continuing. "Yes, I went. I worked hard and received my bachelor's degree in just three years. I've been told I'm an over-achiever," she replied with a look of indignation on her face that slowly softened into a big smile. "I do tend to come off a little…haughty now and then I suppose."

"Oh, you mean snooty?" I quipped. When I saw a sudden look of shock come over her face followed by that pretty smile when she realized I was teasing her, I couldn't help but laugh.

She joined me for a moment of levity. The dimples in her cheeks were deep when she laughed, and her eyes sparkled even more. She had my interest.

"Well, I think that's great. I thought about going once, but it just wasn't my thing. I wanted to see what the world had to offer, ya know?"

The conversation turned a little lighter as we talked a little more about her background. The gravity of the moment could wait a few minutes while we chatted. When the subject of the murder investigation came back around, she sighed deeply.

"I know he's out there and he works for the mob doing their dirty work for 'em. That's who killed the Commissioner at the diner. I just know it. I just can't prove it. Not yet anyway." She looked back down at her lap. Her voice softened, "I'm onto a big story here, but I've hit a dead end," she said as she looked back up at me with a sad, pitiful look on her face.

When I didn't say anything, she hung her shoulders a bit more and turned her attention back to her hands. I watched her silently, giving her a chance to collect her thoughts. The breeze kicked up and blew one of her yellow curls across her face. She reached up with her long delicate fingers and manicured nails, moved it away, and turned to look at me. "Right now, I'm supposed to be doing a story on the Kennels of America Dog Show. Just one of the ridiculous assignments my boss gave me, which is not befitting of a serious newspaper woman, especially an investigative reporter. I'm better than half the reporters on staff, and I shouldn't have to cover a story about some stupid hounds," she said with evident disdain in her voice.

I took the moment as my cue to apologize for laughing. "Hey look, I'm sorry. About laughing. I shouldn't have done that. I know you're just doing your job."

"That's okay. I don't blame you. It all sounds crazy, I know."

She looked at me, pouting, just begging for me to give in and tell her everything she wanted to know; only I was no dummy. I wasn't getting caught up in her little web. A gal like this could sweep most guys away with those gorgeous blue eyes and strawberry red lips - but not this guy. I was one step ahead of her on that little game.

"Nah, you don't sound crazy. This is a big city, and there are a lot of bad people in it. People that will do just about anything and not even blink an eye," I said.

I felt bad that I couldn't help her, but if I told her anything at all it could get me killed, it could get us both killed. Nah, I wasn't going to say anything about what happened. I was as nervous as a long-tailed cat in a room full of rocking chairs just talking about it. If Briana found out I was talking to a newspaper reporter, it could be all over for me. But, I gotta tell ya. I think I was willing to take that chance. Lexi was beautiful, and I liked her. I liked being around her. She smelled great, and when she touched me, I felt something stir inside. Maybe it was because she was the only girl that ever talked to me for longer than the time it takes to order a burger.

"I understand what you're saying. Believe me, I do. But, do you believe you would be safe if you were to expose this…Ghost?" I asked.

"Of course, they wouldn't dare come after a reporter. There must be hundreds of newspapers that would be digging into the murder of one of their own, and the mob wouldn't risk it," she replied.

"I suppose so," I admitted. "But, if this hitman, the Ghost as you call him, is so invisible, what makes you think that he couldn't take you out and no one would ever be the wiser? Sure, it's riskier on his part, but still worth it to protect his identity. Besides, assassins only kill for money."

"That's it!" Lexi exclaimed, as she excitedly turned to me and grabbed my arm. "I've been going about this wrong. I don't need to focus on the killer; I need to find out who ordered the hit finding the money trail! You're a genius, a pure genius!" She leaned over, threw her arms around my neck and kissed me on the cheek.

Now, I felt queasy. I wasn't so sure about what I was supposed to do to help her, but I knew I was going to. It could get me killed in the process, but I was thinking it may be worth it.

***

When I left the park, I didn't want to go straight home, and since I had the evening off, I wandered down the street to the library. I grabbed a book off the shelf and pretended to read it in a seat in one of the comfortable chairs near the back. I couldn't quit thinking about Lexi. The way the wind blew her hair across her face and the way she reached up and pulled it away and the bright, blue eyes hiding behind it sparkling when she smiled - Yeah, I guess I kinda had a thing for her. Who could blame a guy? She was young, beautiful, smart, exciting and - would never see me other than just some guy that works in a diner slinging hash and smelling of grease and pickles. Insert heavy sigh here. I don't usually feel sorry for myself, but right now I wished I had been born to a different status instead of the lousy lot in life I'd been dealt. I know. Too much negative self-talk ain't gonna get me nowhere. I'll snap out of it.

I had agreed to meet her at the park again on Friday. That's typically a busy day at the diner, but I should still be able to make it to the park by 2 p.m. even if the lunch crowd kept us hammered. Lexi said she had to cover her other assignments for her editor and it would be at least a couple of days before she could figure out where to go next with her investigation.

I stayed at the library for a couple of hours before my growling stomach told me it was time to find something to eat. I put my book down, but changed my mind, and picked it up again. It was actually pretty good and kept me interested. That's odd for me, so I decided to check it out. I've been in this library a hundred times, but I hadn't ever checked anything out. The lady asked me for my library card, and when I told her I didn't have one, she handed me a paper to fill out and asked for a copy of my driver's license. I don't have one, but she told me my state ID is fine. She made a copy of it and took my photo. A few minutes later she produced a small plastic card with my picture on it and told me I was now able to check out several items at a time. I just wanted the one book, so she swiped my card and the book and told me I was all set. The book was due back in seven days because it's a best-seller and has a high demand but proceeded to tell me I can check it back out two more times when I bring it back. Why not just let me check it out now for twenty-one days? Policies can be dumb sometimes.

"You also have access to the Wi-Fi, and you can use the computers for up to an hour at a time," she said.

"Thank you, ma'am, but I just want to read the book for now."

I waited for her to hand the book back to me. I stuffed it down into my backpack and bolted for the door. Time to find some chow! I knew I didn't have any food back at my apartment other than a bag of chips and maybe some ketchup so I walked across the street and wandered around until I found an interesting little Chinese restaurant with a bright green awning called the Shanghai Express, and I stumbled in. I'd been there a couple of times before so I didn't feel too out of place. I liked Chinese food and down here in this part of town, that's mostly what you will find. I'd not lived here long, but I was learning my way around. I liked this part of town. There are so many people down here with lots of cars going by and trucks stopping in the middle of the street to unload supplies, different languages being spoken, it's exciting and feeds my need to be around a lot of people while at the same time, completely invisible.

Even though it was early in the afternoon, I still had to wait a bit to get a seat. The place is small, and the seating is tight, but it's good. When I finally get seated, I placed my order; soup dumplings, spicy shredded beef with hot peppers and Shanghai noodles. Sure, it's a little pricey, especially for me, but every now and again, I like to splurge.

After I finished dinner and left the restaurant, I walked toward the bus stop. I'd not had a lot of sleep lately, and I wanted to get to bed early. I figured the next day would be a busy day at the diner. I walked to the nearest bus stop and caught the Q home. When I got off the bus an hour later, traffic was a madhouse, so I cinched my backpack on my shoulders, waited for a gap in the cars and made a dash across the street. Just when I thought I was clear, a car screeched to a stop almost hitting me. I spun around, and my hands slammed down on the hood out of sheer reflexes. My heart pounded in my eardrums when I came face to face with a man sitting in a black Mercedes. He wore sunglasses so I couldn't see his eyes, but I could tell he was highly perturbed; possibly because the jackass laid into the horn and had a disgusted look on his face.

I stepped back and said, sorry, and scurried across the street. Once I was safely across, I turned to look back, and I could just make out the license plate. *CAMGRP7!*

12

The man with the scar across his face and the ugly sneer inched his way toward me with a huge knife in his hand. My back was against the wall in a dark alley, I had nowhere else to run. I would die here, and no one would ever miss me. *I don't have any friends or family*, I kept thinking. Suddenly, Lexi was there. She wore a long trench coat and was holding an umbrella. It wasn't raining so I had no idea why she had it open.

    Bright lights suddenly pierced the darkness. They're coming from a car turning in and lighting up the entire alley. The man with the sneer never looked away; he just kept inching his way toward me. I frantically looked around, searching, but there's nothing to fight back with, not even a loose brick or rock lying around. As he drew closer, I kicked at him trying to get him to drop the knife. Bright blue lights began flashing on top of the car, and the siren wailed and echoed off the brick walls and concrete streets. It was so loud that I had to hold my hands over my ears while I kept kicking. She laughed harder now as it began to rain. Where did that come from and why is he trying to kill me? I didn't have any money so it wouldn't do him any good to kill me. My feet slipped on the slick, wet pavement and I fell hard. All I could hear was a loud buzzing like Mr. Ugly now had a chainsaw instead of a knife!

I awakened in a pool of sweat to the incessant buzzing of my alarm clock. 5:31 a.m.! Whew! I thought for sure I was a goner. I don't usually have nightmares, but this one sure got me jumpy. I guess I must've been kicking in my sleep because the blanket was now lying on the floor at the end of my bed. I reached over and turned off the alarm and laid back a moment while I let the cobwebs in my head fade away.

The soft yellow glow of the lamp allowed me to see my way to the bathroom where I took a quick, hot shower. Got dressed, grabbed my backpack and headed to the bus stop. It was a quiet morning, and the breeze felt good on my face which also helped to keep me awake. When I got home yesterday, I read my new library book all evening and turned in early. I had not been getting much sleep lately, so it was nice. Well, it was, until the nightmare came. I shuddered at the thought, then I smiled. I smiled because even though it was a nightmare, I still had a chance to see Lexi.

The bus pulled up to a hissing stop, and I jumped on, scanned my pass and took a seat beside an elderly lady. The ride to the diner was a good twenty minutes, so I listened to some music to pass the time. The lady beside me indicated she needed up and I watched her climb off at the next stop. I slid over to the window and watched the people pass by when the bus took off again. I saw a black car pass by, it wasn't a Mercedes, but it reminded me of the one I've been seeing. Maybe it was nothing more than sheer coincidence, but something inside me told me otherwise. That was the second time I'd seen it. Scratch that. It was the third time I've seen it. I forgot about the second time that first night. Two times could be a coincidence, but three times? This guy was following me, but why? I was a little worried.

"Where have you been?" Helen asked when I walked into the diner ten minutes late.

"Sorry, the bus was late. I had to hoof it the last couple of blocks." I answered her in my best, don't bother me' voice.

"Sorry I asked," she said sarcastically.

I traipsed back to the kitchen, put my stuff up and tied my apron on. Time to light the fires and kick the tires! I heard that in a movie once.

Sam walked in from the back door, breezed right past me without an utterance, put her things away and scurried to the floor. I could hear Helen talking to her, but I tuned them out. I had more important things to do than listening to a couple of cats screeching around about an old tom.

9 a.m. rolled around, and like clockwork, Greely came waltzing in through the back door.

"Morning Leonard, how's the prodigal?" he said in an almost cheerful manner.

"Morning Mr. Greely."

I had no idea what a prodigal was so I had no idea how else I was supposed to respond.

"Why so glum? It's going to be a great day."

"Not glum, just haven't been getting much sleep lately, ya know?"

He looked at me a moment before turning to the office. "I know what you mean, son," he said over his shoulder. "Try not to think about it too much. Things happen in this world that we'll never understand."

I stood there staring at the big man as he walked to his office. I think that was the first time I'd ever heard him say anything to me that wasn't barking. Could he be getting soft? Nah, not Greely! This is a guy that yells at his eighty-year-old mother for not using enough oil in the knish. I turned back to my work to get my grill cranked up. Not long after, I heard the familiar ring of the front door jingle bells. This day was just starting, and I felt like I had already been up for hours. In reality, I had been up for hours.

***

I worked all day, even through lunch because we were so busy. I don't mind because I was looking forward to seeing Lexi again tomorrow and it helped make the day go by faster. It was 10 p.m. when we finally locked up for the night. When I say we, what I mean is me, Marvin and Helen, because Greely and Sam left earlier in the evening. Greely said his feet were hurting and Sam, well, who knows what her excuse was.

"Good night my young apprentice," Marvin said as he trudged away down the street. "Good night Helen."

"Night Marv, night Leonard," Helen said.

Her no-account boyfriend was waiting for her in a small, gray hoopty in front of the diner. I watched her open the door, and an empty water bottle fell out onto the street and bounced away. She didn't bother to pick it up, just slammed the door shut and they sped away from the curb. People are simply exhausting sometimes. I walked over and picked it up and threw it in a trash dumpster on my way to the bus stop. I slung my backpack up on my shoulder and scurried along. Lightning strikes in the distance lit up the night sky, and I heard thunder only a few seconds later that startled me. *Great!* Just perfect. I took off running for the shelter of the bus stop as the rain began to pour.

I crossed the street and made my way down the block. The rain was coming down in sheets, and the thunder and lightning were even more intense. I never noticed the red sedan following me until the driver suddenly pulled over to the curb in front of me and rolled down his window.

"Get in kid, I'll give you a ride home," the driver yelled.

When I bent down and looked inside, I saw it was the detective from the other night, and I didn't think this day could get any worse. Oh well, at least it should be a dry ride home, so I climbed in and rolled the window up.

"Thanks, wish you would've come along about five minutes ago," I tried to joke.

"Yeah, bad night to be out," he said as if I have a choice. "I meant to come by the diner earlier to talk to you, but I got busy."

"Talk to me?" I asked. "Why so? I already told you everything I know," I replied using my most convincing voice. "Look, Detective O'Conner, I didn't see nothin', I was in the kitchen and didn't see nothin' at all. Honest."

I must've gotten a little shaky because he stopped me before I could say anything else.

"Calm down kid, I believe ya," he said without taking his eyes off the road. "But, sometimes people see things they don't remember at the time. It may not seem relevant at the time, so they forget about it, or it just doesn't register until later."

I could see where this was going. This guy was grilling me for more intel, and I couldn't afford to slip up. I'm no dummy. I knew how these things work. For all I knew, he could be working for the mob and just making sure I wasn't squealing like a pig. No pun intended, of course.

"I wished I could help you, I do, but I told ya everything I know."

"That's okay kid, don't worry about it. I'm sure whoever killed the Commissioner knows you're not a liability because you didn't see them do it. I mean, if you had seen who did it, it would only be a matter of time before they figured out that you're better off dead than to have to worry about you rattin' em out. So, I'm sure you're safe."

Aren't you just a barrel of monkeys, I thought. My heart pounded like it was ready to jump straight out of my throat. I knew right now that my best play was my first play. Say nothing! Briana Fitzgerald saw me see her just before she offed the guy, and I was still alive. That's got to count for something, right? I couldn't imagine why she pulled the trigger, but she did, and if she was the stone-cold killer that she appeared to be, she could've killed me a hundred times by now, but hasn't.

He continued, "But, if you had seen something, anything at all, and you were to come forward with that information, then I could help protect you. You understand, right?"

"Yeah, umm, yes sir," I stammered out of my haze, "I'll be sure to call."

"Here's your stop." He pulled the car over to the curb just as a bright white lightning bolt flashed across the parking lot of my building.

"Thanks for the lift," I said. I opened the door and bolted for my apartment, unlocked my door and stumbled inside soaked to the bone. When I turned back to lock the deadbolt, I suddenly realized I never had to give the detective directions to my building.

13

After dropping Leonard off, the detective drove to the water treatment plant on Berrian Boulevard. The rain was heavy, and the visibility was poor, but he had been here once before and knew where he was going. Frank O'Conner was a hard-nosed detective for the New York City Police Department. He was tough as nails and didn't mind stepping on toes to get answers, even if it meant ruffling feathers on both sides of the law. He could be trusted to do the right thing and prided himself on the fact he couldn't be bought off. A third-generation cop, he was resolute when it came to closing cases, and he was even more so in this one.

The detective pulled into the open warehouse door, shut the lights off on his car and killed the engine. After about five minutes, a car on the other end of the building flashed the headlights three times which was his signal that all was safe and he could approach. He opened the door, stepped out and began walking slowing to meet the man in the middle. Each of his footsteps on the smooth, hard concrete reverberated throughout the building. Even though he had met this informant many times, he kept his hand on his gun anyway. He was not about to let his guard down.

"What have you got for me, Ernie?" Frank asked.

The man he was meeting stood three inches taller than Frank though much thinner. The man pulled his right hand out of his pocket and ran it through his dark hair, smoothing it back. He had an intense stare with dark, piercing eyes and the short goatee he sported gave him the look of the proverbial rogue.

"What? No, how ya doin' Ernie? How's the wife and kids, Ernie?" the man asked sarcastically as he gestured widely with his arms.

"I don't have time for pleasantries so cut the crap," Frank said tersely.

"You got a little…sumpin, sumpin for me?"

Frank reached out and handed the man a hundred-dollar bill.

"Better be worth it."

"Okay, here's what I know. It seems your dead guy made a deal with the devil. Ever heard of the Camden Group?" Ernie asked.

"I've heard of 'em, real estate management or something right? How are they tied to Wood?"

"That's the million-dollar question. Word on the street is, Wood was stonewalling a land deal that would've made Camden millions. No amount of bribe could sway the commissioner's vote, but days after his death, the land deal miraculously goes through," Ernie said with a smirk. "Just connect the dots, detective, and you'll find your killer. Just be careful, big money has lots of power."

Frank got all the information he could from his informant and exited the empty warehouse. He thought about the case while turning onto the city street. He would have to do some digging on this Camden Group and see what he could come up with. *I know the kid seen something that night, but what? Who else had a motive to kill the commissioner besides Camden?* Sometimes things paid off, and sometimes they didn't. This lead could be one of those, but he just couldn't be sure about it. He had other informants, but none of them, other than Ernie, were willing to talk, so this was his first big break in the case. Tomorrow he would find out more about this

Camden Group and go over to their offices and ruffle some feathers until somebody got spooked enough to talk.

14

I didn't sweat the detective. I wasn't scared of him in the least. I haven't done anything wrong, and he can't prove I saw anything. Besides, I didn't believe he was going to kill me and dump my body in some back alley, but Briana Fitzgerald, on the other hand, seemed cold-blooded enough to do just that. If she could off a guy in a diner and never blink twice, it wouldn't be nothin' for somebody like that to get rid of me and not give it another thought. I had more to fear from her than the cops.

After I went inside, I stripped down, turned on the shower as hot as I could stand it, jumped in and out, and then headed straight to bed. I didn't give Detective O'Conner another thought.

When I woke up the next morning, it was still raining so I grabbed an extra pair of shoes and socks and crammed them into my backpack. I knew my feet were going to get soaked, so once I got to the diner, I could change into some dry ones. I had an old raincoat in the closet, so I grabbed it and a small, black umbrella and headed for the bus stop. The whole time I was getting ready, I was thinking about Lexi. I couldn't seem to get my mind off her.

***

Finally! I thought. I was beginning to think my shift would never end! It was Friday which meant payday, but it also meant I was heading to the library to meet up with Lexi. I left the diner before Greely could give me an excuse not to. I had to work the evening shift, so he knew I'd be back anyway. I hit the door running, but forgot it was still raining. I ran back inside, grabbed my raincoat and umbrella and tried again.

I arrived at the library thirty minutes later and headed inside. She was already waiting for me when I arrived.

"Where have you been," she whispered excitedly and albeit, a little loudly. I wasn't sure she had a good grasp of the subtleties of a whisper.

"The bus was crowded, lots of people trying to get off and on at the same time. Jams up the system," I answered while dripping on the carpet. "Public transportation isn't something a person can control ya know?"

"Well never mind about that, I've got something to show you," she said as she grabbed my arm and led me to a table in the back.

I didn't mind being dragged around by her. Like I've said before, she was pretty amazing. Today she was wearing an orange jacket, gray pants, and a cream-colored blouse. She was a few inches shorter than me with loafers on instead of heels. I almost didn't recognize her until I saw her big smile. Nope, can't miss that smile and those blue eyes shining like that. I noticed she had a raincoat and rubber boots sitting beside her umbrella under the table. She had newspapers and printed sheets of information laying all over it.

"I've been here all morning, going through this and look what I came across," she said while pointing at one piece of paper lying on the table. I glanced at the top of it.

COMMISSION AGENDA
March 17 @ 6pm

"Okay, great. What am I looking at?" I asked.

She looked at me like I'm some kind of idiot, which may very well be the case. I'll neither deny nor confirm that, thank you very much.

"This is the Commissioner's agenda from the council meeting two months ago. Look at item number seven in particular. It's buried among several consent items and committee meeting nonsense. Item seven is set for discussion and possible action to be taken on a land purchase," she explained with a look of satisfaction on her face like she just discovered gold or something.

"Okay, you got me. Why is it important?"

"Because," she began, pulling out another piece of paper with *'Council Meeting Minutes'* written at the top and laid it on the table. "This item has been on the council's agenda now for the last five months, but it's been tabled every single time, and now, suddenly, it gets passed in a special meeting, which also happens to be just a few nights after Commissioner Wood was murdered!" she exclaimed, with a finger jab on the paper now lying on the table. "Why would they call a special meeting for the one item when the regular meeting is just a few weeks away?"

I read through the items she pointed out, and when I finished, I was even more confused. "So, let me see if I follow. A land deal of some kind has been on the council agenda for several months, yet keeps getting tabled for some unknown reason. Commissioner Wood is murdered. Two days later, the land deal is passed in a special meeting. You're right, case solved. We're done here. You have cracked the case," I lipped off.

"Don't be flippant, Leo. Don't you see the connection?"

"No, not really," I answered truthfully.

She shuffled through the stack of papers until she found the one she was looking for. "Okay, look here. In the minutes from prior meetings, it has more information about the land deal. Apparently, a company called the Camden Group has a contract with a local landowner to purchase the property. The deal is contingent upon the council rezoning it for commercial use and approving the sale." She pointed at the paper, "But, there isn't anything in the minutes as to why it's being tabled all this time."

"Rezoning?" I asked.

"Yes, I assume it's currently zoned for residential use and this Camden Group wants to develop commercial businesses with it," she explained.

"Where did you get all of this stuff?" I asked while skimming through it.

"The commission is a public body which means the open records act applies to them, and as a newspaper reporter, I can ask to see any of it. By law, they must provide me a copy of everything. I have the agendas, notes and minutes from the commissioner's meetings for the entire last year."

"Oh, I see. I think I follow what you're saying, but that's still not proof anyone ordered a hit on the Commissioner," I replied. "We need to find out more about this land deal and that company."

"I agree, but how? I think whoever ordered the hit could have been someone on the inside of this Camden Group because they clearly have a motive. So, what's our next move?" she mused.

I looked around the room for a minute until my gaze landed on one of the computers. "Let's see what we can dig up on this Camden Group. Maybe we can find something that'll help."

Lexi followed my eyes and quickly put the papers away in the black bag she was carrying and moved over to one of the computers with me in tow. The computers required an access number, so we had to stop at the desk attendant and sign in. After getting a password for access, we both sat down with her at the keyboard and typed in the name, Camden Group. Dozens of articles came up, so we decided to split up. I made my way over to another console and typed in my first search query. I'm not great on a computer as I've had limited access to them in my years, but I knew how to use Google. An hour later we got back together to compare notes.

We learned Camden Group, Incorporated or CGI, is a real estate development firm owned by Lucas Bishop Camden. They're a large company with real estate all over the globe. CGI controls millions in assets ranging from high rises and apartments to luxury residential areas, business parks, and golf courses.

Lexi read through several articles. "On the surface, they look clean as a whistle, everything they do in the public's eye is all about environmental stewardship and making developments greener and environmentally friendly, but when you dig a bit deeper, just under the surface anyway, it seems they'll do whatever it takes to make things happen. Reading between the lines, it's things like bribes of government and city officials to extortion."

"And possibly even murder?" I asked.

"I'm sure of it," she said. "I've found lots of complaints from towns all over where they've strong-armed landowners and bullied city officials into allowing their developments. They've held towns hostage by pitting residents against public officials. They've developed office parks and high-income residential home sites in areas that have progressively fought against the development of what little open spaces they have left."

"Get this," I whispered, "I read one article where they built three new office buildings in a town nearby. The townspeople were upset because the city approved of the development without so much as a public meeting to discuss the use of the land. It seems the parks commission had wanted the land for more baseball and soccer fields, but the city wouldn't approve of the expenditures. They said they didn't have it in the budget, but afterward, Camden comes in, buys the land in question and builds them a park, an office park! Swell bunch this Camden Group is."

"There are lots of examples of that kind of business," she said. "How can a public official tell a company 'no' when they offer them more tax dollars for the town to provide more services for the residents? The residents may want to keep the open space with all the trees and water, but when it comes down to raising taxes, nobody wants that."

"They sound like bad news. Hey, you mentioned you think the assassin may be working for the mob and that he has killed before, right?" I asked.

"Yes, a couple of years ago a city official in Jersey was killed the same way, two shots to the chest and one in the head at point-blank range. Just a year earlier a local businessman was killed the same way. Oh! I see where you're going with this," she suddenly exclaimed with a huge smile. "That may be the link! If we can tie the murders to this Camden Group?"

"Exactly," I agreed, "But we still need proof."

I looked up in time to see one of the librarians approaching.

"Excuse me. You will need to relinquish the computer now. Lots of people need to use them, and we have a strict policy I'm afraid. I'm sorry, but only one hour per user, please. If there weren't others waiting," she trailed off apologetically.

Great! The 'man' trying to cut my groove and keep me down again, I thought.

"So where do we go from here," I asked, as we signed out of the computers and returned to the table.

Lexi stopped to dig in her bag and pulled out a small pad and pen. "I guess I should've brought my laptop, but it's so heavy. This bag is bad enough without having to lug that thing around too. I like to stay light on my feet. We seem to have more questions than answers. How can we tie the Camden Group to the other murders? Also, we need to find out more about this land deal? Who owns it, what's on it, why are they selling it, why is CGI buying it? Just so many questions," she said with a perplexed look on her face.

"Where can we access land records?" I asked.

"We can do that right here too," she said, before suddenly remembering we've been kicked off the computers for the day.

"Do you have a smartphone?"

"Are you kidding me? I don't even have a dumb one," I said a little too loudly.

"Shhhhhhh," a nearby librarian scolded me with a finger over her lips.

I gave her the *I'm sorry* look and continued in a whisper, "You don't have one? I thought for sure a reporter like you would carry one of those things."

"Of course, I do. Unfortunately, I forgot it at the office." She added, "You should have a cell phone."

"Guess I just never needed one. I'll add it to the list. So, what do we do now?" I asked.

She began reshuffling all the papers in her bag, slipped off her shoes in favor of the rubber boots and put on her raincoat.

"We find something to eat. Come on, I'm hungry. My blood sugar is low," she said, grabbing my arm and leading me to the door.

It was still raining when we left the library. Not hard, but enough to get soaked to the bone in no time. Lexi opened her umbrella and invited me under it with her. I gotta tell ya, I was surprised. She didn't seem to mind the smell of the grill I wear as cologne. I know I didn't mind being this close to her. Arm in arm we hustled across the street, careful to stay under the storefront awnings as much as we could and walk down to the Main Street Food Court. She ordered something I couldn't pronounce, and I found a chicken and rice dish that was a little spicy, but good.

"I'm going to have to get back to work soon. I have to close tonight," I said as I munched on my de-feathered fowl.

"And I've got to get back to the office. How about we meet at the library again tomorrow? What time can you be here?" She asked.

"It may be busy at the diner tomorrow so it may be about the same time as today," I replied.

Since Greely's diner is located downtown, we mostly cater to the offices nearby. Corporate America works Monday through Friday, so the weekends are steady with tourists and shoppers.

"Great!" she said. "I can be here too."

15

I left the food court, found the nearest bus stop and grabbed a ride to the diner. My shift didn't start for another half hour, so I went in through the front door. I guess I was lost in thought because the jingle bells surprised me when I opened the door. I kept thinking about Lexi and how pretty she looked with her hair up. I'd only seen her a few times now, but she was getting stuck in my head a lot here lately. That couldn't be a good thing.

"What are you doing here so early?" Helen asked when I walked in.

"I missed your good humor and pleasant company, so I thought I'd come in early and get an earful of it," I lipped off.

"Okay Mr. Wise Crack, keep it up, and you'll have a mighty long day," she said as she wiped down a table.

I noticed there were only a few customers in the place, so I grabbed a seat at an empty table and picked up this morning's paper that was lying on top. I noticed another headline about the commissioner, but there was nothing new, so I flipped through the pages until one, interestingly enough, caught my eye.

CGI Applies for Zoning Variances

It's a small article buried in the middle of the paper that doesn't give much detail, but the title is what caught my eye. *What are these zoning variances that CGI is applying for,* I wondered? *Could it have anything to do with this land deal and could it be related to the dead commissioner?*

"Leo, did you forget something?"

It was Greely hovering over me. I never noticed him walk up, not that he's a ninja or something. He handed me an envelope, and I realized it was my paycheck. Most times, I take it straight to the bank after my shift on Friday's. I took a quick glance at it before folding it and put it in my pocket. I never doubt Greely's accounting, but the IRS? That one always makes me wonder. It seems like Uncle Sam can never get enough of my money.

"Thanks," I replied. Under my breath I muttered, "Someday I may actually make enough to pay my rent," in a somewhat sarcastic tone.

"What's that?" he asked.

"Just said I appreciate it," I replied as he waddled back to his office.

He was in a swell mood today. I hoped he'd stay back there for a while. His office is so tiny that he barely has room to get his carcass behind the desk. I'm sure at one time he could fit into the chair, but now it's like trying to catch a basketball with a catcher's mitt. It just doesn't work. He'd be in there doing whatever it is he did for the next hour, and then he would leave, but not before barking out a few final directives. He plays poker every Friday night at seven. Nothing too big, but I think it's about the only thing he enjoys, plus he gets to smoke his cigars all night.

Since there wasn't but a few customers, I had plenty of time to clean the kitchen and be ready for the evening dinner crowd; if, by chance, we had one. Greely's Po Boy's is a unique eatery in the area. Down here, you will find mostly Chinese and Korean restaurants, so we tend to get an eclectic crowd of business professionals throughout the day and a lot of tourists during the weekend craving a typical fare. I headed back to the kitchen, grabbed my apron off the nail and slipped it on.

"How's my young apprentice?" Marvin asked as I began tying the strings around my waist.

"I'm right as the rain, Marvin. How was the lunch crowd?"

"Busy, busy. Slowed down 'bout two though," he said. "I just gotta finish restocking and I'm gone'uh git. I'm tarred today. My ol' back's been stiff, and this rain has got my knees uh' hurtin."

"I wished it would stop raining. I'm starting to feel waterlogged."

I laughed. I knew he was complaining, fishing, to get me to offer to do the restocking for him, but I wasn't going to bite today.

"Did you see the schedule," he finally asked, though, I could tell it wasn't a question.

I walked over to the board and saw Greely had me off tomorrow. Woohoo! A Saturday off! Was a zombie apocalypse coming or what? Oh well, it didn't matter, all I knew was whenever I closed tonight, I wouldn't be seen back here again until Sunday morning, and that thrilled me to no end. Not sure why exactly. It's not like I had anything else to do. I don't have any friends I hang out with, and I don't belong to the country club, that's for sure.

Soon, both Marvin and Greely left for the day giving me the kitchen all to myself. Helen had a few orders, so I got busy on those, and as I stood at the grill, I heard the back-door open. It was the delivery guy pushing a two-wheeler with several boxes on it. He's supposed to come in the mornings, so this is a bit out of character.

When he handed me the bill of lading, I asked him about it.

"Truck had problems all day; I won't get home 'til midnight, piece of junk!" he complained, while he dragged the boxes into the walk-in freezer.

When the massive door opened, a blast of cold air hit me, and my whole body shivered. I had been standing over the grill sweating for a while, so I guess I was used to the heat. The cold air was a shock to my system. I laughed out loud and turned to walk back to the grill and ran smack into Helen.

"Hey, watch where you're going numbnuts."

"Sorry," I replied. I didn't want a confrontation with Helen, so I just kept cleaning and straightening up my work area.

Helen picked up the paperwork I had just put down, looked it over and signed it for the driver when he came out of the freezer. He gave her a copy, but she handed it back to me and followed him outside. That was a bit strange, I'll admit, but who knew about this woman? She's most likely on the prowl for another sugar daddy.

"Watch the front for me," she said.

Ten minutes later she walked back in smelling like an ashtray. It never bothered me before, the smell that is, until recently.

16

The crowd's applause was enormous for opening night. Rehearsals had been brutal for cast and crew alike, but they had worked extremely hard to be the best they could, and tonight it paid off. The play was sold out, and even the critics couldn't argue the standing ovation that lingered for minutes for the actors. But the biggest applause lasted several minutes for Briana Fitzgerald, the star of the musical hit. The crowd loved her performance and showered her with hundreds of long-stemmed red roses.

When she left the stage some ten minutes after the last curtain call, she hustled straight to her dressing room exhausted yet elated. She loved the euphoric feeling after each performance when the crowd responded as it did this night. She slipped inside and began undressing when a knock came at the door. She hastily pulled on a green silk robe, more out of habit than propriety, allowing it to drape low over her shoulders and opened the door. When she saw who it was, she leaned against the jamb and held the door open leaving her robe to hang open, exposing her naked body.

With her long, beautiful red hair with large, soft curls, bright, emerald-green eyes and perfectly curvaceous figure she seemed delicate, even fragile, at first glance, yet possessed an unsuspecting strength upon closer examination. She was more than fit, and her muscle tone was a testament to her daily workout and dance regimen. She was getting older, but she lied about her age, as was any woman's prerogative, and was never questioned.

Her visitor standing before her was a good six inches taller than she was and never bothered to look at her naked body as she stood in the doorway. After a brief silence, Briana pushed the door open and stepped aside as a nonverbal cue inviting the visitor inside. She pulled her robe around her and tied it.

"Come on in," she relented, closing the door behind her visitor, and locking it.

"You've met with the boy?" the man asked.

"Yes, I did. What's it to you?" Briana answered. She sat down in front of her dressing mirror and began removing her stage makeup. The bright glow of the lights around the mirror was more than adequate to see the lines on her face appear as the cosmetics gave way to the cleanser.

"You realize this is a dangerous game you're playing," his arms were folded tight.

Briana spun about in her chair to face the man. "You realize what I do is none of your business." She softened, "But yes, I know. I'll be careful." She turned back to her vanity and continued removing the makeup as the man unlocked the door, slipped out and shut it behind him. When the door closed, she got up and locked it behind him. She was angry he had come. That was never part of the deal. He was never supposed to - In a sudden fit of emotion, she raked everything off her vanity into the floor with a pent-up growl. When she noticed her image in the mirror, she leaned down with her hands resting on the side of the vanity and stared intently at her half-clean, half-made up face. She laughed.

17

The bus ride home was excruciating. The driver was new, and he stopped at every stop on the route regardless if anyone was waiting or not. At this hour, no one is ever waiting, but he still stopped, opened the doors and just sat for a few minutes each time - and waited. Waiting for whom exactly, I have no idea, but we waited just the same. I usually don't get impatient, but tonight I just wanted to get home.

I saw my stop coming up, so I gathered my stuff and got ready to move. When we finally arrived, I baled off, jogged across the street and made my way down the block. The rain had finally stopped, but there was standing water everywhere so I dodged puddles the best I could along the way. The street was quiet, and I didn't see anyone as I entered my building and headed upstairs. One of the lights in the hallway on my floor was out which made it a bit spooky, not unusual. I turned the key and stepped into my cheerful apartment. Setting my backpack down on the kitchen countertop, I opened the fridge and grabbed a can of Dr. Pepper and popped the top. That was about all that was in it too, I might add. I know, depressing.

"Nice apartment, Leonard," a voice said from out of the darkness behind me.

I was surprised, shocked was more like it, by the voice behind me, and I freaked smooth out jumping clean out of my skin, and I sprayed Dr. Pepper out of my mouth and nose which caused my eyes to water. Not an enjoyable experience, I can attest. I spun around thinking I'm as good as dead, but I couldn't see anything. It took a moment for my eyes to adjust to the darkness as I had just been looking into the bright light of my fridge. I heard a female voice laughing softly.

"I'm sorry, I didn't mean to frighten you so, dear," the mysterious voice said with another slight laugh.

I strained my eyes to see into the living room, but it was somewhat difficult in my current state of Dr. Pepper sinus burn. I wiped the tears away, and I could finally begin to make out a shape of someone sitting in my chair. The voice, apparently a woman, sounded familiar, though, I still was a little uncertain as to who she was. I could smell a hint of perfume.

"It's okay, if I wanted to hurt you, I would have already. Sit," she ordered.

I closed the fridge door behind me and slowly walked into the living room just as Briana Fitzgerald switched on the lamp. I sat down on the sofa across from the chair where I could see her. In my mind, I was screaming, *RUN AWAY YOU IDIOT*, but I was too scared. I doubt I could trust my legs at this point. She looked straight at me, and the smile on her face suddenly turned to a hard, piercing look.

"What's going on?" I asked, looking around nervously. I knew she could see I was scared out of my wits. This whole thing had me worried to the point where I was turning prematurely gray.

"A little birdie tells me you had a meeting with a cute little newspaper reporter," Briana said.

Oh, so that was it. Now I understood. She must have thought I'd rat her out to the first pretty skirt that came by, but that wasn't my style. I studied Miss Fitzgerald a moment, desperately thinking of what to say next. She wore a tight, form-fitting red dress with a short skirt, black stockings, and black heels. The neckline was thin on the sides and plunged way down to reveal just enough of her breasts to make my imagination run wild, and the way she sat with her ankles crossed showed off her long, flawless dancer's legs. She apparently wanted people to notice her, and since I am a people, I noticed. I couldn't help but notice, even though I was about to die…possibly…I still noticed.

How in the hell did she know about my meeting with Lexi? I didn't think anyone knew about it. She couldn't have possibly seen me talking to her. Could she have? Oh God, I'm a dead man.

"Oh, Leonard, I see your little mind just churning away, trying to figure how I might have come by this information. Let me just say this. You can't keep anything from me. I know all your little secrets, I hear everything you say, even if you whisper it," she said, in that low, sultry voice of hers that was almost as if she was purring. "I know where you came from. I know who your parents are. I know your real last name. It's a good thing you changed it, by the way. Nice touch, Valentine, adds a bit of mystery I think, clever boy."

My mind was churning now, but to be honest, here, it wasn't about how she knew I had seen Lexi. Did she just say who my parents are? To be straight up, that statement made my head spin a bit. I was under the impression no one knew who my father was. I was also thinking about that red dress! That, in and of itself, is a major distraction for me but some things are more important, and right now my life is my biggest concern. To me, anyway.

"I didn't rat you out, I swear I didn't. I would never do that."

"Oh, I know. If you had, we wouldn't be having this conversation right now," she said with a gleam in her eyes.

I believed her when she said it. It's discombobulating to think such an incredibly beautiful woman, one that seemed so soft and delicate, could be so ruthless.

"Did you say you knew who my parents were?"

"All in due time, Leonard, all in due time."

"Then, then, why..." I stammered.

"Why am I here?" she finished my thought.

I nodded.

"Oh Leonard, I do like you so. I'm here because you're going to work for me," she said with an ever so slight smile on her face.

That didn't bother me at all. If you believe that, then I've got a bridge for sale.

"Don't look so frightened. It's not that bad. You and I are friends, and friends share secrets. Friends trust one another, right?" she purred again.

I couldn't help but be drawn to her. That sultry voice and the smoking hot body was enough to make my blood boil. She was a beautiful woman that is for sure, but one with dark secrets and I'm certain many more than I could ever imagine and probably several times worse than the one I already knew about. I mean, seriously, I watched this woman kill a man in cold blood and walk away with a smile and a wink. Ruthless doesn't begin to describe it. I'm not sure she has a soul to be honest. Beautiful, but dangerous.

"First thing tomorrow, I want you to get a cell phone and program a number that I'm about to give you into it. If you get a call from this number, answer it immediately. Do not even think about ignoring it. Do you understand?"

"Yes, ma'am, of course," I stammered. She told me the number. I didn't have to write it down - photographic memory honed from working at the diner, remember? I could still see orders and on what dates from months ago. It's crazy, but I'm okay with it. It helped me to survive.

"Enough with the formalities, it bores me. Call me Briana."

"Yes, ma' ... "I began but corrected myself. "Okay, Briana."

"That's a good boy. Don't look so frightened. Am I that scary? There are some dangerous elements in this city much scarier than I am. Those are the ones you should worry about. Especially, if they were to ever discover your secret. Besides, I may never have need of you, and you may never hear from me again, but more importantly, if you ever find yourself in a bind, and I mean a real bind, call that number."

Wait! My secret? What secret? Why should I be afraid of it? My mind was racing. She must've noticed my confusion again.

"If people were ever to find out who your father is - well, let me just say it wouldn't be a good day for you and even I couldn't protect you," she said.

Wait! What? Okay, bombshell! This lady seems to be full of 'em!

"Umm, what was that?" I asked her. "My mother is dead, and no one, not even she knew who my father was."

"I know all of the secrets in this city. I know every player in the game. The reason you don't know who your father is - was by design, and someday when the time is right, I'm sure you will understand. It was all for your protection, I suppose."

"Okay, wow! I'm confused," I replied, shaking my head like it was full of cobwebs.

"Of course, you are, but that's to be expected. Right now, all you need to know is, outside of this room, trust no one. Oh, I know all about your little quest with your newspaper girlfriend, and I applaud your efforts. Just keep one thing in mind, nothing, and I mean nothing, should ever point back at me. Just know if I'm ever implicated for any reason whatsoever – even Satan himself couldn't save you from me," she smiled wickedly at me with her eyes narrowing much like that of a reptile. "Now, I must be going. Remember, this visit never happened." She stood to leave at that last comment.

I got up from my perch on the couch, though not nearly as graceful. She leaned over and kissed me softly on my cheek. There wasn't much more conversation afterward even though I tried to ask more questions. She wouldn't have it.

Miss Briana Fitzgerald smoothed her dress and gracefully strolled out of my apartment affectively leaving me breathless. Not only because of what she had just said but because of the dress, she wore. The back of it plunged even lower than the front. Her thick red locks flowed effortlessly down over her shoulders and stopped midway down to reveal her lower back. Maybe I shouldn't have stood up, no pun intended. I closed the door behind her and locked it. This time I put the chain on too.

I must say, I was beyond shocked at all this information. Was she just telling me all of this to keep me quiet or so I'd stick around only to find out more about my father? Did she truly know who he was? Wait a minute – how could I be so stupid? She said she knows who my father *is*, meaning he was still alive? Oh okay, now I was confused. Why wouldn't he want me to know who he is and why would it be to protect me? Protect me from what? How could she know any of this anyway? The whole thing is kinda scary for me, but to be honest, the scary part that will keep me awake nights was I was supposed to work for her. Doing what, pray tell? That's the last thing I freaking need in my life. A job working for a stone-cold killer! I was not about to get into that racket. No way! Jeez, just when I thought it was all clear sailing ahead, I found myself smack dab in the middle of a storm. What else could go wrong?

18

I awakened the next morning with a start. The alarm didn't go off, but when I looked over at the clock, I suddenly remembered I didn't have to work today. I fell back under the security of my blanket and just laid there watching it tick down. I didn't get much sleep and what sleep I did get wasn't all that restful. When I finally rolled out of bed, I went straight to the bathroom and turned on the shower. It takes a few minutes for the water to get hot, but once it did, I jumped in and stood under it for what seemed like a half hour. In reality, it was a half hour! It felt good blasting down on me while I tried to knock the cobwebs out of my head and wake up. I'm a light sleeper and don't have any trouble getting up, but the last few nights had been long ones. Nothing like a good hot shower to get the juices flowing again.

The whole time that I was in the shower, I kept thinking about the visit from Briana. After she left, I went to bed and thought about everything she said. The lady scared me - Scared the hell out of me honestly, but at the same time, she seemed like a person that kept her word, no matter the circumstances. Funny as it sounds, I trusted her. She gave me explicit instructions, and I didn't have any problems with it. I kind of like living and breathing, to be honest. That's something I do well, breathe that is.

When I reached down and turned the water off, it continued to drip, but it would eventually stop when the building gets torn down. I reached out, grabbed a towel and dried my hair. I should get it cut soon. I got a little rest last night, and after the shower, I felt pretty good. I stepped out on to the mat to finish drying off, and when I did, I noticed the steam from the shower on the mirror. Someone had written on it with their finger in giant block letters.

TRUST NO ONE

***

The sun was bright when I left by the front door of my building and caused me to squint until I had time to adjust. I was on a mission. I had a few hours before I was to meet Lexi, so I decided to walk instead of taking city transportation. I walked to the drug store a few blocks away and went inside. It was a big place and already busy, but I found the aisle I was looking for. Once I stood in front of it, I realized I honestly didn't have a clue as to what I wanted. There were dozens of different prepaid cell phones hanging on the wall behind the counter. Jeez, like I needed any more complications in my life. I must've had a confused and pitiful look on my face because a lady came up to me and asked me if she could help. With an exasperated sigh, I surrendered to her.

"Yes ma'am, as a matter of fact, you can. I need a cell phone. One with the internet would be good," I replied.

"Not a problem, let me show you what we have."

Half an hour later, I finished paying for the overpriced gadget. The lady was kind enough to help me get it set up and showed me how to use it. I had considered getting one after Lexi had mentioned it before, but last night gave me a little – nudge. I wrote my new number for it down on a small piece of paper and put it in my pocket. I've never had one before, so I kind of felt important, yet, I had no idea what I was supposed to do with it. Did this mean I was a real grown up now? I wasn't so sure I wanted to be a grown up yet. I don't know, but I have to tell you, the women in my life sure come with a price.

I left the drug store and walked across the street to a small pizza shop and ordered my favorite, medium Canadian bacon, and mushroom with extra cheese. This place had the best pizza ever, in my humble opinion. It didn't take me long to devour the pie before I bolted for the library to meet up with Lexi.

The library was several blocks away, so I opted to take the bus for the trip over. I found a good seat at the bus stop and sat down to wait for the next one. I reached into my backpack and took out my new handy dandy cell phone which I had no idea how to use. I knew what the internet browser icon looked like so I pulled it up and surfed the web. As I sat there playing with it, a stoic-looking guy in a tan suit sits down beside me.

"Whatcha got for me kid?" Mr. Sunshine asked without looking at me and kept a straight face.

I reached into my pocket, pulled out the piece of paper with my new number on it and handed it to him without saying a word as per my instructions from last night.

The guy took it from me, got up and walked away without saying another word. I went back to the business at hand of playing with my new phone and took the time to plug in the number Briana gave me last night. The bus rolled up to a stop, but before I got on, I clicked a picture of the Broadway play advertisement on the side of it. I don't think I was cut out to be a secret agent at all, but what else could I do? Oh yeah, get killed! That's what. I grabbed my backpack, slung it over my shoulder and got on. I found an empty seat, finished inputting the number and attached the new photo to the contact listing.

***

A few minutes later, I stood in front of the library. Before I had a chance to walk in, I saw Lexi hustling over to me with a look of excitement on her face.

"I found something!" she exclaimed. A little too loudly for my benefit as I looked around to see if anyone was watching.

"What is it?"

She had her bag hanging over her shoulder and was holding a piece of paper in her hands waving it like a flag. "This is a print out from the county assessor's office. Henry Allister owns the land the council approved for sale, and it's a seventy-acre dairy farm at the edge of town. We have to take the Metro over there, so we need to hurry." She was talking so fast I could barely keep up.

"Whoa, slow your roll girl, come again?"

"Okay, but let's walk to the train station, and I'll fill you in on what I've uncovered," she said, grabbing my arm and pulling me along.

I knew then that I shouldn't have followed, but there was no way I was going to tell her no.

"The county assessor's office has their records online where anyone can find out who owns a particular parcel of land. After searching, I found out a man named Henry Allister owns the land in question. Well, *owned* the land anyway. Remember the Camden Group had been given the council's okay to purchase it," she said.

"Oh, that reminds me, I read an article the other day that said CGI had applied for rezoning permits, but it didn't say much else," I said as I struggled to keep up.

I had no idea how a woman could walk so fast in the boots she had on. They didn't look that comfortable though they did look great on her with the skin-tight jeans tucked down inside the boots. Today, she was wearing a red t-shirt form-fitted to her body, and I have to tell ya, she looked like a million bucks.

"I saw that same article. They sure didn't waste any time, did they? The ink's not even dry on the council's approval or the commissioner's death certificate," she said excitedly.

She seemed to have more pep than an energy drink.

We finally arrived at the Metro station, and once we figured out exactly where it was we're going, we get our passes. It shouldn't take too long to reach the farm, though I'm not sure what it is she expected to find once we got there.

"Come on Leo, where's your sense of adventure?"

"Sense of adventure… It's an adventure every time I leave my apartment. Besides, I'm here aren't I?"

"Sure, you are, but you're dragging your feet," she said. "Besides, when's the last time you were on a real adventure?" she asked with her eyes lit up with excitement.

I suppose I may be a tad bit apprehensive about taking the Metro out to some stranger's farm on the edge of the county, but she did have a point. I should try to be more engaged. I knew I liked being with her and, to be honest, I'd rather have been on a wild goose chase with her than being lazy in my apartment.

"You're right. I guess I'm just overly cautious. I might as well go along and keep you out of trouble," I laughed.

The train pulled up and stopped. When the doors opened, dozens of people scurried off and made their way down the platform and off to where ever it is they were going. Lexi and I were finally able to board, and we found a seat near a wall with a route map marking all the stops on it so we could study it and make sure we didn't miss our stop. We knew this train wouldn't take us all the way there. We would have to get off and get on another one, not an easy task, mind you, but we could manage. The trip back should be better as we could jump on a bus and ride most of the way back before we have to change buses.

"Hey, I almost forgot about it, but I picked up a new *smartphone* this morning," I said.

I reached into my bag and pulled it out.

"That's great, now we can text and communicate like normal people," she laughed.

She gave me her information to add to my contacts and let me take a photo of her so I can see it's her when she calls me or sends me a text. When we finished that, she took a picture of me and put my number in her phone. That kind of felt nice.

"There, now we're all set."

An hour later we were hoofing it down the street looking desperately for a cab.

"I don't think we're going to have much luck finding a taxi out here. We might as well figure on wearing out some shoe leather to get there and back," I said as we continued walking.

"I think you're right, I wished I had worn different shoes."

I glanced down at the boots she had on again. The heels on them sounded like a horse clomping along the street, and it made me laugh out loud.

"What's so funny?"

"Nothing, just thinking about your boots."

"In my defense, I didn't consider we would be hiking all over this city," she said indignantly.

I chuckled and said, "It's not that. I was laughing because you sound like a horse walking in a parade in those things, but I guess we are going to a farm."

"Hey, I resent that," she said, and slugged me on the shoulder and laughed too.

I liked hearing her laugh. It's soft and infectious. We both stopped walking for a moment and just enjoyed the moment of levity. She grasped my arm with both of her hands, leaned against me and we ambled along. When she touched me and held onto me I felt somewhat overwhelmed, and my heart threatened to jump right out of my chest, but I didn't dare let on that she had that effect on me, maybe in time.

"You make me laugh. I do enjoy your sense of humor." She giggled. "You're a good friend to have around."

Fan-freakin-tastic! Just what I had hoped for, the good old *friends* line! Not that I expected anything else. I guess you could say we were friends now, and at the least, that's something I hadn't counted on. We did get along well, but who am I trying to kid, she would never, in a million years, ever consider a guy like me. Uneducated, minimum wage earning, no family having, no roots or sense of belonging anywhere - Oh well, I've always heard the way to a woman's heart was to make her laugh. I'll have to keep it in mind.

***

Half an hour later, we began to see fewer buildings and more open land. We had to be getting close. Lexi took her cell phone out and pulled up a map.

"All of the land on this side of the road looks to be part of the Allister Farm," she said.

"How do you know that?" I asked.

She showed me the app she had on her phone and explained how she used the coordinates from the assessor's office to find the farm.

It didn't take long before we arrived at the farm's front entrance gate. The gate was wide open with a sign hanging from an unmanned guard post that explained tour times, but with a hastily painted sign hanging over it that just said, *CLOSED*. Even though it was a working farm at one time, the owner also operated an agri-tour business catering to schools throughout the city. I'm sure many of the inner-city kids had never seen cows in person before, so it must have been exciting for a kid to have a hands-on experience with a real working farm. Come to think of it, neither have I.

"Look, here is an information guide on the farm," she mentioned as she picked it up and perused it. It was weathered and faded in areas, but we could make out most of the details. I moved a little closer as she held it open where we could both get a better look.

"It says here the owner is Henry Allister, a fifth-generation dairy farmer. That confirms what I found at the assessor's site. It is also nearly seventy acres with several ponds, a milk barn, a large hay barn and several outbuildings," Lexi pointed out.

"Yeah and here's a picture of the dairy barn. It looks huge."

"Come on, let's see if anyone's around."

I had to jog a few steps to catch up and walk beside her. She was bold, fearless even, and that's kinda cool. She had the kind of personality that's infectious, you know, it just draws you in, and by you, I mean me.

The road winding up to the farmhouse was paved but in disrepair. I also noticed the lawn needed to be mowed and the hedges looked more than a touch shaggy.

"Maybe this Henry Allister no longer lives here?" I suggested.

"Sure doesn't look like it, does it?" she said, hurrying her pace.

We were still a few hundred yards from the sprawling farmhouse when she pulled up short right in front of me and stopped me with an open hand to my chest.

"Look, we're in luck!" she exclaimed. "There's a pickup truck parked near the house. Let's go up and knock." She turned and hurried toward the home.

Luck? I'm not so sure about that, but we did come all this way. It would be ridiculous not to go up and knock. When I looked up at the truck, I also noticed a black Mercedes parked beside it sporting a familiar license plate.

19

"Holy cow," I nearly shouted. My obvious concern stopped Lexi in her tracks, and with a worried look on her face, she spun back around to look at me.

"What is it?"

"That car, it's the same one that almost ran me down the other day."

"Are you sure? Maybe it just looks like it. Besides, why would they be following you?" she asked.

I realized at this point it wasn't random. No way could this be a simple coincidence. This guy had been following me, but who was it and why was he following me? I explained to her all the sightings I'd had.

"I'm positive it's the same car, there's no mistaking it. See the license plate? We can't let them see us here."

"We don't know for sure. Maybe you're just paranoid?" she suggested.

"Once or twice would be a coincidence, but not this many times."

"Wait, the license plate, I know who it is! Quick, let's find somewhere to hide."

The house was three stories tall with several gables and an enormous wrap-around porch. The steps leading up to the, once upon a time, grand entrance front door was wooden and looked to need repair as a few of them were broken. I was noticing a common theme around the place that reminded me a bit of my rat-trap apartment. The house itself overlooked a large pasture where the main hay barn sat with its tremendous doors pulled shut. Even as far away as we were, it was huge, but there was a small, walk-through door on the side hanging open. There were lots of trees lining the drive, so I suggested we use them as cover and make our way to the barn.

"Maybe we can hide in that big barn until whoever's driving the Benz leaves," I suggested.

"Sounds good," she said and moved off the drive to make a beeline for the barn door. I followed closely behind.

The barn was dark inside beyond the entrance forcing us to stop for a moment to allow our eyes time to adjust. Once we could see better, we carefully moved further inside. The barn must have been fifty-feet tall, and I could see stairs leading up to the next level.

"Let's find a spot up there where we can watch the house," I whispered a little late as Lexi was already two steps ahead of me.

"Come on."

I have to admit something, reluctantly, of course, and certainly not to her, but I was just a little scared. This wasn't our property, and we could get arrested for trespassing. Oh well, you only live once I suppose. I followed her up the stairs, and when I got to the top, I could see it opened into a huge hay loft. It was mostly empty, but stacked in one corner were several big square bales of hay. We made our way over to it and climbed up to a window where we could see the house.

The brochure we had picked up earlier said the farm was dedicated to environmental preservation and used as an educational classroom, but it didn't look like it had been operational for quite some time now. I said as much.

"Maybe that's why it's being sold now. I mean look at this place, it's huge. All this open land so close to the city must be worth a fortune!" she said in amazement as she looked out a barn window. "You can see nothing but trees, grass and open fields."

"I bet that's why the Commissioner was killed," I suggested.

Lexi turned to me with a thoughtful look and said, "This whole thing has me puzzled. I mean, what do we know for sure? First, we know someone killed the Commissioner in the diner where you work. We know the council had been tabling a land deal for several months now and just two days after Wood was killed, they passed it. Coincidence? I think not, Leo. And I don't believe it's a coincidence that this land deal has something to do with the Camden Group, the same people that have apparently been following you since the night of the murder!"

"I dunno, maybe we should go to the police?"

"We can't. Not yet anyway. We don't have any solid evidence. All we have are leads. We need much more than this to break this thing wide open, and when that happens, this is going to be huge!" she said.

"Ok, you told me you know whose car that belongs to?"

"Sure, it's quite simple," she said walking over to the window sill. Once there, she got down on her knees, took her bag off and laid it on the floor, and wrote the plate letters in the dust. CAMGRP7. She turned and looked up at me staring at her with a confused look on my face.

She wrote the letters separated by big spaces, so it looked to be in three pieces. CAM   GR   P, another quick glance at me with a sly smile, she filled in the rest of it. CAMden GRouP!

I stood there in amazement. I don't know why I never put it together before. I suppose it was too simple, too obvious and I wasn't looking for it. Either that or I'm too simple. Jeez, I can be dumb sometimes. Okay, whatever, I may not be the sharpest tool in the shed, but I'm not the dullest one either.

Suddenly, we heard voices below in the barn. They must've come outside while Lexi was explaining the car tag.

"We have to hide. If they come up here, they'll catch us for sure."

I looked around and saw a place we could use. I grabbed Lexi's hand and whispered, "Come on."

I led her across the top of the hay we're already on and climbed up and over one of the hay bales where we ducked down into a gap so as not be seen by anyone on the floor. It was a tight fit for both of us, and it was quite hot and nasty in there, but it was better than getting caught. As we scrambled into the hole, we kicked up a lot of dust and hayseed. Lexi grabbed her mouth and nose to stifle a sneeze. When she couldn't hold it back any longer, she buried her face and hands on my chest and sneezed twice before sheepishly pulling back.

"I'm so sorry."

She had the look of an apologetic puppy on her face.

"Shhh," I whispered back, "It's okay."

And it was. I don't mind a little sneeze on my shirt. The best part was getting to hold her close to me. So, what if the circumstances weren't what you might call the best situation? From my view, it's not the worst either. I could smell her perfume, and her hair brushed my face and tickled as we lay hidden, hunkered down behind the huge bale of hay.

We couldn't tell who the voices below belonged to, but they didn't seem to be coming up the stairs. That wasn't necessarily a good thing for me, as I'm sure you can figure out why on your own. Lexi whispered she wanted to hear what they were talking about and crawled back over the hay bale and tip-toed over to the staircase. She looked back at me when she got there and motioned with a frantic wave of her hand for me to come over. I stumbled out of our hidey-hole and made my way over while she held a finger over her lips to indicate she wanted me to be quiet. I wasn't sure if she thought I was dumb enough to trod like a lummox across the floor like an idiot or she's just making the gesture as a general warning. I'm hoping she doesn't think of me as her bumbling side-kick. I pictured myself more of the Batman to her Robin, to be honest, and not the other way around, though I could be mistaken in that assessment.

She was crouched down next to the staircase and peering intently below. I could hear the voices as they moved from beneath the stairs to the interior of the barn and she moved silently along the floor so she could listen to the conversation. At one point, she got down on her hands and knees and put her ear to the floor. I followed suit, but I couldn't make out but a few words here and there. One of the men with a deep, authoritative voice was talking.

"Demo......thirty days."

At that moment I heard two, maybe three doors on a vehicle all close about the same time, but they were definitely car doors slamming closed. Lexi heard it too and turned to me with a questioning look on her face. I just shrugged my shoulders. I had no idea either, but I got up out of my crouch on the floor and crept over to the barn window. From there I saw three men in business suits walking up to the farmhouse. As they walked, the two men from the barn walked out and headed up to greet them. There, they stood and talked for a few minutes before going inside.

"Did you hear what they were saying?" she asked.

"No," I whispered back. "I couldn't make out the gist of their conversation at all. A few words are all I could make out. I heard Allister's name come up, but I didn't know if the guy was calling him by his name or they were talking about the Allister fellow?"

"Yes, me too. I think I understood them to say they're going to start demo work in the next thirty days," she explained.

"I suppose it only makes sense. If this group bought the place just so they could tear it all down and build offices and stuff, I guess they would start on it as soon as they could," I replied.

The three men walked back out of the house a short time later followed closely by a man with salt and pepper hair trimmed short, a chiseled jawline and a face full of stubble. He was wearing a navy-blue suit, red tie, and black shoes and seemed to be the man in charge as the other three all looked at him when he spoke and nodded in agreement at the same time. I knew right away he was the guy that almost ran me down in the street. I could never forget that face even though he was wearing sunglasses at the time. Scary guy, that one was, and I knew we couldn't be seen by him.

Within a few minutes, the three men left together in a black sedan as the man giving the orders watched them drive away. Once they were headed down the lane, he opened the door to his black Mercedes and started to get in when his cell phone rang. It was an odd tune he used as a ringtone, but it could be heard even as far away as we were in our hiding spot in the barn. I could see him put the cell to his ear and say something quickly before hanging up and climbing in. He was driving away when she nudged me in the ribs with her elbow.

"Let's go knock on the door now. The pickup truck is still here, and I'm betting it's Allister's."

"Okay, but you're doing the talking," I insisted.

We walked down the stairs and were just about to exit through the door when she suddenly turned to me with a worried look on her face.

"What's wrong?"

"My bag," she said. "I must've left it in the hay."

"Wait here, I'll get it."

I ran back up the stairs and over to the hay bales. I found it right away, grabbed it, and ran back down and handed it to her.

"Thank you," she said appreciatively. "I could never lose this bag."

"I would guess you have everything in it like your i.d. and stuff huh?"

"Yes, but the bag is more valuable than that. It's a Kate Spade you know. A Cobble Hill Mayra to be exact. It's expensive," she said with mock haughtiness.

"Well aren't you important," I joked.

She laughed.

"I'm truly not a superficial person. Please don't think that of me. I'm only joking with you because I'm sure you have no idea about ladies' handbags. Yes, it is expensive, but it's the kind of thing I would never buy for myself no matter how much money I had. It was a graduation gift from my father. It's large enough to carry my tablet and still stuff all of my things in it."

"I wouldn't think that about you, but you're right, I have no idea about handbags as I'm sure you can tell with my old beat up backpack."

We traipsed up the cobblestone path and made our way up to the farmhouse. Just as we stepped up on the porch, the front door opened and a tall, elderly man stepped out.

"Excuse me, I'm sorry to barge in on you like this. Mr. Allister, I presume?" Lexi said in greeting the elderly farmer.

"Yes, who are you and what do you want?" Allister asked, somewhat startled and seemingly put out by the intrusion.

Lexi extended her hand and the old man took it in his.

"I'm Lexi Osborne, Mr. Allister, I'm a reporter with the Daily Grind, and this is my friend, Leonard. We were hoping to talk to you for a minute about the farm if you don't mind."

20

The man looked to be in his late sixties or early seventies, thin with a slight stoop, graying light brown hair and wearing bib overalls, boots, and a blue plaid shirt. After Lexi introduced us, his demeanor softened.

"I'm sorry," he said, "You'll have to forgive me. You just caught me off-guard. I thought you were with the vultures that just left."

"Oh, no sir. We're not with them at all, but we saw them leave as we came up. They didn't look like a friendly crowd," Lexi said.

"No. No, they're not. Pure vultures if you ask me - greedy vultures." He paused for a moment. "I'm sorry kids, I forget my manners, how 'bout we have a seat here on the porch and we can talk. I'd offer you a glass of tea, but I'm afraid there's not any left in the house."

"That's okay Mr. Allister," Lexi said. "We're fine."

Allister turned and walked over to some chairs on the porch and invited us to sit.

"What can I do for you?"

"The guy that left alone, who was he? I assume he was one of the vultures you speak of?"

"Oh yes, he's the head vulture, Matthew Schofield the *third*. Pompous ass if you ask me."

"What's that?" I asked, apparently a little too enthusiastically, because they both suddenly stopped and turned to me. "Sorry, that name just rang a bell or something, but it's nothing. Sorry."

They turned back to their conversation.

"We've been curious about the farm," Lexi began again. "I realize you just sold it, but do you have any idea what the plans are for the place now?"

"Unfortunately, I do. And, yes, I just sold it, but not for half of what it's worth I'll tell you that," he stated rather fervidly. "They had me over a barrel though, and they took advantage of it. If it weren't for my son, I wouldn't have sold it at all."

"Your son?"

I could see the look on his face turn from anger to one of disappointment as he talked. I felt sorry for him. He was such a charismatic man that I couldn't help but take an instant liking to him.

"Yes, he's a businessman out in California. When it came time for me to retire, I had hoped he would take over, but he wanted nothing to do with this place. Never has. This farm has been in my family for generations. My great, great grandfather emigrated here with nothing more than the clothes on his back, worked hard and bought a few acres. Wasn't much at the time, but with hard work, time and determination my family built it into what you see today. Well, that's not entirely true. It used to be something until a few years ago. Now it's in sad shape."

He paused again, but this time a sad look came over his face as he looked around.

"The sound and smells of livestock, kids laughing as their teachers try to keep them corralled, tractors, hay…" he trailed off with a distant look on his tired and weathered face. "It's all gone now and won't ever be heard or seen again."

"So, what happened?" I asked.

"Time happened, son," he said quickly, turning to look me in the eyes. "I got old. Just couldn't keep up with the work anymore and the place gradually declined. It was time for me to retire and my son urged me to sell it for what I could and retire comfortably. I didn't want to retire, but I had to face facts too. Unfortunately for me, I signed a contract with those vultures you saw leaving at the urging of the real estate company and, of course, my son!" he said stridently. "Good kid, but unreliable. Anyway, they offered far less than what this place is worth, and I laughed in their face. I had several offers for far more than what they were willing to pay, but, the funny thing is, every one of the other offers was mysteriously pulled off the table. All except one I guess, but her offer came in after the deadline."

"What do you mean?"

"The real estate company I signed a contract with set a deadline for open bids so when the lady came by to talk to me with her bid in hand, it was too late. The deadline had passed. But, you see, it wasn't after the original deadline at all, and that's what she was upset about. It seemed Camden, and his cronies got the real estate company to move the deadline up by two days early. She was angry when I told her, but there was nothing I could do since I signed a contract with the real estate company to sell it for me. It was their deadline. Not mine. So, I was left with the one offer from the vultures. Now you tell me if they're playing by the rules!" the old man said with a sour look on his face as he looked back and forth at Lexi and me. "You can't tell me they didn't have something to do with all the other offers being rescinded I thought at one-point Schofield was going to work with me after all, but when it came right down to it, I knew he couldn't be trusted."

I sat quietly, listening to him and watching his reactions. He seemed like such a nice guy, it was too bad someone would take advantage of someone like that. Lexi leaned in closer to hear him talk. I think she could've sold a plane to a bird with her charms. He warmed up to her quickly.

"I wonder why the other lady wasn't scared off like the others. Who was she?" Lexi asked.

He leaned back in his chair and thought a moment before replying.

"I believe she said her name was Richards if I recall correctly. I have her business card around here somewhere. She may be a pretty lady, but one with an undeniable dark side. She was angry about it all, but it was out of my hands. She stormed out, and that's the last I saw of her."

"What did she look like?" I asked the old farmer.

"Oh, about average height I suppose, long black hair and her eyes were just as dark. Wore too much makeup for my taste though." He chuckled. "She was much too pretty to be so angry. I have milk cows with more personality than her," Allister said as he fumbled through a few business cards in his wallet. "Here it is,"

He handed us a glossy, black card with gold writing on it, but stuck to the back of it was his son's business card as well. I pulled it loose but looked it over carefully before handing it back. I had my suspicions about this Michael Allister. He sounded like a real weasel.

Michelle Richards, CEO Jade Development, Inc.

"My thought is since she was a late player in the game, Camden either didn't know about her or knew she wasn't a threat at that point and left her alone. I never heard from her again," Allister said.

"Oh, I see. Since the deadline was up, she wasn't allowed to bid anyway?" Lexi said.

"Right, and that's when the real problems started. I had to sign a six-month contract with Camden after the bids closed. Apparently, the county has control of major sales of open space land, and the only way I'm allowed to sell it is by approval of the County Commissioners. Camden had a six-month window to meet all the commission's regulations and get approval. If not, the contract was null and void, and I could open it back up for bids again. Since they scared everyone else off, paid 'em off or whatever they did, I was left with no other choice!" Allister exclaimed, getting worked up again.

"Wow, that does sound like vultures. To take advantage of someone like that isn't right," Lexi said. "So, what happened next?"

"The six months was almost up, and I thought I'd get out of that contract, but that's when the head commissioner was killed. He seemed to be my only ally in this fiasco. He must've known they were snakes and had been stalling the vote on the sale for months. A few days after he was killed, the commission met and approved the sale just like that," he said, as he snapped his fingers. "I'm not sure what happened. It's all a mystery to me, but darn convenient. It was just darn near null and void, and they had to meet in the middle of the night and approve it. They were deadlocked for months, just kept tabling the vote. Wood was the only one that opposed the sale, and I was glad of it. My son, on the other hand, was furious about it. Said it wasn't any of their business who we could or couldn't sell to. If we wanted to sell the place, it was our right to do so. I tend to agree, but at the same time I understand why they would want some control over it."

Lexi touched the man's arm gently.

"I'm sorry Mr. Allister. I wish there were something we could do."

"Why would your son care if you sold the farm or kept it? Didn't you say he lived in California now?" I asked.

"Yes, he does, but I'm sure he's thinking about his inheritance. I made him part owner of the place many years ago thinking it would entice him to stay. It didn't work, of course. As I said, he doesn't want anything to do with running a farm. He never liked living here, and I guess I could see he always had a wandering spirit. Growing up, he always found things to do that took him away, and when he went to college, it was as far away as possible," the old man explained with a sad look on his face. "I have always hoped he would eventually come back home and take over. I'm just too old to take care of the place, and I'd like to retire."

The old man looked at us with a sheepish grin before he continued his story.

"To be honest, I'd like to travel and see what's out there. I've never even been to the Grand Canyon, and I'd like to see it."

I saw in the old man's face he was both happy and sad or maybe the happiness was faked as he tried to convince himself, but I could also see he was between a rock and a hard place. He was too feeble to take care of a farm this big and his son wasn't any help either, apparently. As a matter of fact, I was beginning to not like his son at all, and I'd never even met the guy.

"Well, Camden owns it now, and they're ready to take possession. That's what they were here to tell me today. That I have exactly thirty days to find somewhere else to live before they start tearing everything down," Allister said, forlornly. "I don't mind having to find somewhere else to live, I have plans already, but what breaks my heart is to see this place get torn down. The house isn't the original of course, but the barn is. My great, great grandfather built it with his own two hands. Used to be hundreds, if not thousands of school kids would tour this place every year just to see it in all its glory."

I could see his eyes begin to light up again.

"Yes, those inner-city kids would ride the bus out here, and we'd take 'em on a tour of a real-life working dairy farm. I can see still how their little faces would stare in amazement the first time they saw a cow up close or the first time they got to pet a calf. I'll miss it, but I suppose all good things must come to an end."

Lexi turned and gave me a sideways glance like she had honed in on something. She leaned in a little closer and asked him, "Mr. Allister, is your son, Michael, here?"

"Oh no, I mean he was last week, but once the place sold, he went back to California. Said he had investments to shore up. I don't know much about the business world he works in. All I know is farming."

"Oh, so he was here?" she asked.

"Yes, he was here all this last week, but I drove him to the airport just yesterday. He didn't have enough cash to rent a car. He said he lost his wallet, but I know he's broke. He's just too stubborn to tell his old man."

She looked at me again with that same look. I think we both had the same idea. Maybe Mr. Allister's son, Michael, had something to do with the death of the commissioner. He had a motive.

"What are you going to do now Mr. Allister?" I asked.

"I'm going to buy the RV I've always wanted, and I'm going to go see the Grand Canyon, Mount Rushmore, Crazy Horse Monument and after that who knows? I'm going to travel," he said with a matter of fact attitude.

"That sounds wonderful, Mr. Allister, simply wonderful," Lexi said.

"Please kids, call me Hank. All my friends do, and I like you, two kids. How long have you been together?" he asked.

"Oh, we're not together Mr. Allister, we're just friends," Lexi quickly stammered with a shocked look on her face.

"Uh huh," Hank said questioningly, as he looked us over.

Great, just fabulous, I thought. She was quick to point out we weren't a couple to the old man. I mean, I realized we weren't a couple, and we were just friends, but wow, I'd never seen anyone jump on a denial wagon so fast and throw out the 'we're just friends' thing so seriously like. I guess that told me I needed to get those thoughts out of my head. She was just too far out of my league. I think sometimes I forget my place.

"Mr. Allister, we're going to have to get going, but thank you so much for visiting with us," Lexi said.

"You two don't have to leave so quickly, do you? And I told you, it's Hank. Not, Mr. Allister."

"I'm sorry… Hank," Lexi laughed as she stood and extended her hand again. "It's a long walk back to the bus station and a long train ride home so we really must be going."

"Let me give you a lift down to the bus stop at least. I just have to lock up."

"Oh no, we wouldn't want to trouble you."

"Nonsense, young lady, It's no trouble at all. I'll just lock up and grab my keys."

After a few minutes, we were loaded up in Hanks pickup, and he was driving us to the bus stop. It only took about twenty minutes to get there by vehicle. It seemed so much further away when we were hoofing it. Lexi sat in the middle so that I could sit by the door. I have to say, for a farm truck, it sure was a nice one. I never learned to drive, though I can ride a dirt bike. During the ride over, he said we could call or come by anytime at all…or at least until he moved. He said he had a moving crew set to come out next week to get everything packed and loaded up on big trucks. Camden didn't want anything left behind because they were going to be tearing everything down with bull-dozers anyway he said. In other words, only leave anything he didn't care ever to see again.

We waved goodbye to Mr. Allister as he drove away. When he got out of sight, Lexi turned to me, and I could see her face was clouded with her thoughts.

"I hate to say this out loud, but I think his son may be our killer and not a hired assassin after all."

"From what Mr. Allister told us, I don't like the guy that's for sure, but I don't think he was the triggerman, and honestly, it doesn't sound like he had the money to hire your ghost. I mean, he had motive and opportunity sure, and he didn't stick around."

The bus pulled up and stopped, so we climbed on. It was a long trip back into the city. When we got onboard, I took a window seat about halfway back, and Lexi sat down beside me.

"I don't know. I feel so sorry for Hank. His only son might be a murderer. How's he going to take that news?" she asked.

21

"Good afternoon Mr. Camden, thank you for meeting with me, I know you're busy," the detective said, as he shook hands with the CEO of Camden Group, Inc.

Lucas Bishop Camden was an imposing figure at six feet four inches tall, dark hair, crystal blue eyes and thin lips with a well-tailored, custom fit business suit complete with gold Rolex watch encrusted with diamonds. The detective guessed he was in his mid-fifties judging from what he had read about the man and his first meeting with him, though he didn't look mid-forties.

"Please come in and have a seat," Camden said as the two men shook hands.

O'Conner surveyed the luxurious office as he entered and let out a low whistle. He walked over to the dark burgundy leather chairs sitting in front of Camden's desk and sat down. He had a quick thought that the two guest chairs alone had to cost more than his entire office budget. Several photographs hung on the wall and Frank studied them with a keen, well-trained eye. Some were of Camden playing golf or having dinner with dignitaries, congressmen, senators and a plethora of celebrities. One frame sitting on his desk was strikingly plain which seemed irregular. It looked to be a young Lucas Camden, a woman just a few years younger and what he surmised to be their parents. Seemed Camden had aged well. He couldn't have been more than twenty-five years old in the photo, just out of college most likely. The celebrity photos didn't bother O'Conner. That type of thing did not intimidate him. After many years in law enforcement, he had seen and heard it all and was oblivious to the bluster and peacocking by men who bought and paid for friends and used them as they needed. Frank knew the type and knew them well.

"Nice looking family," Frank suggested, indicating the photo on his desk as he picked it up.

"Thank you, Detective, my father founded this company and ran it for several years before I took over after his death."

"I see. My condolences on your father."

"Thank you, but it was a long time ago."

"Your mother still with us, I presume?" Frank inquired casually.

"No, both of my parents have passed. It's just me now."

Camden took the frame from Frank's hand and turned it back around to form a straight line with the blotter, arranging it perfectly.

Frank noticed the man's desk was in perfect order with straight lines and right angles just as all the photographs on the wall were perfectly centered and squared away. He had picked the picture up purposely to see how Camden would react. Just as any person with the obsessive-compulsive disorder would behave, he concluded.

"What can I do for you, Detective?" Camden asked.

"Seems your secretary keeps you busy," Frank smiled. "I've phoned your office a few times. Thought I'd take my chances and stop by and catch you in."

"My apologies, yes, she does keep me busy."

"I won't take much more of your time, Mr. Camden," Frank said. "I suppose you are aware of Commissioner Wood's unfortunate passing."

"Yes, I am, a terrible thing. This city just doesn't seem too safe at all these days. No offense, of course," Camden replied tersely.

"None was taken," the detective said, without missing a beat. "I understand as President of the Board of Commissioners he alone held the tie-breaking vote on a large tract of land your company had a contract to purchase?"

"Right to the point, eh Detective? I respect that. I'm not going to try to lie to you and tell you his vote didn't matter because, obviously, it did. Camden Group has hundreds of land deals going at any one time, and we have millions of dollars in developments and projects requiring more attention than one little land purchase. This one was important, but he was not blocking the vote, only tabling the vote until we had everything in line just the way the commission wanted. The biggest hurdle they demanded of us was to submit a proposal that included green initiatives such as a park for the community to use, trees, plants, flowers, even green technology in any buildings or houses to be built," Camden continued as he reached in his desk drawer and pulled out a folder. He tossed it on his desk in front of the detective. "This is the final proposal, and as you can see here, all of the commissioners agreed including Commissioner Wood. So, why would I want to kill him?" Camden concluded with a smugness that waned on Frank's nerves.

Detective O'Conner glanced over the proposal and saw all the commissioners had signed off on it just days before Wood was killed.

"I never said you did Mr. Camden, merely inquiring as to the nature of your association. Can I get a copy of this?"

"Certainly, Detective. I'll have my secretary get it to you if you would be so kind as to leave her your card," Camden said, standing to indicate the meeting was over.

The detective thanked him again for seeing him as he walked out the door of the office. Just before he exited, he stopped and turned back.

"Oh, one last thing Mr. Camden, just a matter of protocol you understand, but where were you the night he was killed? You can account for your whereabouts?" Frank asked watching Camden's face carefully.

"Of course, I can. I was in the company gym that evening playing racquetball with one of my account managers, Tim Westfield. We have security footage that will show that I never left the building until after 1 a.m.," Camden said.

"I'm going to need that footage as well," Frank replied. "Protocol, you understand?"

"That won't be a problem. I'll let my Chief of Security know you will be stopping by on your way out."

"Thank you for your time, Mr. Camden."

Frank heard the door close behind him a moment later. He was sure he had ruffled Camden's feathers, even if only a little. He made his way over to Camden's secretary and left his card with her before making his way out. He turned down the hallway, found the elevators and pushed the down arrow. Just as the elevator stopped, the doors opened, and before he could step in, four men in business suits stepped out brushing past him without a word of greeting. Frank shrugged it off and went down to the first floor where he met with the security officer and asked for the Chief of Security. He was escorted to an office where he met John Strauss. He showed him his badge and told him what he needed.

"Yes sir, Mr. Camden phoned just a moment ago. Not a problem. I've already burned a copy for you. Everything is digital nowadays, so it's quick and easy to manage," Strauss replied, handing Frank a shiny thumb drive embellished with CGI, Inc. on it.

The detective thanked the man and left the building to head back to his office. Something was going through his head about Camden, but he couldn't quite put the finger on it yet. He thought something was off, but not exactly sure what it might be.

22

It was late when I finally got home. We had stopped and eaten at a restaurant near the bus terminal after the last leg of our trip back from the farm. I had to work in the morning, so as soon as I walked into my apartment, somewhat apprehensively mind you, I stripped down and jumped into bed. As I laid there awake staring at the ceiling in the quasi-dark room, something began gnawing at me about all of this. First, this Schofield guy that's following me seems to have me in his sights for some reason, but I honestly don't know why. Maybe this was something I should mention to the detective - well, never mind. I'd better not say anything to anyone other than Lexi right now. Jeez! I have to get some sleep.

Being a bit paranoid when I left my apartment building for work, I exited through the back entrance and scoped things out first. I was dressed in a dark hoodie, and it was pulled up over my head with sunglasses on like I was some kind of movie star dodging the paparazzi. I suppose my ratty backpack would've given me away to anyone who knew me being that I'm never without it, but that didn't mean everyone knew me. Few people knew me. I had what you might call a small circle of friends. Let's see, there's

Lexi and - okay, so I can't even make a full circle. Sue me captain obvious.

I left extra early in the morning so that I could take a different route to a different bus stop. At that hour, there weren't many people out and about on the streets yet, but there were still plenty enough to keep me jumping at every sound I heard from car horns and screeching tires to slamming garage can lids. I'm familiar enough with the area, so I wasn't worried. I knew how long it would take to get there and which bus to take that stopped nearest the diner, but it still seemed a bit strange. Becoming a covert operative was not in my wheelhouse.

When I got to work, I reached into my pocket for the keys, but when I put it in the back-door lock, I noticed it was already open. I was on time, even early, so I wondered, *who would be here this early?* I pushed the door open, walked into the kitchen and immediately saw Helen sitting on a stool behind the counter leisurely drinking a cup of coffee.

"Good morning Helen," I greeted her with a chipper voice. Or what I thought was chipper. Apparently, she didn't think so.

"What's eating your shorts," she asked sourly.

"What do you mean, I'm in a great mood."

"That's exactly what I'm talking about," she said, before turning back to her coffee to ignore me.

I didn't want her sourpuss, *"I hate the world, and the world hates me"* attitude bringing me down, so I shrugged it off and went to work prepping my kitchen. It wasn't long before Greely came in and he seemed to be in an excellent mood too.

"Leonard, make sure you clean out the freezer today. I swear there are dead animals in there," he said gruffly, passing through on his way to his office. I heard his door close. He rarely closes his door.

Considering the freezer was full of meat, I'm reasonably certain he was right. But, I'd clean it out; after all, he was the boss even if he was a grumpy tub-o-charm!

The morning went by fast, and before I knew it, Marvin was staggering in for his shift. I finished cleaning the freezer and helped him get ready for his lunch crowd. When I finished, I grabbed my bag and headed for the library. I didn't feel like going home to my apartment because frankly, there was not a thing to do but stare at the walls. At least at the library, there were lots of people around, but I could still be alone.

No sooner had I walked out the back door than I heard a weird sound. I looked all around me, but I was alone in the alleyway. After a few seconds, I realized it must be my new cell phone, so I quickly dug it out of my backpack. I've got to change that sound. Besides it being annoying, I'd never been able to hear it unless it's quiet where I'm at. I looked at the caller id, and I saw it was Lexi.

"Hello, this is Leonard," I answered. I tried to sound professional and important, but I think I came off as sounding more like an idiot. I better stick to a simple, *hello* from now on; I can pull that off much more natural than professional and important.

"Hi, Leo," Lexi greeted me with her silky voice with a bit of a chuckle. "Why haven't you texted me back?"

"Oh, I never realized you had texted me. I must not have heard it go off. I'm sorry."

"It's okay," she laughed. "I was just checking on you. It was a long day yesterday, and I'm exhausted. I can only imagine how tired you must be. You have to get up so early."

"Yeah, I'm exhausted. How about you? You sound like you're bright eyed and bushy tailed, ready to challenge all on this battlefield of life," I laughed.

"Well – I did get a few more hours of sleep than you."

We talked for quite some time, and I have to admit, I liked it. She told me she had been at work all morning and hadn't given much thought to everything we learned yesterday because she was just too busy with all her other work. To be honest, neither had I. It was a long day, and I still hadn't gone over everything in my head yet. The morning shift at the diner kept me hopping, and the freezer took it out of me. I never even thought about the farm or the murder for that matter.

I loved hearing her voice on the phone. I felt my face growing tired as I listened to her. Not because I was tired of her, but because I was smiling and laughing with her like a giggly school girl. *Jeez, man-up Leonard*, I thought.

"What are you doing with your time this afternoon? You have to work later, right?" she asked.

"Yeah, I gotta work the evening shift, but right now I'm headed over to the library to read for a while. I didn't feel like going home and to be honest, I think you were right."

"About what?"

"About being a little paranoid," I laughed.

"Oh, I understand. But, now that we know what we do, I think you have a right to be a little worried, and I'm sure after what you witnessed in the diner last week, it can be rather scary when you think about it," she said.

That's the last thing I want is for her to think I'm scared because she doesn't seem to be afraid of anything. I guess I'm just a worrier.

"Maybe a little," I replied. In my head I was screaming, *a LOT*!

"Hey listen, I'm tied up here all day and will be working late, but I'd like to do a little reconnoiter later tonight. I know you'll be working late too, so I wonder if I could meet you at the diner afterward and you could go with me. I want to check something out," Lexi said.

That didn't leave me much time for sleep since I had to open the diner again tomorrow, but if I had another chance to be with her, I'm willing to make the sacrifice. I may be a little grumpier at work, but that would only help me fit in with my co-workers.

"Sure, it's slow in the evenings, and I can probably lock up by nine or so," I answered.

"Perfect, I'll see you then - and Leo?"

"Yeah?"

"Text me back when I text you."

She laughed and disconnected.

I clicked the phone to the red *end conversation* icon and clicked open the messaging icon to read her text.

Good morning sunshine, hope you got some rest. Thanks for tagging along and making me feel safe, Dr. Watson! ☺, *Lexi*

I texted her back,

Anytime Mr. Holmes. ☺

I hope that wasn't too…goofy of me, but no sooner had I hit send she replied,

☺ *See ya 2nite*

I laughed. Again, much like a giggly school girl, but I honestly didn't care. I was in a great mood, and nothing was going to bring me down from this euphoric high!

***

"I'm outta here, Leo. You got this. See you in the morning," Helen said, grabbing her purse to leave the diner.

I could see her latest man-toy waiting for her in his pimp-mobile outside. We hadn't had a customer in the last twenty minutes, so I knew she'd be flying the coop soon. It wasn't even nine p.m. yet. I didn't mind at all. I was eager to see Lexi and since I talked her earlier today, the rest of the day had been dragging by. I'd been on cloud nine since and I think Helen and the rest of the crew had their concerns about me.

"Good night, Helen. See ya tomorrow," I said. "I'll be locking up behind you anyway."

When she left, I turned the lock on the door and began cleaning up. There wasn't a lot to do because when it's slow in the evening, it gives me a chance to catch up. I hate when it's slow because time drags by, but it does allow me to get finished faster and ready to get out of here.

I had been thinking about everything Lexi, and I learned from Mr. Allister. It seemed like his son may have had a good motive to have the commissioner killed, but I just didn't think he had the means to do so if what Henry said was true. It was also a far stretch for me to believe Briana Fitzgerald was a paid assassin.

I had gotten a text from Lexi about twenty minutes earlier saying she was on her way. I was antsy waiting for her to get here.

After about ten or fifteen minutes, I heard a knock on the front door. When I looked up, I saw Lexi smiling through the glass, so I walked over and let her in.

"Come on in, I'll just be a minute to get my things, and we can go," I said.

I closed and locked the door behind her.

"No hurry, it's still early."

There was a sparkle in her eye and a mischievous little grin on her face. She was up to something. That comment, along with the whole recon mission she alluded to earlier, got me wondering what exactly she was up to.

"How much trouble are we going to get into now?" I asked. I laughed just a little but worried a lot.

"Oh, don't worry. I won't let anyone hurt you," she snickered.

Okay, call me a wimp, but I worry about that kind of thing. The farm trip wasn't too bad, but this mysterious late-night mission of hers could be a little more - complex.

"I'm not worried about myself," I said with feigned indignation, "but someone has to protect you from, well… you." I laughed.

"Haha, Leonard P Valentine, very funny."

I put my apron on the hanger, grabbed my backpack and ushered her out the back with me as I turned out the lights and locked up. The street light above us in the alleyway buzzed loudly overhead as we stood there while I put my keys away in my pack. The light shined down in a weird cone shape against the dark, red bricks of the buildings on all three sides illuminating the two green dumpsters. It was eerily quiet.

She whispered, "I know you have to work early in the morning so I'll try not to keep you out all night. I have to be at the office at 8 a.m., and after the long day yesterday, I'm feeling a little lethargic today myself."

"No worries, I don't mind at all. Besides, what else do I have to do, but run around playing Batman and Robin? Or being Mr. Watson to your Sherlock Holmes," I reassured her. "Where exactly are we going?"

"To the Camden Group offices."

23

Detective O'Conner sat at his desk going over the reports and evidence they had collected when his long-time partner walked over. They were among the last ones still on the floor as everyone else had gone home for the night. His partner broke the silence causing Frank to look up.

"See anything new in all that?"

"No, nothing new, Mike, but there's something about Lucas Camden that's been bugging me. I just can't put my finger on it yet. The whole CGI angle is flawed somehow," Frank replied.

"There's more than just *something* about the guy. From what I can tell, he has every politician in the state in his back pocket. He has all the power money and influence can buy. We can't prove any of it, of course." He sighed.

"So, what's our next move?" Mike asked.

Frank was the lead detective on the case, and even though the partners had several other cases to work on, this one was high profile and took precedence. They both knew it. They had been working every possible angle and had delved into the commissioner's agendas and discovered the tie their murder victim had with Camden Group, but many questions remained to be answered.

"Camden said he had no reason to want Commissioner Wood dead and, of course, his alibi checked out. He was without a doubt in the gym working out the night of the murder. Forensics confirmed the video as legitimate, and they clearly show him in the gym at the time of the murder. They also show him leaving the building early the next morning. No way he could've gone out and come back in without the surveillance cameras picking him up," Frank said.

"Maybe there's another way in and out that's not covered by video. Besides, it doesn't mean he's innocent; maybe he hired someone," Mike replied.

"Thought of that, but it was checked out thoroughly by our team. The hiring someone though, that's what I'm thinking, but getting a warrant for his bank records to see if he's paid out any large sums of cash to hire someone ain't gonna happen without more evidence, especially if he has judges on the payroll. Any motive he had to have killed him falls apart with Wood's signature signing off on the sale."

Mike sat down on the edge of Frank's desk with one leg and leaned down with his elbow resting on his knee. He was lost in thought while Frank kicked his feet up on the desk and leaned back in his chair in silent contemplation.

A door closed to an office down the hall, and a few other officers talked among themselves further away, but they were oblivious to it all. After a few minutes, Frank looked up at the whiteboard where they had the murder plotted out with all known connections and variables and stood up.

Mike turned to see what he was looking at, "So what do we know for certain?"

"Well," Frank began, "We know Camden had a land deal that was being held up by the County Commissioners. The sale was tabled for several months. Camden said it was only tabled until they had an agreement in place about the use of the land after the sale. Wood's datebook shows he had a meeting the night he was killed. There was nothing more than that, and his secretary had no idea what the meeting was about. Wood's wife also had no idea who he was meeting or why. If Wood was on board with CGI buying the land and was set to approve it, why was he killed?"

"To keep him from approving it," Mike pondered.

"Possibly, but who would do that?" Frank asked. "Who had an interest in the land other than Camden? Who would benefit from CGI not being able to purchase that piece of property?"

"Someone that wanted it for themselves. The land has to be worth a fortune."

"That's my theory. Someone didn't want it to go through," Frank said.

Mike stood and walked around to the front of Frank's desk looking at the board as if willing it to point out the killer.

Frank leaned on his desk, "We need to meet with the real estate company that had the contract on it. See who else made offers on it besides Camden, and we need to talk to the landowner and see what we can find out from him? We're missing several pieces to this puzzle and the longer we wait, the harder it will be to track down. Hell, for all I know, we could be barking up the wrong tree."

"Maybe so. What do you want to do next?"

"Let's split up in the morning and run down some of these leads. I'll head over to the real estate company first thing, and you can check out the owner," Frank replied.

"Sounds good. Right now, I'm gonna go get a little sleep. I'm beat. Good night."

Frank watched Mike walk out of the office while he continued to think about the case. He knew the answer was right in front of him, but he just didn't have enough of the pieces put together yet. He decided he should follow Mike's thought and head home to get some rest.

24

I stopped short and gave her a questioning look when I heard where she wanted to go. It must've come off as a more worried look though - or was it a scared one standing there in that dark alleyway behind the diner? Either way, I thought she'd flipped her lid.

Lexi laughed and grasped my arm. As she led me down the alley to the street, she explained she wanted to go check out the offices and see what we could dig up.

"It may be a wild goose chase, but we know CGI has something to do with the murder," she said.

"I don't know about this. Do you think we can get in and even if we do get in, what do you hope to find? And what happens when we get caught?" I asked.

"Well, for starters, they have to have files on Mr. Allister's property. I don't know, but what I do know is, CGI is bad news, and I'm betting we can get some answers there. Who knows, we may not be able to get in anyway, but I still want to snoop around."

"Okay, but for the record, I don't like it."

A short time later we stepped off the bus, and she looked at her cell phone for directions.

"This way," she said and took off walking at a fast clip.

When she was several steps in front of me, I noticed she was wearing black yoga pants, a black shirt, running shoes and her hair was tied in a ponytail. It never occurred to me before now, but she was dressed like a cat-burglar! Trust me, I noticed the yoga pants right off. I just didn't put it together until now. She was one crafty lady – and fearless.

At this hour, there wasn't much traffic in this part of town so when a vehicle approached from any direction it made us both a little jumpy. Maybe it's the paranoia that does that, but it sure makes you aware of your surroundings when you're about to do something illegal. It didn't seem to bother her as much, but it made me as nervous as a cat in a room full of Rottweilers.

The street lights shined down on the sidewalk like spotlights, which we skirted around so that we weren't easily seen as we continued our journey to perdition. We passed by a small park where a homeless man was sleeping on a bench. He had on an old overcoat that looked ragged, torn and dirty. It always made me wonder how they ended up where they were. What were their circumstances behind their current state? I silently said a little prayer being thankful for what I have. It puts life into perspective sometimes.

Eventually, we ended up standing in front of a tall building with beautiful windows lit up in a soft blue-white glow up the sides. The mostly glass building was a stark contrast to the all brick parking garage standing equally as tall beside it. A large sign out front, also well lit, read, Camden Group, Inc. letting us know we had the right place. My stomach didn't have butterflies at all. Nope, not even close to what I was feeling. I think I had pterodactyls flying around in there, but I couldn't let her see my fear. Good thing it was dark. We stopped on the opposite side of the street where we could see inside the front doors well. The entire front lobby entrance was lit up.

"Look, a security guard is sitting at the reception desk. There's got to be a way around him," she said.

"When I was young, I lived in a state ran boarding house and we had a guard there at night too. One thing I learned is they get bored easily, and there's always a way around them if you want to bad enough. Let's go over to the parking garage. Maybe we can find a way in from there. People in a building this big don't know everyone so they may look at us funny, but they're just going to think we work in a different department," I said.

I'm not sure where my delinquency came in to play, but a few minutes later we were standing in the parking garage looking at the entrance door. The door required a badge to scan for entrance, but when a tall, lanky guy in a dark suit came strolling out carrying a briefcase and looking intently at his cell phone, texting furiously, we had the perfect opportunity. We pretended we belonged there and waltzed right in before the doors closed. The man barely even glanced up and kept right on walking.

Once we were inside, we could see the guard at the desk in front, but he never looked up at us. We immediately ducked down the hallway and out of sight. There were video cameras in the corners, but we kept our heads down and didn't look up any more than we had to. Just outside the elevators was a big sign on the wall that listed all the floors and the occupants of the offices.

"Here it is, Lucas Bishop Camden, *CEO Office Ste 1001*. It looks like he's on the 10th floor. Schofield's office is up there too. He's the attorney that's been following you. Maybe we should start there?" she suggested.

"I'm sure you're right, but this one here is labeled file clerk. Do you think all of the company's files are kept in one room?" I asked as I held my finger above the up-arrow button of the elevator.

"You may be on to something. Let's check it out first," she said in a rough but hushed voice.

Still hasn't got the whisper thing down yet, I see.

I hit the button and waited for what seemed like forever. In reality, it was forever. When the doors finally opened, we quickly stepped on. Lexi glanced down the long hallway at the guard before she reached over and hit the button for the 2nd floor.

"He's probably checking his Facebook. He never bothered to look up."

The elevator stopped on the 2nd floor, and directly across from the open doors was a sign pointing the way to the file clerk's office. When we walked down the hall to the office, we found the big, heavy door was locked, and there didn't seem to be any other way in. We resigned ourselves to getting back on the elevator and checking out the top floor. The elevator doors closed, but before I pushed the button, I had a thought and turned to Lexi.

"Maybe we should take the stairs in case the guard noticed the elevator going up and down?"

"Yeah, you're probably right. Let's go."

I opened the elevator doors and did a quick look around to make sure it was clear before we got off. It didn't take long to find the stairwell door at the end of the hallway. It was a long climb up, but soon we saw ourselves opening the door to the tenth floor. I peered out into the corridor cautiously to make sure no one was around before we got off.

"Which way now?"

She looked around the hallway for a moment, "No idea, let's try this way," she said, leading us out and to the left.

The entire building was glass so even though the lights in the hallways were off, we could see well from just from the ambient exterior lighting that lit up the building. As we moved down the hall, we heard a door close somewhere up ahead that froze us in our tracks. After a few seconds without any further sounds, we continued. The marble-floored hallway came to an end, and we had to turn left or right. I noticed a light shining from underneath a door down the left, so I signaled to Lexi to be quiet as I pointed out the placard. Matthew Schofield III.

She pointed to a door just down the hall and mouthed the word, bathroom. I understood what she meant, so I led the way over to the door and pushed it open.

"Let's hide in here for now, and when he leaves we can sneak in," she suggested.

The motion sensor turned the lights on as soon as we walked in. I located the wall switch and turned it back off.

Lexi cracked the door open just barely enough to see out and watched for the man to leave. After ten minutes of watching through the crack in the door, we decided to sit down in the dark executive washroom and settle in to wait him out.

"Are you scared?" she asked.

"No, why? Are you?"

"I'm fine, but I can feel you shaking," she giggled quietly.

"No. I'm not scared. It's just cold in here. They must have the A/C turned to subarctic," I replied, trying to sound manly - if that was possible at the moment. It must've worked because she moved closer to me. I wasn't going to complain about that.

A short time later, we heard the attorney's door open, so we peeked out through the crack and saw a man walk out. I couldn't see his face, but I guessed it was Schofield since it was his office. The hallway lights were off, and the only light was the dim glow of the outside lights through the windows.

"He's leaving. Let's go check it out," she said.

We watched the man walk out of the office, down the hallway, and around the corner toward the elevators. I know he pushed the button because I heard the ding when they opened. When it closed, we made our way out moving as quickly down the hallway as we could to the previously occupied office. The light we saw from under the door earlier was off now, so I reached for the knob and carefully opened it. When I had the door open wide enough to slip through, I noticed there was a light on in the back office. I motioned to Lexi to wait for me while I checked it out. She understood my gesture and held the door so that it didn't make any sound. I crept over to where I could peek around the corner at the inner office and saw it was merely a light from a desk lamp that someone forgot to turn off. No one was there. I walked back closer to her.

"All clear," I whispered.

The office was more than I imagined it would be with its plush décor and design. It was spacious, so we decided to split up to search it. I stayed in the outer office and Lexi went into what I gathered was the attorney's private office where the small desk lamp was on. After a few minutes of looking around, I heard her call out to me in her restrained, whispered yell.

"Hey, Leo, come in here for a sec."

She was trying to whisper, but she really needs work on it. She sounded like she had laryngitis or something. When I walked into the office, I saw her looking at a book lying open on the desk.

"What is it?" I asked.

"Looks to be some ledger."

I let out a low whistle as I flipped through it. "Was it just lying open like this?"

"Yes, it was the only thing on the desk," she said, pointing out several city officials, judges, and even high-ranking law enforcement officials. It had several pages in it, and it dated back several years.

I was looking at the same names she was, but I didn't recognize them at all.

"This is a senator, and I know this name too, he's a congressman. There are even judges I recognize and city officials. It looks like payroll or something."

"Um, Lex, do you have any idea what this is?" I asked, somewhat rhetorically. I was beginning to have a bad feeling about this.

"You don't think…," she trailed off with a look of shock and horror on her face.

"Yeah, that's exactly what I think," I said. "This is an accounting ledger showing payoffs and bribes to a lot of influential people. This is the kind of thing that gets people killed."

I flipped to the last page, "Look at this last entry. It's the same date the commissioner was murdered, and it's for fifty-thousand dollars."

"Wow, if Commissioner Wood were paid off then they wouldn't need to kill him," she pointed out. "That's odd."

"Yes, it is. So, who else had reason to kill him if not them?" I asked.

"Maybe it's a payoff to vote yes on the land deal, but they were too late," she speculated with a trace of disdain in her voice.

"Look at the payoff just a few days earlier. It doesn't have a name, just a set of numbers," I pointed out.

"That's weird. And here are the names of two other commissioners above his but dated months earlier."

"This isn't the kind of thing someone would just leave lying out on their desk for the whole world to see. It doesn't make any sense."

It suddenly occurred to me, whoever this guy is; he's coming back!

"I don't like this; we better get out of here. This could get us both killed," I whispered.

"I agree, but I want to check out Camden's office first. Let's just take a quick peek and then we'll get out of here."

Against my better judgment, I let her talk me into going down the hall to Camden's office. There were no signs of anyone in the hallway, thankfully, so we made it there unseen. I opened the door carefully and quickly slipped inside first. When I turned on my flashlight app, I knew immediately something was wrong.

"Oh boy," I said.

"What is it?" she asked.

I looked around the room and could see there were papers all over the place and things knocked off tables. Books had been pulled off shelves and thrown on the floor. A vase with a plant of some kind had been knocked off a shelf near the secretary's desk and had spilled water and dirt on the floor. The place had been ransacked. It was a complete disaster. Whoever had done this was careful not to have stepped in it and leave any tracks.

"Looks like someone broke in and trashed the place. I said I didn't like this earlier; now I'm more than certain I don't like this."

"Me either. I think you're right. We should probably get out of here."

I didn't think she meant it by the way it sounded.

I could see she was more curious now than ever. She had her flashlight on and was walking around the office checking it out when she disappeared into the inner office. I followed her to see what it looked like inside. It was just like out front except there were photographs of Camden all over the walls with famous people and celebrities. This guy was hung up on himself to the point of ridiculous vanity. Dozens of photos lined the walls and shelves. Camden had the same look in every picture. Not a single hair out of place and the same sick smile. He seemed as phony as a three-dollar bill to me.

"I think we should go now. This is obviously a break in and if we get caught…" She trailed off.

"I think you may be ri… - wait a minute, what's this?" I asked.

I picked up a photo with a shattered frame. It appeared to be Camden and his family. I picked Camden out easily enough as I had seen his mug in all the articles I had found about CGI. I carefully moved some of the glass shards to get a better look. It was taken several years ago when he was in his mid-twenties or so, but it was the same unmistakable sick smile. It was a typical family portrait; what I assumed were the parents sitting in front of two siblings, a young man, and woman, standing in the back - the all-American family. They were all pretty, especially the girl. My eyes rested on her a moment. Something was familiar about her. Long dark hair, discontented smile, dark eyes. It suddenly came back to me where I had seen her before.

25

"Wow, someone was upset from the looks of this," Lexi said. "They trashed the place."

I put the photo frame back down where I had found it, and shut off my flashlight, but something on the wall caught my attention. A picture hung at a weird angle and looked slightly off.

"Hey, check this out."

I clicked my flashlight back on. There were several hanging around it, but this one was different. I walked over to it and pulled on it. It swung out on hidden hinges to reveal an open safe behind it. I shined my light into the safe. It was empty.

"They've been robbed."

We stood in silence for a moment just looking around and taking it all in.

"Curious they don't have an alarm system," Lexi said.

"Who says they don't? And guess who's standing here now?"

Our eyes met with the same understanding. We hurried back to the door, slowly opened it, and peered out into the hallway. It was empty.

"Let's go, head straight for the stairs. I'll be right behind you." I whispered. "Whatever happens, just keep going."

"What are you going to do?" She asked.

"No time to explain. I'll be right behind you."

We both ran down the hallway in a panic. As soon as Lexi opened the stairwell door, I repeated myself and told her to keep going.

"I'll catch up with you at the bottom."

I ran back to Schofield's office and quickly ducked inside. Once there, I grabbed the ledger, and tucked it into my jeans just under my shirt-tail and bolted for the door. I caught up to Lexi on the 7th-floor stairwell landing.

"Where did you go? What'd you do?" she asked.

"I'll explain later."

"I just hope we make it out of here," she said as we navigated the steps.

Suddenly, as if on cue, we heard one of the large, steel doors several floors below us as it opened and closed heavily and echoed up the enclosed stairwell.

"Oh no, we're trapped," she whispered frantically.

I tugged at her elbow, and we crept back up to the 8th-floor landing. I opened the door as quietly as I could and pulled her along with me. Once we were through, I let the door close softly behind us, and we waited in the darkness of the hallway.

"Was it a guard? Did you see anyone?" she asked as we held steady by the door waiting and watching.

"I couldn't tell, never saw 'em."

I know I was breathing hard. I have got to start working out and get in shape, especially if I'm going to be an international spy and all.

"I hope they didn't hear us," she whispered.

I listened with my ear to the door.

"You and me both. Whose bright idea was this anyway?" I tried to make light of the situation.

"Okay, so maybe this wasn't such a great idea," Lexi said while panting for breath. Feeling dejected, she slid down the door and sat down. "I'm so sorry. I shouldn't have gotten you mixed up in this."

"Don't worry, Lex; it'll be fine. I promise," I said, kneeling down beside her.

A ledger with names, dates, and payoffs like this could get a lot of people put away for a long time. We were wading out into some deep water, and I'm not so sure we could swim. Finally, we heard a door open and closed again on the stairs. I cracked our door open just enough to see and make sure it was all clear. Once I determined it was safe, we ducked back in and continued making our way down. When we got to the first floor, I opened the door slowly and looked outside. Not seeing anyone, I opened it and let her out first. I could see the garage door entrance to the building where we came in not far away, but the front entrance where the guard was earlier was much closer. Suddenly, we heard the elevator door ding open and footsteps walking down a hallway around the corner.

"Oh no, we're going to get caught for sure," I whispered emphatically. "Got any other ideas? I don't look good in orange jumpsuits!"

"Just one… *RUN!*"

26

Frank sat in his living room watching the television and sipping on a cup of hot tea. He couldn't sleep so he thought he could take his mind off the case for a moment, but as he flipped through the channels he couldn't find anything worth watching. He was halfway through his cup when the phone rang.

"Yeah, O'Conner here."

"Frank, this is Joe from dispatch. A silent alarm was triggered, and the call just came in, thought you'd want to know right away. It concerns one of your cases."

Possibly a break in the case, Frank did not bother turning the TV off. He grabbed his car keys and hurried out the door to make his way over to the CGI offices. He didn't want to tip his hand just yet by barging in on the beat cops checking it out, but he wanted to find out all he could. He would at the very least do a drive by.

27

I heard someone shout from somewhere behind us as we made a mad dash across the lobby, out the front door, through the parking lot and ducked into a nearby alley. An alarm blared and echoed through the darkness as we ran.

As we got further away from CGI, our panting for air slowed a bit and we breathed a little more comfortable, but we didn't slow down. We wanted as much distance between the CGI offices and us as we could get. At least if they chased us this far, we could slip into a backyard or an alley and hide. I could tell Lexi was struggling to keep up.

"I think we're safe now. Maybe we can slow down a little."

"Don't say that for my sake, I can keep up," she said defiantly.

We plodded along, jumping at every sound we heard.

"I've been thinking about something," I said.

Without turning to look at me, she asked, "What's that?"

"The empty safe in Camden's office," I replied. "I think I know what was in it. I mean, think about it."

She mulled it over for only a few seconds when she had an *aha* moment and suddenly stopped walking. She grabbed my arm and spun me around.

"Schofield must've been the one that trashed Camden's office and took the ledger out of the safe," she said.

"Exactly, but why? Why would he trash his boss's office and steal it from his safe?"

"Maybe he's going to try to use it against him. Could be he's trying to hide his tracks and put the blame on someone else."

"It's possible. These people are snakes. From everything we've been reading about them, they don't have a lot of fans. He may be planning to use it against Camden to take over the operation?" I replied.

"Maybe the old saying is true; there is no honor among thieves."

We walked along for another five minutes or so in silence when we heard a police car siren echoing through the night. We picked up our pace to a slow jog and ducked down a dark alley. Another vehicle sounded like it had joined the other one, which made us even more nervous. When we came out on the other side, and onto the sidewalk of the street, a car passing by suddenly spun around and turned their headlights on us before we had a chance to run.

"Hold it right there you two!"

That voice was familiar. We started to bolt back into the alley, but there was something about the voice that held us in place. With the bright headlights shining in our eyes, we couldn't see him, but it became evident to me - we were either in a lot of trouble now, or we were in big-time trouble now.

"Detective O'Conner, it's not what it looks like I promise," I said.

"What do you think it looks like Valentine?" The detective asked. "Looks to me like you're running away from something in the middle of the night…or someone?"

Just our luck! There is no way the detective was just driving by. That told me he had contacts. When the guard triggered the alarm, it must have gone straight to the cop shop, and someone that knew he was investigating the place had to have told him. Not sure if I felt better about that or not.

"Okay... so...maybe it is what it looks like," I replied. After all, the guy did have a point. "Ya gotta believe us. We didn't do anything. We were just in the wrong place at the wrong time. It wasn't us I swear."

"What are you talking about? What did you do?" O'Conner asked.

"We don't have time to explain right now. We didn't do it though. They're right behind us. Please, Detective, you've gotta help us," I pleaded, knowing it was only a matter of seconds before the security guards caught up with us if they were combing the area.

"First, get over here and tell me what you've done and who's after you," the detective ordered us.

We walked over to his car where we could see him clearly. We were still panting for breath, and he knew we had been up to something.

"Detective, I'm Lexi Osborne, and I'm a reporter for the Grind. I'm afraid we don't have a lot of time to talk. Leo is right; we were in the wrong place at the wrong time. We've been investigating the murder of Commissioner Wood which led us to the CGI offices. We went there tonight to see what we could find out, and now they're after us, and I'm afraid they're in no mood for talking," she explained.

I could see the look on the detective's face as he considered our story. He seemed hesitant, but finally said, "Hurry, get in the car!"

We moved fast and jumped into the back seat. He did a U-turn in the street, hit the gas and sped away

"You two have a lot of explaining to do!" he growled.

She gave me a pinch on my knee, and when I looked at her I saw her give me the, *'I'll do the talking'* look.

"Out with it!" he ordered.

Neither of us said a word.

"Not everybody speak up at once, please."

His sarcasm wasn't easily missed. He was miffed and wanted answers, guess I couldn't blame him.

"Now, one at a time starting with you, Miss. I have a feeling I'll get more information from you than this one anyway," he said, as he hooked a thumb in my direction. "Tell me why I shouldn't arrest you and haul the both of you's in right now?"

Lexi began, "We went to the CGI office's tonight because we've been investigating the murder of Commissioner Wood. As I said, I'm an investigative reporter for the Grind."

"That remains to be seen," he said.

She dug out her press card she had around her neck and tucked into her shirt. She continued her story and held the card for him to see.

"The building wasn't locked when we got there, so we just walked in. We didn't break in at all, Detective. I swear we didn't, but when we went up to Camden's office we saw the place had been burglarized so we got out of there as quickly as we could, and that's the truth," she said.

"Did you see anyone else there or did anyone see you? You said the guards were chasing you?" he asked.

"No, we never saw who did it. We just walked in on it after the fact. I don't think anyone saw us. Not our faces anyway."

"What does that mean?" he asked glancing back at her.

"I think they may have spotted us as we ran out," she said.

"Just great," he said. "Did it ever occur to you that if they killed someone as important as a commissioner in cold blood, they wouldn't hesitate to get rid of a couple of kids?"

She sat back in her seat with a defiant look on her face and faced straight ahead with her arms crossed.

"What makes you think CGI had anything to do with the murder anyway?" he asked.

Lexi explained our theory that the commissioner's murder had to be tied to Camden and how we went there tonight to look for evidence to solve the case. She also told him about our research on

Camden and that there have been other murders in the past that had to do with the purchase and development of land that they were involved in. She also spoke of our trip to the farm and the visit with Allister. I cringed in my seat, however, when she told him about her theory of the Ghost assassin.

"Oh, I see," the detective said, "So what I'm hearing is you believe Michael Allister had something to do with the murder, so you thought you'd find evidence of his involvement at the CGI offices? That makes perfect sense. There's also a ghost assassin loose on the streets knockin' people off, and then there's Camden. Is there anyone you don't suspect?" he asked sarcastically. "I think I've heard all I need to."

"No sir, well, maybe, but we also think Schofield had something to do with it, and there's also the matter of…"

The detective cut her off sharply.

"Oh, now I see. It's clear as day. It's a conspiracy. What motive would CGI have to kill the commissioner?"

"We know from the papers that Wood had tabled the vote for the past five months. Once Camden had a contract with Henry Allister in place, the commission allows six months for the purchaser, CGI in this case, to complete a land use proposal. If they meet all the criteria the commission requests, then they would vote to allow the sale to go through. If not, the contract would be nullified, and the land would go back on the market. With Wood out of the way, it passed only a few days after he was murdered," Lexi replied triumphantly.

The detective gave her musings brief thought. "Maybe. It is a theory. I'll give ya that, but who's to say that eliminating Wood prompted the sale being approved by the commission?"

"Who's to say it didn't? After all, it did pass two days after his death during an emergency meeting. I don't have to tell you that a meeting of urgency isn't the place for a public body to be transacting business as huge as that land sale was. There are laws about what type of activity can be transacted during an emergency meeting," she said. "I still have more questions than answers at this point, Detective."

"Exactly," O'Conner declared. "That's why from this point forward, you're going to allow me to do my job and stay out of the way. Got it?"

We kept our mouths shut and shared a worried glance. I could tell he was getting more annoyed with us, but I hoped he wasn't going to take us to jail. Lexi tried explaining all our different theories so far, but when she finished, even I was confused. The detective suddenly pulled the car over, put it in park and killed the engine. He spun around in his seat and gave us a stern look.

"Okay, spill it. I know there's something you're not telling me. Now out with it," he ordered.

"No, there's nothing else," she said.

"I'm taking you both home, and I want you to listen to me and listen good. You are both to cease with any more investigating," he said. "Furthermore, if they press charges you could both go to jail for breaking and entering. There's not much I can do to help you there I'm afraid."

"But, we didn't break in. The place wasn't locked," she replied emphatically.

"Secondly," the detective ignored her to continue his rant, "did you stop to think about the security cameras and that they may have you on video surveillance?" he asked, glaring at us.

Neither of us said a word. I wasn't about to lip off. I didn't want to go to jail, not tonight anyway. I had to work at the diner in the morning.

"I didn't think so. Therefore, you are not to continue interfering in police affairs, got it?"

"Yes sir, but…"

"No buts. I mean it. You two stay away from this case!" he said sternly. After a few minutes of silence, the detective softened a little.

"Do you not see how dangerous these people are?" he asked, clearly understanding we weren't the bad guys he was after here.

He had a point. We looked at each other, me with a look of fear and her, indignation that turned to hurt and dejection.

The detective turned back around, started the car and pulled back out onto the street. We drove along in silence for several minutes watching the street lights pass by when he suddenly pulled the car over again.

"Okay, look you two. I understand what you're trying to do, but this is just too dangerous, and it's my job to protect people especially when they aren't smart enough to protect themselves. Say I believe your story that you didn't break in or steal anything, CGI may not, especially since the place had been ransacked as you say. They'll be looking for whoever did it."

"We understand. Honestly, we do, but it's my job as a reporter to get the story. I'm not afraid of them."

"No, I don't think you are, but let me say this. It may be your job to get the story, but that doesn't give you the right to break the law, and trespassing is breaking the law. If they want to press charges, they have every right to do so," O'Conner said.

"No sir, I mean, yes sir," she said.

She seemed disappointed at that last statement. She slouched back in her seat and looked down at her lap. I didn't like to see her being so down on herself because I knew how much this story meant to her. The detective turned back around and pulled back out into the street.

"Tell you what, if you kids will stay out of the way, or at least arm's length, and don't get into any more trouble, I'll make sure you get the first shot at the story from my end. Deal?"

"Sure. Thank you," she said. "But what about…" She trailed off not sure if he would be angry if she continued.

"What about what? What is it? Am I missing something?" the detective asked.

"Yes!" Lexi exclaimed. "Well, no, but well…"

"Well, what is it?" he asked.

"There *is* something else, someone else rather. A woman. Her name is Richards, with Jade Development. Apparently, she tried to bid on the Allister property, but she was too late. Camden pulled some strings and got the real estate office to close the bidding earlier than originally planned. When she found out she became angry," she explained.

"So, is that the entire list of suspects now?" the detective asked. "What about you, Valentine? Got anything to add? You've been pretty quiet back there."

"No sir, I'm just trying to keep her out of trouble," I replied.

She gave me a dirty look, and I just smiled back with a shoulder shrug. Besides she didn't want me to do the talking anyway, remember?

"Oh well, I think that's enough anyway, it's more than sufficient. You seem to have the suspect list narrowed down to half the city. Are we clear on your involvement on this now, you two?"

We both nodded our assurances.

"Good, now that we have that straight, I'm going to forget this little event tonight, and I'm taking you both home. With any luck, CGI won't press charges being that you - *didn't break in*." He emphasized that last part.

The detective asked Lexi where she lived so that he could drive her home first. We arrived a short time later, and he warned her again about staying out of police business before he would let her out.

Her apartment building was a much swankier place than my poor excuse of an abode. She said bye to us both and thanked the detective when he dropped her off and escorted her to her building door. I climbed into the front seat and waited to make sure she got inside safely. Once she had gone safely inside, he came back to the car, got in and pulled out for the drive to my place.

"What are you not telling me, Valentine?" he asked.

I had been mulling it over since the detective first picked us up. There's no way I would ever rat Briana out. I'd end up on the losing end of that deal real fast, but she didn't say anything about doing what I needed to stay alive, and I think that's exactly what I needed to be thinking about right now. I had to trust someone, but just how much is the question. I decided to tell O'Conner about the ledger. What I wasn't going to tell him was that I went back to Schofield's office and snatched it.

"Are you sure kid?"

"Yeah, I'm sure. I know my way around a payoff sheet. I've learned a few things living on the streets ya know. That ledger had hundreds of names and hundreds of thousands of dollars in payoffs listed. It had names, dates, times, locations, and bank accounts. You name it, it's in there, and get this, it goes back years. That thing can get a lot of people sent to prison for a long time, not to mention get a lot of people killed."

"Holy hell, that's dangerous stuff! It's not hard to figure how these companies become so powerful. If that book ever fell into the wrong hands, there's no telling at the hell that would be unleashed on this city."

"You're telling me," I said.

"The only problem is I don't have a valid reason to pick Schofield up or to search his office. Not yet anyway," the detective replied.

"Not even if you had an eyewitness and evidence placing him at the diner the night he was killed like, say a credit card receipt for his order?" I asked.

Detective, Frank O'Conner smiled.

"That may very well do it, kid."

28

Matthew Schofield stood at the security reception desk speaking with the two police officers that responded to the alarm.

"I'm sorry fellas. I must apologize. It was a false alarm. My security officer was being overzealous and didn't realize it was me that had returned to the building. He thought I was an intruder."

"Not a problem, Mr. Schofield, better safe than sorry, eh?" the taller of the two cops replied. "We'll just be going, but if you need anything at all, don't hesitate to call."

"Thank you again, officers. Pardon me if I don't show you out, but I must get up to my office and get some work done so I can go home."

The two officers turned and exited the building. When their patrol car was pulling out of the parking lot, Schofield leaned over the guard's shoulder, picked up the phone and dialed his boss. When Camden answered, the attorney was short and blunt, "We had a break-in at the office tonight. You better get down here."

While he waited for his boss to arrive, the attorney visited the security surveillance office with CGI Chief of Security, John Strauss, who arrived moments after the alarm went out. Together, they watched the videotape stop at precisely 10:07 p.m. and not start back again until 10:37.

"Dammit! Whoever broke in tonight was sophisticated enough to hack our surveillance system, power it off, and back on again once they got what they came for," Schofield said.

"Yes sir," Strauss replied. "The guard never noticed because it was set to playback a continuous loop of an empty building. These were professionals."

The attorney stood and walked out just in time to meet Lucas Camden rushing into the building. Together they took the elevator to his office on the 10th floor.

***

Lexi typed in the passcode to her apartment building and rushed up the stairs, down the hallway and inserted the key to her door. Once inside, she closed the door and locked it behind her. The only light in the apartment came from a small nightlight in the hallway. It was more than enough to illuminate the pervading darkness of the room, but she flipped the overhead light on and put her things down on the table in the entryway. She stopped long enough to stare into the mirror hanging just above it and let out an audible groan when she saw the smear of mascara and matting of unruly locks of hair from the sweat of the evening's clandestine activities. She grimaced and headed for the bathroom to wash up.

Twenty minutes later, she lay in bed staring at the ceiling trying to fall asleep, but no matter how hard she tried, her mind just couldn't rest. The night's events kept playing out in her head. First, Schofield had the ledger in his office that was clearly an accounting book showing payoffs and bribes to so many people. The commissioner's name was on it and dated on the day he was killed, so why would they need to kill him, she wondered. Maybe he threatened to expose them, or possibly he refused the bribe, so they had no other choice for them to be able to purchase the Allister land?

Second, why would Schofield be following Leo around if not for thinking that Leo saw something the night the commissioner was killed?

She couldn't shake the feeling that Schofield was a snake in the grass. What seemed to bother her most is that she didn't like him when she didn't even know him, but she couldn't figure out why. There was just something about him that she couldn't quite put a finger on.

Lexi was the only daughter born to Pete and Jennifer Osborne. Her parents married just out of high school. They both doted on their daughter and were, perhaps overly protective. Lexi was headstrong, much like her mother, and not afraid of anything. She viewed the world as one in which everyone was good, even the worst of the worst.

When sleep wouldn't come she picked up her cell phone, scrolled through the contact list, found Leo's number and clicked the green call button.

29

The detective finally cut me loose, but not before reminding me to stay out of the way as he worked on the case. He also asked me to call him if I remembered anything else or felt threatened. I assured him I was done with police work and closed the car door when I got out. I knew I was taking a considerable chance trusting him with as much as I dared, but one thing I knew for sure from skimming through the ledger from Schofield's office, Frank O'Conner's name wasn't on it.

    I raced upstairs, down the hall and quickly disappeared inside my apartment. I turned on the sad, pitiful excuse of a lamp, broken too mind you, walked to the crippled old fridge and grabbed a soda. After a long gulp, I reached behind me and pulled out the ledger, sat it down on the small table in front of me and just stared at it. This was the kind of thing that gets people killed, but it may also keep someone alive. That someone would be me. I looked through it and checked out some of the names. I didn't know but a few of 'em being that I don't keep up with who's who in this city, but I used my phone and googled a few - politicians mostly. They seemed to be the ones with the big money payoffs anyway. Not only big numbers but regular payoffs too. The book was loaded with information. It even had bank account numbers, cash payouts, and drop off locations - a veritable gold mine of bad-guy activity that any cop would love to get their fingers on; any honest cop anyways. I still couldn't figure out why the commissioner was killed if he was already in their pocket. It had to be a way to identify someone, and I'm more than certain who that person was, but I would also bet they had no idea who she was. She didn't strike me as being an idiot. I knew the numbers weren't bank accounts either. As I said, I know my way around an account sheet. If these numbers were a way to identify her, someone had to know what they meant, or there'd be a key to unlock it somewhere. I scanned through the entire book and noted that it went back for almost ten years amounting to hundreds of thousands of dollars in payouts. I had to find a safe place to keep this thing.

I put my soda down on the table, picked up the ledger and opened it on the countertop under the overhead light. It took me about twenty minutes, but I photographed every single page with my new handy dandy cell phone, uploaded them to the cloud, then deleted 'em all, leaving only two photos on my cell, one of Lexi and the other of Briana. After I finished the last page, I picked the ledger up, carefully wrapped it air-tight in plastic wrap from the kitchen and carried it outside to my window ledge. There, on the fire escape, I keep an old grill which seemed like the perfect place to hide the thing. Once it was securely hidden under the charcoal ashes, I came back inside and jumped in the shower, jumped right back out and threw myself on the bed. I never thought I could be so tired. I'd have to get up and go to work in a few hours, but I was wide awake now, wired up with adrenaline - and worry.

Dammit man! I couldn't believe it. As tired as I was and I couldn't freaking sleep! With help from the ambient light coming through my window, I laid there and counted spots on the ceiling. Just as I finally began to get drowsy and fall asleep, I heard a loud jingle playing. It startled me so badly that I sat straight up out of my bed.

"What the hell…who…"

It took me a second to realize it was my cell phone ringing. I picked it up and saw it was Lexi calling.

"Hey, what's wrong? Are you okay?"

"I'm sorry, I couldn't sleep, and I wanted to check on you and make sure you're okay. I thought you'd be awake. I'm sorry," she said.

"I was. I mean…I am. It's fine. I was just staring at the ceiling. Are you sure you're okay?"

"I'm fine. Really. I've been thinking. What bothers me most is there doesn't seem to be a motive for Schofield to have murdered him which leads me to believe that it must've been Allister's son, Michael, as much as I hate to admit it. But he had a clear motive, and he was here during that time according to Hank."

"I know right," I agreed. "Schofield seems to be a snake, but I'm not sure exactly what his involvement is. It seems to me he would have more to lose if something happened to Wood than he would gain from it," I replied.

"You're right," she sighed. "So, listen, we'd better get some sleep. I'm sorry I called so late."

"Don't worry about it. You can call me anytime at all, day or night."

"Thanks, Leo. Will you call me tomorrow?" she asked in her soft, lyrical voice that always seemed to make me feel all swoopy inside. Jeez, what a sap I am.

"You bet!" I said, grinning like a great ape. I bet if you could've seen my face right then, I'd have looked pretty much like a lovesick idiot grinning like that, but I couldn't help it. Hey, I'm an emotional guy.

30

Frank watched Leonard walk to his building in the glow of the streetlight. Once he saw the kid get inside the building, he called the station. The dispatcher answered after the first ring.

"Police station, front desk."

"Joe, Frank here. Hey, listen. Have you heard anything about that break-in reported earlier tonight at CGI?"

"Yeah, it was nothing. Timmons called it in a while ago. Said it was a false alarm. One of the managers was working late or something and tripped the alarm."

"Is that right? Okay, Joe, thanks."

Frank clicked the end-call button on his cell phone and turned the car around. Twenty minutes later he parked across the street from the CGI offices. If Leonard and Lexi were right about what they saw, they could be in a lot of trouble, the kind of trouble that could get them killed. He would have to keep a close eye on CGI, particularly one Matthew Schofield.

***

"The guard up front is new, only been on the job a few weeks. He hit the silent alarm when he heard someone running out of the building during his rounds. He chased them, but they were gone before he caught up to him. He didn't see anything, only heard their footsteps as they ran out of the building; probably had a car waiting outside," Schofield explained.

"What about surveillance?" Camden asked.

"Strauss is in the surveillance room right now. The time lapse of the video is missing the twenty-two minutes the thief or thieves were in the building. He's trying to discover how they hacked into the system now. He said, whoever it was, knew exactly what they were doing, a professional job."

"Interesting," Camden acknowledged. "What did you tell the cops?"

"I told them it was a false alarm and sent them away. Didn't think we needed to advertise it."

Lucas listened attentively even though his eyes were staring at his office. He considered his next words carefully before replying, "No, you did right. These were professionals. No other explanation. This…" He paused with a look of anger and disgust. With a gesture at his ransacked office, he completed his thought, "This was a message."

"Yes, I agree, but by whom?"

"I have no idea, but they were good enough to hack the alarm system and crack my safe. They didn't even look at the priceless paintings hanging everywhere. No, they knew exactly what they were after and could've done so without all of this," he said. He pointed out the room again.

"Looks and sounds like a professional job to me."

John Strauss walked into the office and joined the two men.

"What did you find out, John?" Camden asked.

"Not much, a total breach of security systems. Surveillance was rigged to loop an empty building, so the guard monitoring the video feeds never knew differently. What I can't figure out is how they were able to do so through our firewall. If I didn't know any better, I'd say it was an inside job. At this point, we have nothing."

"I figured as much," Schofield said.

"Was anything taken from your office, Mr. Camden?" Strauss asked.

"No, nothing is missing," he lied. "It's just trashed."

"Maybe it was protesters from one of those free-space, tree-hugging, civic groups," Strauss suggested. "At least nothing valuable was lost," he said as he looked around the office indicating the valuable paintings and sculptures in the room.

Camden glared at the man but knew he shouldn't say anything about what was missing from the safe.

"No, I have a feeling this was much too sophisticated for any of them. Keep searching and let me know if you find out anything further."

"Yes, sir," Strauss said and exited the room.

Lucas Camden watched his Chief of Security leave and then turned his attention back to the office. He studied the disaster, picking his way around overturned chairs and scattered files to pull the hinged painting from the wall. He stood in front of the empty safe. He had made the drive to the office in half the time as normal when he got the call from his attorney about the break-in. He did not need to worry about being stopped by the police as he most likely owned any that may have pulled him over for speeding anyway.

"I don't have to tell you what's at stake. Whoever has the ledger will want to use it!" Camden said with his cold eyes glaring intently at the attorney. His face flushed with anger – and fear.

"I'm betting we'll be hearing from whoever took it soon," Schofield said.

"You can count on it. I want answers. I want to know who it was, where they live, who their families are and everything about them. I want some answers, and I want them now!" Camden shouted. He was seething.

"I'm already on it."

"Good, in the meantime, make sure we can't be connected with Councilman Wood in any other way than through the legal channels. We can't afford the negative publicity right now," Camden said as he sat down at his desk. "I've got phone calls to make. Close the door on your way out."

The attorney turned and walked out of Camden's office. Just as he reached back to close the door, Camden growled, "And tell the new guard he's fired!"

Schofield exited the building through the parking garage entrance doors on the first floor. When he got to his car, he looked around. Seeing no one, he pulled the handle, opened the door, and sat down. He reached over and hit the button on the shifter to start it, put the car in drive and left the garage. He wouldn't be working out at the company gym this morning. He had to figure out who took the ledger. The guard couldn't give him anything to go on so it could've been anyone. He had his suspicions though, but nothing concrete.

Across the street, Detective Frank O'Conner started his car and followed the black Mercedes as it exited the parking garage of CGI.

31

It was a long night, but a short one in regards to rest, and the morning wasn't much better. I had just finished cleaning the kitchen and restocking for the day when the boss, one Mr. Horace Greely, walked back in after an extended smoke break in the alley, blew past me and headed straight to his office without the chaotic utterances most associated with his wonderful disposition. Suited me just fine, I didn't want his sour mood to spoil my good mood. I glanced up at the clock and saw it was almost time for me to skedaddle out of here anyway, and I would too, just as soon as Marvin showed up to relieve me.

I'd been jittery all morning, and more than a little surprised no one had shown up asking for me yet or to lead me away in cuffs. Lexi and I getting caught by the detective last night was dead last on my bucket list of things I wanted to do before I died. I honestly figured it would be either him or some random mob hitman that would be walking in every time I heard those jingle bells ringing on the front door when customers came in. It took me all morning to settle down.

The back door opened again, but this time it was Marvin.

"Ooo wee, place sho' lookin' good this moanin' my young apprentice."

"It was crazy busy early this morning, but slowed down the last hour or so. I had plenty of time to get it cleaned up and ready to go again," I replied with a look of satisfaction.

I still wasn't sure why he called me his young apprentice. The only thing he'd ever taught me was how to fake looking busy when the boss was around. Oh well, I'd let him have his fantasy. It was no skin off my nose.

After a brief chat, I took my apron off, hung it up and let him know I'd be back for my evening shift a little early. I grabbed my backpack and bolted for the door. It'd been a pretty quick morning, and I was thankful for that. I'd been anxious and nervous about talking to Lexi. I'd never called a girl before. Sure, Lexi may have given me the kiss of death with the whole 'friend' thing, nothing more, nothing less, but it was still different. As soon as I walked out the back door, I felt myself grinning like the goofy cat in that kid's story. You know the one – yup, I felt that foolish, but I didn't care if anyone saw me like this. I was in a great mood, and nothing was going to change that.

I reached into my backpack, pulled my cell phone out and hit the call button next to Lexi's photo. I heard it ring several times before it finally went to voicemail, but I nervously hit the *end call* button before it got to the part about leaving a message. She could see I called and I was sure she'd call me back when she could. That wasn't going to cut my groove. Right now, I was off to the park to kill a few hours reading and take a break from Greely's slop shop.

When I arrived at the park, I found a nice shaded bench and sat down to read the book I had checked out at the library a few days ago. I started reading, but something kept gnawing at me. I finally gave in to it when I realized I had come to the end of the page and had no idea what I had read. I pulled out my cell phone, opened the web browser and typed in the name, Michelle Richards. A few seconds later, I was staring at a newspaper article with a photograph of the lady. It was black and white and being that it was on my tiny screen, it was a little difficult to make out her features well, but it didn't take me but a split second to know exactly where I had seen her before. I took a quick screenshot and saved it, and I hit the call button for Lexi again. After the first ring, it went straight to voicemail again. This time I left her a message.

Dr. Watson here, I have just made a startling discovery Mr. Holmes, umm, Miss Holmes, an interesting piece of information. Call me as soon as you can

I tried my best to mimic an English accent, trying to be funny. I put my phone away and grabbed my book again. An hour later, the sun moved around, and I lost my shade, so I moved over to a grassy spot under a tree. The next thing I knew, I was waking up. I laughed at myself when I realized just how tired I must've been. I slept for almost two hours. I didn't wear a watch, but I knew it was already time to head back for the evening shift. I checked my cell phone and saw that I had missed a call from Lexi, but there was a text from her too.

Sorry I missed your call, Mr. Watson. Was away from my desk. I'll try you again later. S. Holmes Hugs :)

I quickly hit the reply button and texted her back. I'd have to be sure to check it now and then when it was slow at the diner in case she called. I crossed the street to get back to the diner and passed by, what seemed like, a million vehicles along the way. I was used to all the horn honking, the banging and clanging, the shouting and every other indistinct sound. It was just a part of life here in the city. A person learns to tune it all out and worry about their own business.

When I got to the alley behind the diner and turned the corner, I noticed a black SUV with tinted windows parked next to the dumpsters. It was blocking the way to the door forcing me to walk around it. Just as I passed by, the door flew open, and a big, ugly bruiser of a guy jumped out of the passenger side and put a gun in my face. I froze instantly, thinking I've never even had a girlfriend! I may have just wet myself – again.

"Put this on and get in!" he demanded, handing me a dark hood indicating I was to put it over my head at the same time he ripped my backpack off and threw it in the vehicle.

"What's going on? Where are you taking me?"

Big ugly punched me in the gut, efficiently limiting my ability to talk by knocking the wind out of me. I doubled over in pain desperately trying to breathe. Jeez, what the crap was this all about? I'd no idea who these idiots were, but they were starting to piss me off.

"Keep your mouth shut, and you might live, keep asking questions, and you'll discover what the bottom of the East River looks like," he said and roughly shoved me into the back seat.

I felt big ugly slide in beside me, grab my hands and tie them with a zip tie. A little too tight, but seeing that I needed to focus my efforts on breathing... I let it go. I tried to sit up, but the driver took off fast and slammed me back into the seat. It suddenly occurred to me – I'd dropped my cell phone in the alley.

32

"Good morning, I'm Detective O'Conner, NYPD. Need to see Lucas Camden."

Frank kept a close distance to Schofield as he exited the building and followed him to his home. When it was apparent the attorney was finally settled in for the night, Frank made his way back to the CGI offices and waited until regular business hours before announcing his arrival.

"One moment, Detective," the guard at the reception desk replied.

After a brief conversation on the phone, the guard escorted Frank to Camden's office. He had been giving a lot of thought to what Lexi and Leonard had told him, and he had to admit, CGI seemed to be right in the middle of the investigation. When the two men entered the office on the 10th floor, Camden's secretary told Frank he could go right in. The guard exited at that point to head back to his post, and Frank met Camden in his office.

"Detective O'Conner, what can I do for you?" Camden asked.

"Maybe not much at all Mr. Camden, I'm just following up on the break-in report that came in last night," Frank said.

He observed Camden's face to see if and how his facial expressions changed, looking for any indication of deception. If what those two kids told him was true and he had no reason to believe otherwise, then the office would be a mess, but as he entered, the room looked as it should. No overturned chairs, no papers littered the floor, no broken lamps.

"I've already explained to the officers that came in last night that it was merely a misjudgment on the part of my overzealous security guard. You see, there was no break-in at all, it was one of the company executives working late, and the guard didn't realize it. That's all. I appreciate your concern, Detective, but honestly, I feel like this was a waste of your time and time is a valuable resource we can't get back you know."

"Yes sir, that's true," Frank replied. "I was just in the neighborhood and had heard it on the radio. No worries. I just wanted to make sure everything was alright."

"I appreciate your concern, Detective, but I assure you, there was no break-in."

Camden smiled reassuringly as he began to usher Frank toward the door.

Camden's face never seemed to hint that he may be telling a lie or indicate any deception that Frank could spot. When he turned to leave, he noticed a glint of something shiny on the floor. Frank's shoe suddenly needed to be tied.

***

An hour later, O'Conner walked into the precinct office with a tall cup of coffee in one hand and a pastry in the other. He quickly slalomed through the maze of large gray-metal desks and made his way over to his own where he met his partner, Mike Freeman.

"Morning sunshine, glad you could join us today," his partner, greeted him.

"Ha, very funny, but in my defense, I had a late night last night," Frank replied.

"Business or pleasure? Wait, who am I talking to? Of course, it was business."

"Aren't you just a regular comedian. But, to alleviate your fears of losing a partner to debaucheries and leave you to solve this case all by your lonesome, let me just say that it *was* business. But first, what did you find out about the farmer's son?"

Mike laughed at his usually stoic partner's attempt at humor.

"His alibi checks out, solid even. I think we can rule him out as a suspect," Mike said.

Frank took a quick bite of his cream cheese Danish and devoured it.

"I'm waiting," Mike replied impatiently.

Frank swallowed his breakfast and took a drink of his coffee. "Sorry."

For the next half hour, Frank filled Mike in on the events of the last twenty-four hours including the eyewitness statement from Leonard placing Schofield at the scene of the crime.

"Camden's good. He looked me square in the eye and lied about the break-in. When I was leaving, I found this."

Frank held the small glass shard up for Mike to look at.

"What's this?"

"I believe it's a piece of the photo that sat on his desk. He had the place cleaned up, and everything was in order - except a photo of his family on his desk. It was missing. I saw it the first time I was there. My guess is it was broken, and he hadn't time to replace it yet."

"Yeah, that could be."

They agreed the next step would be to bring Schofield in for questioning, but they also knew the captain might not approve of such a risky move with the little amount of evidence they had and the shaky eyewitness account. They had to shake things up and see if they could make people nervous. When criminals get nervous, they make mistakes. This case was high profile and had stayed on the front page of every newspaper in the city. Frank didn't care whose toes he stepped on though; he was all about solving the case and putting the bad guys away. He would never compromise his integrity by treating the rich and powerful any differently than he would the poor working stiffs. A criminal was a criminal in his eyes.

The two detectives poured over each other's notes and carefully constructed a cause for a search warrant of the CGI offices based on Leonard's eye-witness statement. It wasn't much to work with, and they may not have any luck finding a judge to sign off on it, but it was a risky move they were willing to make at this stage of the investigation. Even if it didn't pan out, it might be enough to make the killer show his hand and allow the detectives to pounce.

***

"It's not much your honor, we know, but we have reason to suspect Schofield is tied up in all of this beyond what we can put on paper right now," Frank said to Judge Henry.

"It's thin fellas. I'd like to help you out, but there's not much in the way of evidence here to tell me he's involved with anything. So, he drives by the diner the night of the murder. I'm sure a hundred people drove by that diner that night. You can't suspect all of them, can you?" Judge Henry asked.

"Well, no sir, but a credit card receipt places him at the scene not to mention the fact that his business has close ties to the Commissioner, and those ties weren't exactly on the up and up. We spelled it all out in the request, sir," Frank said.

Judge Henry looked back down at the search warrant request the detectives prepared and read for a few more minutes. He was known to be a bit eccentric and even been called a lone wolf at times, but he knew the law and was never one for nonsense. When

Frank needed a search warrant signed that was a little too political for most judges, he would come to see Judge Henry.

"Yes. Yes, I see that you have laid it out quite well. Tell you what. I'm going to sign off on this warrant, but you had better find something, or it may be the end of a career - for all of us. But, there's enough here to warrant a look," the judge said.

He signed the paper and handed it back to the officers.

Twenty minutes later, the two detectives, along with two squad cars and four other officers, pulled up to the front entrance of the Camden Group offices and walked inside together.

The security guard at the reception desk suddenly jumped up when he saw them come in and stopped them immediately.

"What can I do for you officers?" the guard asked as he held his ground firmly. It was evident his job was to stop anyone from coming past the front desk, and he seemed adamantly opposed to the intrusion, even by the police.

"Here to see Matthew Schofield," Frank said tersely.

There was an awkward silence as Frank and Mike stood in front of the guard, who hesitated.

"Now!" Frank demanded.

"Yes sir, but I'll need to phone upstairs first sir. I have strict orders," the guard said.

"You go right ahead son," Frank said with a smile in his eyes. He knew someone *upstairs* had already spotted them. He pushed past the guard and headed for the elevators not waiting on the results of the guard's phone call.

The man quickly hung up the phone and scurried to catch up.

"I'll show you up."

They were prepared to enter with or without an invitation, but Frank liked to toy with his prey just a bit. The guard pushed the button on the elevator without another word. When they exited on the top floor, they were greeted by none other than Lucas B. Camden.

"Good morning gentlemen. Please follow me where we can talk," Camden suggested.

Frank paused for a moment, looked over at his partner with a somewhat amused smile, and replied, "Sure thing Camden."

Mike and the officers followed the two men down the hallway to his office. When they arrived at his doorway, Frank instructed the officers to wait outside a moment. He knew Camden had to be aware this wasn't a simple Q and A. The man had to be stalling for Schofield and trying to find out everything the police knew.

After Frank introduced his partner, Camden asked them to have a seat. They sat down in the same plush chairs Frank sat in last time he visited with Camden.

"So, what can I do for you? I'm afraid I only have a few minutes to spare then I really must get back to a conference call," Camden said with a wisp of a smile passing his lips on their way to a perturbed scowl. "I told the officers last night it was a false alarm. Apparently, my Chief Council forgot to let security know he was back in the building."

"It's not about that, Mr. Camden. This won't take long," Frank began. "For starters, I need to know some details about the Allister property. I understand that in the beginning, several interested parties had put in bids, but soon retracted them leaving only Camden Group. Any reason the others would have pulled their bids?"

"Honestly, Detective, I've no idea why the others retracted their bids. Perhaps they couldn't put the financing together in time, or they decided it wasn't what they were looking for. I am at a loss as to why you would bother asking me that when you could have talked to them yourself," Camden said smugly.

"Oh, we did, Mr. Camden," Mike said, leaving the comment hanging for interpretation. When he received no response, he asked, "Did your Chief Council, that you mentioned earlier, have any business dealings with these other companies by chance?"

"Well, of course, he did. We have dealings with numerous companies from all over the country, from all around the world, so yes, I'm certain we've visited them on occasion. What are you getting at detective?"

"No implication at all Mr. Camden, simply trying to understand the dynamics of a business deal that apparently led to the murder of a prominent county commissioner. That's all," Frank said.

Camden bristled with the statement, and his eyes blazed with anger, but he held his tongue. The detective knew he was getting to him, so he pushed ahead.

"Mr. Camden," Frank began again, standing as he spoke, "Were you aware your attorney was supposed to meet with Commissioner Wood at the diner the night he was killed?" he asked carefully watching Camden's face.

"Yes, of course, I am. I'm aware of everything to do with this business. He was to have gone on my behalf to iron out a few details, but he was delayed here at the office and had to cancel the meeting," Camden said.

"To iron out a few details, concerning the Allister property?"

"Yes, precisely."

"Forgive me if I'm wrong here, but being that Wood was representing a public office, isn't an offsite and out of public view meeting concerning business with the board…illegal?" Frank said, looking sternly at Camden.

"Certainly, it would be, if they were discussing business that would have come before the board, but, I assure you, the business to have been considered at the meeting was concerning only items previously approved by the board. Therefore, conflict of interest would not apply. Now, if you'll excuse me, gentlemen, I must get back to my conference call."

"Oh, I understand, Mr. Camden, but before you do that, you may want to see at this," Frank handed him the search warrant.

The detectives watched the business mogul's face turn red as he read the warrant.

"Would you be so kind as to direct us to your attorney's office, please? I'm sure that once we look around and have a word with him, we can clear this whole thing up," Frank said with a slight smile.

As Camden stood, in what the detective surmised as feigned self-righteous indignation, Frank stopped him cold with an off-topic question.

"Who is the lady in the photograph with you and your parents?"

Caught off-guard, Camden had to refocus to answer, "That's my sister, Michelle," he replied with a befuddled look.

"Is she involved with the business?" Mike asked, sharing a look with his partner only the two of them could understand. The lady in the picture had dark hair, dark eyes and was quite attractive.

"No. No, she's not. She and my father thought it best she had nothing to do with it and she left a long time ago. I've not seen her in years."

Frank thought he detected a trace of bitterness in Camden when he spoke of his sister.

"Oh, you were going to show us to your attorney's office."

The detectives left with Camden leading the way. When they reached the outer door, Frank suddenly turned to Camden, "If you don't mind, Mr. Camden, I need to ask you to wait here a moment."

"What? Why?" Camden asked indignantly.

"Simply a matter of procedure," Mike replied.

A secretary inside greeted the two detectives when they entered the office.

"Good morning, gentleman. How can I help you?"

"Good morning," Frank replied, as he and Mike moved quickly to the back office. "We need to speak with your boss."

"I'm sorry sir, but you can't go in there," the secretary said as she tried to stop them.

"It's okay Irene," the attorney said from the open-door way to the back office.

Frank walked up to Schofield, offered his hand and introduced himself and Mike to the attorney. The attorney asked them to have a seat.

"We're fine," Frank said succinctly to put Schofield on edge as quickly as possible, hoping to rattle him. "Where were you the night Commissioner Wood was killed?"

"Um, well – I was at home that evening," Schofield replied.

"Can anyone corroborate that?"

"Excuse me, Detective? What did you say your name was again?" Schofield asked.

"Detective in charge, Frank O'Conner, NYPD. Can anyone corroborate your whereabouts?"

"Well - no, I was home alone," the attorney stammered.

"We're going to need you to come with us down to the station to answer some more questions."

Camden barged in, "I don't believe that'll be necessary, Detective."

"Mr. Camden, we need to take a look at all your files on the Allister land purchase if you don't mind," Frank said.

"Actually, I do mind. I'm afraid that's privileged information."

"And you still have the search warrant in your hand that gives us access to that privileged information," Frank said as he snatched it away from him. "I'm sure you understand what it means?"

"Let me see that," Schofield demanded.

Frank handed over the search warrant for the attorney to read and watched the color drain out of Schofield's face. The exact look he had hoped to see. Even if they found nothing, at least they were making them nervous now.

"You have nothing on me. You can't possibly try to pin this on me," Schofield blurted out.

"We don't? This warrant says we do, and with your business ties, let's just say we've been digging into those here lately, and they don't look all that positive. We have reason to suspect you have more involvement in the murder of Commissioner Wood," Mike piped in.

Schofield bristled, "Still, you have nothing to go on, and we all know it. This is preposterous. I'll have your badges for this!"

"Just relax; I'm sure you're all too familiar with how this works. We look around, if we find anything, we tag it and bag it, and if it's incriminating, we bag you too. So, sit down and relax," Frank said with a warning look.

"I told you, you have nothing. You don't have probable cause, and we both know it. You can't arrest me, but I promise you that even if you try, I'll be out before you finish typing out the report!" Schofield stated hotly.

"That may be, but not before I turn over every rock in the city and gather every piece of evidence I can find on this case," Frank replied.

Two of the uniformed officers walked into the front office; one carried an evidence bag, the other a large manila folder. Frank had sent them to secure Schofield's car before they entered the building. The first officer opened the items and showed the contents to O'Conner and said the items were found under the seat of a black Mercedes registered to the company and checked out to Matthew Schofield III.

Frank peered inside the bag, and let out a long, slow whistle.

"This - this represents some of those proverbial rocks I just told you about. There's got to be..." He pulled out a stack of cash and flipped through it, "I'd say at least forty or fifty grand in here."

The attorney stood silently trembling with a look of shock and horror on his face as the detective continued.

Frank pulled a pistol from the evidence bag.

"From the smell, it's been fired recently," Frank stated as he used the plastic bag to pop the clip out. "Look here boys, seems exactly three rounds are missing." Frank held the weapon up for all to see.

"How many times was the commissioner shot, Mike?" he asked.

"Uh, that would be three, Frank," Mike replied.

"Hey, what the hell is this? I'm being framed! This is a setup!" The attorney shouted, his face turning a bright red.

"Mathew Schofield, you are under arrest for the murder of Commissioner Wood."

"I've never seen that gun before. You planted it on me!" he shouted.

"Calm down Schofield. You're going to have a coronary if ya don't but makes me no difference," Frank said as he handed the evidence back to the uniformed officer.

Schofield bristled. "No, that's not mine. I'm telling you I'm being set up!" he shouted. "This is a big mistake."

"I'm sure forensics will match this to the bullets they pulled out of the victim. I'm betting the mistake here was yours," Frank said.

"You can't do this. You don't have anything on me. I didn't kill Wood. I never stepped foot in that diner!" Schofield bellowed. "That's not my gun I'm telling you! I've been set up! You don't have enough evidence to hold me for jaywalking let alone murder, you morons. I'll be out before the ink dries. How dare you?"

"How dare I? I dare pretty damned easily Schofield. Please, resist arrest and let me show you just how daring I can be," Frank said sternly as he took out his handcuffs, roughly spun Schofield around and cuffed him. After reading him his rights, Frank turned to the uniformed officers and said, "Take him downtown fellas. I'll book him in as soon as we wrap up here."

Frank asked the other officers to stay while the cyber-forensics team began working on the computers.

"Now look here Detective, I'll have my team of attorneys working on this and he'll be released before you can get back to the station and you know it," Camden said. "You have nothing more than circumstantial evidence and no motive. It was a setup. You'll be doing yourself a favor if you stop with all this nonsense and look in other directions, like towards who actually killed the commissioner."

The detective knew people like this, powerful, wealthy and narcissistic, could never tolerate the lack of control. That's what he was counting on. When he turned over rocks and found all the pieces, he could put the whole puzzle together and discover the truth. Schofield's arrest was just the beginning of a hailstorm of problems for the CGI officials. Camden, the head of the empire, looked shocked and disarrayed with his shirt collar unbuttoned, tie dangling loosely and sleeves rolled up.

"That may be, Mr. Camden, and that's your right of course, but not before the press gets ahold of it first," Frank said with a sparkle in his eyes. "You might want to put your jacket on and fix that tie when the cameras start rolling, you know…so you look good on the news," Frank said, glancing out the office window. "It sounds like they've arrived just in time to see your hotshot attorney being escorted out. Now, about those files?" Frank said as he gave him a no-nonsense look.

Frank rather enjoyed this part of his job - making criminals squirm. He was a clean-as-they come cop and had been his entire career. His loyalty to the badge was unequivocal and well known among both cops and criminals. For that, he was both praised and despised by criminals and fellow cops. He didn't care.

***

Detective O'Conner entered the dank, stark room, closed the door behind him and threw a file down on the table across from where Matthew Schofield sat in handcuffs.

"We have the murder weapon used to kill the commissioner. We also have your prints, and the bullets will most likely match the ones pulled from Wood's body. You also lied about your whereabouts the night he was killed. Not only do we have an eyewitness that can place you at the scene, but we also have a credit card receipt, so you can do us all a favor now, Schofield, and write out a confession," Frank said, pushing a pad and pen in the attorney's direction.

"That's impossible. You can go to hell. I'm not saying a word until my lawyer gets here," Schofield replied. His voice was shaking with anger. "I've been set up. This is a frame job."

"Right, you realize, of course, that's what everybody says," Frank said with a slight chuckle.

"I'm telling you, I've been framed and that's all you're going to get from me!"

"Fine, fine. I'm sure he'll be along any minute now. Just know this Schofield - we have all the evidence we need. The D.A. won't have a choice but to prosecute you. Your money, power, influence - none of it will bail you out of this one. You've already perjured yourself. You murdered one of the most prominent men in the county. You're going away for a long time, that is, unless you start cooperating. Just think about it. Murder one can put you on death row," Frank said. He stood up to leave, "If you change your mind, you know where to find me."

Frank walked out of the interrogation room and met his partner in the hallway.

"Now what?" Mike asked.

"He's lawyered up already and not saying anything else. Did we get all the bank records yet?"

"Yeah, and there's a lot of 'em too. It'll take a little digging. So, Frank, you know that gun was wiped clean, right? There were no prints at all on it. A guy that smart? It doesn't add up. He'd never leave the murder weapon where it could be found that easily or that kind of cash either."

"I know, Mike, but he's guilty of something. Besides, he doesn't know that. In the meantime, let's go pick up Valentine and have him identify Schofield as the one he saw that night. One thing at a time 'eh?"

***

"What in the hell do you think you're doing O'Conner? You're the lead on this case; you're experienced. You're supposed to be a professional. Have you taken a blow to the head lately? I expect you to have a little more sense about you than to arrest Mathew Schofield. You better have video proof this guy did it, you better have rock solid, video evidence or eyewitness testimony, or both!" Captain Ramirez shouted at Detective O'Conner and his partner as they sat in his office.

The entire office floor could hear the captain shouting at the detectives. They all knew the captain's temper as most had come under it before and knew it was better to be on the outside of his door during one of his tantrums than it was from where Frank and Mike were sitting.

"As a matter of fact, Captain, we have something just as good," Frank said emphatically. "We have an eyewitness placing him at the scene at the time of the murder, and we have the victim's calendar that shows they had a meeting. We have a credit card receipt that he signed that also places him there. He had a motive. We exercised a warrant, and during a search found what appears to be the murder weapon in the trunk of Schofield's car."

"What judge did you roust up in the middle of the night to get to sign off on it?" Ramirez asked, heatedly. "I can't imagine anyone would be crazy enough to do it."

"Judge Henry signed it, and we executed it all legal and proper. Since when have I ever failed to follow the book?"

The captain seemed to have calmed down some once Frank explained all the evidence they had to hold the attorney.

"Not to mention the lawyer lied about his whereabouts when we questioned him," Mike said.

"I've already had three calls, and one was from the Mayor's office. He's not happy. Tell me everything you've got because we will have to go out there for a press conference in twenty minutes...don't leave anything out!" the captain demanded.

Frank explained, "We have copies of the file on the Allister property, and we're going over it with a fine-tooth comb. Also, we have the commissioner's agendas, notes, and meetings for the last year. But our witness that places him at the scene is solid. No criminal history or any kind of trouble."

"Who is this elusive eye-witness?"

Frank bit his lip a moment before he spoke, "The kid that works at the diner."

He noticed the captain's face begin to turn red and jumped back in quickly.

"The kid was scared and didn't think it was important at the time," Frank stated. "Com'on, Captain. We also have the receipt. Slam dunk. This is good stuff. Even if he isn't our killer, this will surely help to smoke 'em out."

"Thin as hell, but it will at least give probable cause validation," Ramirez relented.

The captain listened to the rest of the story from his detectives and ordered them to accompany him to the press briefing. The three men were met in the hallway by the Mayor. After a quick briefing, they all walked outside together, down the steps to the building entrance where a podium had been set up and with a grim determination, the Mayor stepped up to the microphone and began. The two detectives stood behind their captain and stared straight ahead at the cameras.

33

Lexi sat alone at her desk working when she noticed everyone in the office gathering around a television at the front of the newsroom. She quickly joined them when she saw the mayor giving a press conference concerning the Commissioner Wood killing. The headline read, "Accused Killer Arrested." The mayor spoke about the murder for ten minutes before handing the mic over to the captain. Lexi recognized Frank standing in the background right away. The same detective that had picked her and Leonard up the night they broke into the Camden Group offices.

"Oh my God," she blurted to no one in particular, yet everyone turned to look at her. "Sorry."

That was my scoop! She thought. *How could this have happened?* She wanted to cry, scream, or kick. It didn't matter. She needed to vent. She wanted to call Leo. This was her big chance to break a story wide open and show her boss she had what it takes to be a real investigative reporter, to prove herself. Now, she may not get the opportunity. They were so close that she could almost taste the Pulitzer. When the press conference was over she quickly made her way back to her desk, found her cell phone to call, but as she turned on the screen she noticed he had sent her a text.

'No worries, starting my shift now. Closing up @ 10ish if you want to talk after? ☺*'*

"Darn," *He must've just gotten my voice message from earlier. I'll have to try to call tonight when he gets off work,* she thought.

***

Horace Greely stood at the grill next to Marvin wearing his greasy white apron and chef's hat. Leonard hadn't returned for his evening shift, so Greely filled in at the grill. Everyone knew it wasn't like him to miss work. Greely checked the schedule twice just to make sure he had Leonard down.

"I swear, that boy's been so flighty here lately I don't know what I'm gonna do with 'em," Greely said to anyone within earshot.

"Well, boss, we was all young once too. I think he's prob'ly got a girl on the brain," Marvin replied.

"A 'girl on the brain' warrants fifteen… maybe even twenty minutes, but not an hour," Greely stated.

Marvin laughed a deep, long chuckle shrugging his shoulders, "Maybe she's a real purty girl."

Greely harrumphed and dropped the conversation. Helen slammed two more orders on the counter. "Order up!"

Sam was hollering for someone to make more coffee as she refilled a handful of soft drink glasses.

Detective O'Conner and his partner walked into the diner just as Helen cleaned off a previously occupied table.

"Excuse me ma'am, NYPD, I'm Detective O'Conner. This is my partner, Mike Freeman. We're looking for Leonard Valentine, he around?"

"Join the club fellas, he was supposed to be here an hour ago, but he never showed," Helen said, carrying a tray full of dishes to the back.

"Is that right?" Mike asked.

"Yeah, he works the morning shift then off until he comes in for the evening shift about five o'clock or so, but as I said, he never came back; comes and goes through the alleyway in the back. He likes to go up to the library or the park to read awhile. If you ask me, he's up to no good that one," Helen said with a contemptuous bite.

Frank indicated with a head nod for Mike to go check out back. A few minutes later, Mike came back with a cell phone in his hand.

"Found this out back, Frank. It belongs to the kid. It was lying beside the dumpster."

"Are you sure? Let's have a look."

Frank scrolled through the text log, "Yeah, looks like his alright."

***

Lexi looked up at the clock and saw it was getting late. A few other people were working throughout the office, but the newsroom was strangely quiet. She was working on a story about a homeless shelter downtown that had been having a difficult time keeping its doors open. She finished the piece, emailed it to her editor and logged off her computer. As she prepared to go home for the night, her cell phone rang. When she looked at the caller id, a smile crossed her face as she slid the icon across her screen to answer.

"Hi, Leo, I knew you'd call soon," she said with a laugh, as she grabbed her purse and began walking to the elevator door of her office building. She suddenly stopped and froze in her tracks when she heard the rich baritone of another man's voice.

"No ma'am, I'm afraid this isn't Leonard. It's Detective O'Conner."

Lexi's heart began pounding when she heard the detective's voice instead of her friend's.

"Detective O'Conner? Has something happened to him? Is he okay?"

"I was hoping you could tell us, Miss Osborne, we stopped by the diner to speak with him, but he never showed up for his shift. We found his cell phone in the back alley, so I'm afraid we suspect something's happened, but no idea what. Where are you?"

"I'm at the newspaper office. I was just getting ready to walk out the door and go home," Lexi replied.

"Not to alarm you, but you may be in danger as well," Frank said as he and his partner climbed into their vehicle and left the diner behind. "We're on our way now. Stay put until we get there. Got it?"

"Yes sir," Lexi said, but the detective had already disconnected.

***

"Step on it Mike, I have a bad feeling about this," Frank said as they raced down the street to get to the newspaper building. "There are only two contacts in the kid's phone."

"Oh? Who's the other one?" Mike asked.

"I can't tell if it's some joke or not, but the photo next to the number is that redheaded Broadway actress, Briana Fitzgerald."

"You're kidding me, no way - got to be a joke. It's probably a fake number just trying to impress somebody. I bet you anything it's his mom's," Mike laughed.

Frank studied the phone while Mike navigated the busy New York streets. It was easy to know whose phone it was as Leonard had put all his information in it and even had a picture of him next to it.

"Glad he didn't have a passcode on it."

Leonard P Valentine

34

I had no idea how long I'd been sitting there tied to the chair, but I can tell you I was hurting all over. The zip ties around my wrists and ankles were cutting off the circulation, and the hood covering my face made it hard to breathe. It smelled like a combination of greasy fried chicken and week-old gym shorts. I couldn't see anything through it, including light, but I'm pretty sure that was the point. I could hear voices every so often, though I couldn't make out what they were saying. They were muffled like they were behind a wall or something. Finally, I heard a door open and footsteps coming nearer.

"Mr. Valentine." I heard a man's voice say, "It seems you have taken something that does not belong to you."

"Nope, not this guy. You must've mistaken me for your high school boyfriend, and just for the record, I don't think you ever get that back. It doesn't work like that," I lipped off.

"Very funny, I like that. A sense of humor will go a long way. You, on the other hand, may find the situation isn't all that funny in the end," he said, with more than a hint of severity.

"I'm here all week. Two shows a night on the weekend. What do you want from me?" I asked though I didn't feel that I was in any position to get answers from these clowns.

"I want what you took from CGI. The ledger. I want it, and I want it now!" he demanded.

"We've looked through your man purse, Valentine. It's not here so, where is it?" I heard another man's voice ask. From the tone, it sounded like big ugly that put the gun in my face earlier.

"Man purse? Do I detect a hint of jealousy there, chuckles? You too can own an excellent, luxurious canvas murse for only $19.99 from your local drug store. Available in various colors to make it easy, even for you, to accessorize. Free lipstick and nail polish with every purchase while supplies last," I said sarcastically.

CRACK!

Big ugly punched me across my jaw. I wasn't expecting it, and it almost knocked me smooth out. I could taste blood, and I'm sure one of my teeth was loose now. When I'm backed into a corner and scared, I tend to lip off. I guess it's a self-defense thing, but it wasn't working out so well in this particular situation.

"Look, I don't have any idea what you're talking about Buttercup, I swear. If I did, I'd give it to you right now."

THUD!

The jackass nailed me in the back of my head with his palm.

"Son-of-a-bitch that hurt! Was that necessary ya bastard?" I yelled.

"It's up to you to make it stop. Just give us the ledger, and all your troubles are over," the big brute said as he hit me again, snapping my head back.

I had no idea which direction the blows were coming from, so I couldn't even deflect them by turning my head. That last punch must've knocked me smooth out because the next thing I knew, somebody was slapping my face, coaxing me to wake up. Against my desire and better judgment, it worked. I woke up with my head pounding and jaw hurting like nobody's business. It may be broken, so I gingerly moved it around. It hurt, but it was still working. I hoped it wouldn't need wiring shut. I don't think I could contain all my years of wisdom behind a wired shut mandible.

"We can do this all-night Valentine, up to you."

I answered him the best I could in my groggy but conscious state, "I swear I don't know what you're talking about. I'd give you anything you want, but I just don't know anything about a ledger."

"Let's try a different route. Who is your partner?" he asked.

I drew a deep breath and slowly began talking, "Now, look fellas that would make me a snitch, and you know what happens to snitches." I took another deep, slow breath. "You're obviously in the business to know these things. There's just no way I can rat someone out."

"Have it your way," big ugly said, punching me square in my nose. I felt the blood splatter as my head snapped back again. This jackass was starting to piss me off.

"That's enough," I managed to eke out. "There's – no – need – for all this – violence."

"Then start talking. Give me a name! Who's your partner?"

"Okay, okay. Her name is Amelia - Amelia Earhart."

"Where can we find this Amelia Earhart?" I heard the sadist ask, quickly followed by an "Oomph! What was that for?" But, this time, it wasn't me that got hit.

"Amelia Earhart was a pilot that crashed in the Atlantic Ocean in the 30's you moron," I heard his partner say.

CRACK!

Another punch to the face, but it wasn't nearly as hard this time. Still, it was enough to make me hurt again. I could taste even more blood, and I think my eye was cut pretty good. I could feel the blood dripping down into it, stinging.

"Com'on fellas, my modeling career?" I wheezed.

"Keep the wisecracks up kid, and you'll end up in the river even sooner," big ugly said.

"Seriously fellas…. haven't you heard……. you catch more flies with honey?" I said, gasping for air and the strength to push it out in a literary form these idiots could understand. "Just ask nicely, and I'll tell you everything I know, which isn't any more than what I've already said. There's just no need for all the violence."

I heard big ugly suck in a breath and sensed he was going to hit me again. I tensed, waiting for the blow.

"Wait, please - don't hit me again. I'll tell you… everything. Just take this hood off so I can breathe. It smells like what I imagine your underwear would. It's just nasty!" It hurt to talk, but I believed if I didn't give them something soon, I wouldn't be doing any talking at all. I had to figure a way out of this, but I'd never give Lexi up to these idiots.

My plea was met with silence for a few seconds before a pair of large, meaty hands grabbed my head upright and ripped the hood off. As luck would have it, I'm blinded by cliché! These morons had a lamp aimed at my eyes so that I couldn't see them. I've already seen big ugly so what's the problem?

"Okay, the hood's off. Start talking."

"Listen, fellas - yes, I admit, I was there," I took another deep, painful breath. "All I did was look around the place and…the only reason I went there…is because the lawyer guy has been following me." My words came a little more manageable now as I got my breath back. Big ugly was so gonna get it whenever I could get my hands on him!

I continued my story, "The guy's been stalking me for days, and I'm just trying to find out why. If he's worried about what happened at the diner, he needn't bother because I didn't see anything, and that's exactly what I told the cops. I'm nobody's rat!"

Once again, I'm met with silence. I could hear someone else open a door and walk into the room, but I couldn't turn my head enough to see who it was, my neck hurt too badly from all the slapping around these two ass-clowns have been having fun with. I heard the new person talking to the goon squad, but I couldn't quite make out what they were saying. I did hear the name Richards come up. A moment later, a chair scooted across the room, and someone sat down just at the edge of the darkness where I couldn't see their face.

"Leonard P Valentine," a man with a sharp voice began in a slow, deliberate manner, "Occupation, a short-order cook at Greely's Po Boy's. Before that, washed cars for a living, before that, street urchin. No family, no friends. No one to miss you. No one will even care when your body is found floating in the river."

"Com'on man," I pleaded, "I don't know anything. I didn't steal anything, and I didn't say anything. No way I'm a rat."

I heard the man take in a deep breath and exhale slowly. I couldn't make out his face with the bright light aimed at me - and the swollen eye.

"I don't believe you, Mr. Valentine. That may not be a good thing for you, however. Lock him up; he'll start talking soon enough. If he doesn't, make it look like an accident when his body is found floating in the East River."

I got a bad feeling in the pit of my stomach after hearing that statement. Not that I'd been feeling good after being treated like a piñata', but the whole, *make it look like an accident* thing, referred to how they meant to dispose of me...that was no bueno. I needed to find a way out of this mess and fast!

"Wait a minute. Maybe we can work something out?" I pleaded.

I didn't have a clue as to what I could work out with this jackass, but I had to try something. It was a matter of life and death - mine!

"Is that right?" the guy asked. "What is it you think we could work out?"

"Well, for starters, if anything happens to me, that ledger gets delivered straight to the cops, and that doesn't benefit anyone."

I was taking a big chance that this wouldn't get me killed on the spot!

"Keep talking kid."

"Okay, so you know I took the ledger now, but I'm the only one that knows where it's at and can get it back."

I hoped that if I offered my services up, I might be able to get out of this thing alive.

"Why should I believe you? Why shouldn't I just kill you right now? Maybe I could start filleting you, and you tell me where my men can retrieve it?"

"As I said, I'm the only one that can get it. If I don't show back up, it gets airmailed to the cops and posted all over the internet. The way I figure, I'm betting that little book can also tie somebody directly to the killing of the commissioner, not to mention payoffs to dozens of judges, politicians and city officials. I doubt any of them would want it in the hands of the cops. I'm more than certain bribing officials is pretty illegal."

I made my case the best I could.

"Go on," he said.

"If I get it back for you, you let me live, pretty simple bargain. I have no stake in this game. It's all way above my pay grade, so I don't care about any of those people." I tried my best to sound convincing. It was my only play at the moment. "Just give me a couple of days to arrange it."

I heard the guy amble back around, and this time he stepped into the light where I could see his face.

"Tell you what, you have until midnight to get it back to me, or you're a dead man. Not only do you disappear, but so does your little girlfriend," he said. "Do you understand?"

"Yeah - yeah, I can do that... Mr. Schofield."

35

Lexi sat at her desk intently reading the article she had pulled up on the computer. She needed to occupy her mind while she waited for the detectives to arrive instead of speculating on what may or may not have happened to Leo. She wasn't scared for herself, but she was worried about him because she had dragged him into it and felt responsible. Instead of waiting around, she wanted to do something about it, and the best way for her to do that now was by learning as much as she could about the situation and all the people she suspected of being involved. She had to get to the bottom of all this and soon.

The article she had pulled up was one that involved the Richards lady and her company, Jade Development. The report didn't have much in it to help identify who she was, but it did mention that even though her company was headquartered in another state, she was originally from New York which made her even more interesting. She closed out the article and did another search for her. Several more popped up and Lexi scrolled through them one by one until she came to one that mentioned the Michelle Richards' name alongside the name Camden which she thought odd. Could she have a relationship with Camden Group, she wondered? She immediately opened the article and was shocked to learn Michelle Richards was Michelle Camden before Richards. *Was she married to Lucas Camden?* There would be a record of it in the court documents. She hurriedly pulled the online court records up and searched. She found nothing that indicated she was ever married or divorced in the state of New York.

Reluctantly, she closed the court records search out and went back to the internet. After a few minutes of scanning, she found another article that looked promising. A Michelle Camden had competed in a business course several years ago in high school where it appeared that she led a team against other groups in a city-wide sustainable business venture competition. There was a newspaper photo of her team along with a listing of the names involved. Could this be the same person, she wondered? The article showed a picture of the top three teams along with their names in the cut line. Lexi gasped when she read the names of the first-place team. Lucas Camden was the leader of the winning team while Michelle Camden led the second-place team!

The elevator dinged open, and when Frank O'Conner and his partner walked into the newsroom, Lexi stood and met them halfway across the floor.

"Ms. Osborne?" Frank said when he spotted her.

"Yes, Detective," she answered, jumping up to meet them in the hall. "Did you find Leo yet? Is he okay? Is he in trouble? I've been worried sick."

"Sorry, nothing yet. We rushed over here first to make sure you were okay. When was the last time you spoke with him?" Frank asked.

"About an hour or so after you dropped me off. I called to check on him. He was supposed to have called me this morning, but we missed each other. I did get a text today just before he went back to work."

"Yes, ma'am. We saw that," Frank said.

Lexi's phone rang in her office cubicle at that moment, startling her. "I'm sorry, I better get that in case it's him or my boss."

"Sure thing."

Lexi rushed across the room to her cubicle to answer it. "Daily Grind, this is Lexi."

***

Frank's cell buzzed while they waited on Lexi. "Uh huh, I understand thanks. Appreciate the heads up."

"What was that all about?" Mike asked when he hung up.

"When Schofield posted bail this morning I had a guy tail him. He lost him a few hours ago," Frank told him.

"That can't be good," Mike replied.

"No, I can't imagine how it could be," Frank said. "I'd hoped we could've held on to him longer, but it could push him to make a move and slip up!"

***

The man in the navy-blue suit returned to the limo and stood by the back door as his boss slid the window down.

"The kid's not here. The waitress said two detectives came by to talk to him this afternoon, but they took off when they found his cell phone out back in the alley. They don't know what happened to him, and they never came back."

"Curious indeed," Briana Fitzgerald purred thoughtfully. She sat in silence for a moment before coming to a conclusion. "Get in the car, Victor. We have places to be." She pushed the button, and the dark tinted window rose slowly.

36

"Lexi, It's me, Leo."

"Oh my God, Are you okay? Where are you? What happened? The detectives are here now looking for you, and I've been worried something bad has happened to you. Detective O'Conner and his partner," she whispered frantically. "They found your cell phone in the alley behind the diner and thought something had happened to you. Don't you know that…?"

"Lexi, stop! Please?"

I knew she was worried, but I didn't have much time before I was to become a permanent fixture in the footing of a new high rise or at the bottom of the river and I didn't want either of those things to happen. I heard her gasp for a breath of air before I continued.

"I'm sorry, but I don't have much time, I'll explain later. You can't let the detectives know you're talking to me, not yet anyways. Can you meet me at the library in twenty minutes?"

"I don't know. The detectives are here now, they've been looking for you and thought something happened to you and came over to make sure that I'm safe. They had me worried."

"Well, something did happen, but I don't have time to explain right now. I think I know who had the commissioner killed. Do you think you can ditch the Mod Squad?"

"Sure, but they've already caught the killer. It was Schofield. They found the murder weapon in his car and arrested him earlier today."

"Is that right? Well, he's out now, but that sure explains a few things. Just meet me at the library in twenty minutes?" I tried to hurry her along.

"I'll do my best," she said in her all too familiar coarse whisper.

"And, Lexi…be careful."

"But, Leo… "

"No time, Lexi. I'll explain as soon as you get here. Make sure you're not followed," I said before hanging up.

37

"Is everything okay Miss Osborne?" Frank asked when she returned from her phone call.

"What's that? Oh yes. Yes, of course. I'm sorry. It's just that I'm so worried about Leo," Lexi replied.

"I understand. For now, I think you should come with us until we can find out more about your friend. We believe he may be in trouble and you could be in danger as well."

"Of course, if you think it's best, I understand. Let me grab my stuff off my desk first. I'll just be a moment," she said as she walked back over to her cube. She went to gather her things, though she had no intention of leaving with the detectives. She had to trust that Leo knew what he was doing. Her heart pounded as she picked up her cell phone and dropped it in her bag. Glancing back at the two men who waited on her, she saw they were deep in conversation, so she saw her chance to scamper out the back door and down the stairs to the street below.

Mike turned to his partner while they waited for the reporter. "I had hoped the gun we found in Schofield's car was the murder weapon. Case closed!"

"We could only get so lucky," Frank said. "It may not have had his prints on it, but it was still found in his car along with the bundle of cash. Unfortunately, I agree with him. It's a plant, but by who is the question."

"Still, I think it rattled his cage a little. You think he nabbed the kid?"

"That's what's been eating at me. If it was him, there's no telling what he might do, and I'm afraid he may go so far as to come after the girl too. Hey, speaking of the girl – what in the world is taking her so long? Surely she's had enough time to get her stuff."

The detectives hurried over in the direction of her cubicle but found no trace of Lexi Osborne. She had vanished.

***

"She gave us the slip!" Mike exclaimed.

Frank reached into his pocket and retrieved Leonard's cell phone and hit redial. Lexi didn't answer, and no ringing nearby could be heard. The two men hurried to their car and called dispatch to put out a BOLO for the newspaper reporter. Frank told his partner to cruise around the area for a bit before leaving.

"She couldn't have gotten far on foot," he said.

"No, and she should be easy to spot with that red dress."

After driving around for half an hour, the cell phone buzzed. He pulled it out, looked at the caller id and answered it. "Miss Osborne, glad to hear you're okay," the detective said. He looked at Mike with a concerned look on his face.

Mike watched his partner curiously as Frank listened intently on the phone. He could tell from his partner's look that he was more than annoyed. When the call ended, Frank put the cell phone back in his pocket and relayed the conversation.

"It seems our Miss Osborne has located Valentine. He was taken at gunpoint but got away. Now, apparently, they need our help. Claims to know who killed the commissioner and we have to meet them at this address tonight at midnight. Not a minute before or a minute late."

"It sounds like they've gotten themselves into something. Do you trust them?" Mike asked.

"I think so. Just not sure if these two kids know just how dangerous their little cat and mouse game is. Hopefully, we won't find them in the river tomorrow. Let's get down there now and stake the place out and watch for 'em."

38

Twenty minutes later, I watched Lexi as she paid the cab driver and stepped out onto the sidewalk in front of the library. I looked around to make sure she wasn't followed and watched her enter through the front doors. When I was satisfied she was alone, I quietly made my way over to meet her.

"Lexi, it's me," I said as I sat down beside her. I had on a dark hoodie pulled down low over my head to help hide my face. It wasn't pretty with all the black and blue beauty marks dealt by Schofield's goon squad.

"Where have you been? What's going on?" she asked frantically.

"Schofield had his guys nab me on my way back to the diner. He knows it was me that snuck into his office the other night and he grabbed me just as I was about to go back to work."

"That makes sense now. Like I said on the phone, the detective that saved our bacon the other night arrested Schofield for the murder earlier this morning. There was a big press conference, and apparently, they found the murder weapon in his car."

"They dang sure didn't keep him locked up long. He was there tonight with his men," I said.

Lexi reached over to move my hoodie back, but I caught her hand before she could complete the move.

"It's not pretty."

"What do you mean?" she asked, pushing my hand away.

I wasn't sure how she would react to my current condition, but when she sets her mind to something, there's no stopping her.

"Oh my Gosh, what happened to you?" she cried out when she saw my face. "I've been worried sick about you, and it's obvious why now. Who did this to you?"

Her voice was soothing but shaking. I could tell she was worried and no doubt conflicted with anger - and guilt.

"There was three of 'em!" I said. "Look, I don't have much time. I'm perfectly fine. It looks worse than what it is, but I have to get some things in order. They only let me go because they believe I have something of theirs. Once they get it back, they won't need me anymore. But, I have a plan."

"What is it? What do they think you have?" she asked reaching up and tenderly touching my forehead.

I had tried to clean up my wounds the best I could, but a lack of anything other than soap, cold water, and paper towels made the job somewhat difficult.

"The ledger we saw on Schofield's desk," I said.

"But we didn't take it. We left it there on his desk, remember?"

I stuttered for a second, "Well…I uh, …I took the book when I went back." I felt just a little more than ashamed.

"What? But why would you do that? And why didn't you tell me what you were going to do so that I could've stopped you? You said it yourself, that's the kind of thing that gets people killed. You're lucky to be alive right now!"

"I know, I know. Trust me. The detective gave me the riot act for us even being there, but that's not the point. Right now, I've got to get that ledger back to Schofield, or they're going to kill me."

"But you can't do that. Once they have it back, there's no guarantee they will let you go."

"I have no intention of doing that, but I have a plan that should keep us both alive and land Schofield right in the place he needs to be - prison!"

"Great," she said. "Just what is this miracle plan you have brewed up?"

I smiled, the best I could anyway considering how swollen my face was from the beating I just endured and held up the burner phone Schofield's people gave me to contact them.

"A simple phone call or two and a little ingenuity," I replied.

***

"Leo, I don't think I like this plan at all," Lexi said.

We had just made our way out of the library and were walking up the street just as it was closing.

"I have a key to the diner because I open and close - on most days anyway. We just have to find a place to lay low for a few hours until Greely closes up and goes home. No worries," I reassured her.

"We both know if you give the ledger back to him, he will need to get rid of you so that he doesn't leave any witnesses," Lexi said worriedly.

"I know, but trust me; nobody wants to live more than me. He's not going to kill me."

We took a longer route back to the diner so that we could go over the plan and cover any contingencies. The street traffic had slowed considerably by now, and not many pedestrians were out, so we had the sidewalk mostly to ourselves. I had on a dark navy hoodie pulled up over my head, and my backpack hung on both shoulders. Lexi walked next to me holding on to my arm as we talked quietly.

"What bothers me is the timing. This is going to be tricky and what happens if you get killed? They could chop you up into little pieces and feed you to the fish! What about that?" Lexi asked with a concerned look on her face.

"I'd rather that didn't happen, thank you very freaking much. Let's not mention the small details like death and dismemberment, shall we? Just stop worrying so much. It's the only play we have right now."

Lexi gave me a worried look, "This is my fault. I dragged you into this."

I stopped and stared back into her sensitive eyes, "I'm a grown ass adult, and I am fully capable of making my own decisions. You didn't twist my arm or threaten to maim my cat or boil my bunny rabbit alive, so you're off the hook on that one! I'm a big boy."

"I realize that, but I still feel guilty. I'm so sorry you got beat up and dragged into this. You're lucky to be alive right now."

She reached up and tenderly stroked the bruises on my face with her soft, velvety hands. The touch of her hands felt good. Maybe I should get beaten more often.

"I know it, and you know it," she sighed.

"But I am alive, and that's what matters right now. Well, that, and *staying* alive!" I gave her a light-hearted laugh. "First, I need to stop by the drug store and pick up a few things."

39

The streetlights cast an eerie glow on the sidewalk as I made my way out of the drugstore and down the back alley. I had instructed Lexi to wait ten minutes after I left and then to take a different route. The wind was blowing at a good clip, and though it wasn't raining yet, I could see a storm was working itself up into a frenzy. In the distance, lightning crackled and splintered the dark, cloudy night and the smell of ozone was heavy. I kept to the shadows the best I could and looked for anything that might mean I had been spotted, but I didn't see anything. No one was out this time of night, not that it was unusually late, but with the storm moving in regular folks would stay inside. I couldn't believe what I was about to do, but here I am, trying to be all slick and pull a Colombo on some very dangerous people. If I could get an admission out of Schofield on a recording, I may be able to get out of this thing alive. Lexi's job was only to have the detectives at the right place at the right time – the right time would be before my death of course! I just hoped it would work out in my favor. I put my head down and plodded along at a little quicker pace.

The diner was dark inside when I slipped in through the back door. I didn't need to turn the lights on because I knew my way around well enough to see without them. Once inside, I made my way through the kitchen and into the dining room. I moved some tables around to get set up and then unlocked the front door just as the rain started beating down. I almost took the bells down off the door but thought better of it. Who knows, it could work as an alarm when someone came in.

My plan wasn't all that complicated. I mean, as far as plans go, I suppose. I figured it would be better keeping it simple, and not confuse the situation - too many players and too many chances. If I was lucky, and I mean *really* lucky, I would walk out of this thing alive. If I was not lucky, I could get killed. It only took a few minutes for me to get everything ready, but once I was set, I made three phone calls. Now the hard part was the waiting in an empty diner in the middle of the night with a storm waiting to let loose at any time.

***

I knew Schofield would show. He was early when he opened the front door and walked in, but I suspected he would be. Even though I was ready for him, the jingle bells on the door still startled me, and I jumped almost out of my seat. He wanted that ledger in a bad way, and I didn't think he would trust any of his gorillas to do it; he was way too narcissistic for that, but I was pretty sure they were close by. I slowly stood up and slid the cell phone into my pocket. I had hoped the guy didn't catch the move in the darkroom, but I anticipated that. When I turned, I saw the glint of something shiny in his hand. He had a gun trained on me. Just peachy. Apparently, there's no trust in this line of business.

"Let's have the cell phone, kid," he said, holding out an open hand.

I slowly reached into my pocket, retrieved the cell phone and handed it to him. He took it from me, tossed it on the floor and stomped on it.

"You have the ledger? Care to hand it over – now?" he demanded more than asked, as he waved his gun at me.

"How do I know you won't kill me just as soon as I do?" I asked.

"You don't," he growled.

"Well that sounds like an excellent idea," I said with a touch of sarcasm and more than just a little fear.

"All that matters right now is the ledger," Schofield prodded.

"I don't have it on me. I'm not that dumb, Mister. Soon as I was to hand it over, you shoot me. No dice. That's not good for me."

"Maybe I'll just shoot you in the knees and let you bleed out slowly. How about that? In this storm, no one will hear a gunshot, and if they do, they'll just think it was the thunder."

"As I said before if something happens to me, it goes straight to the cops. Not only does it incriminate you and your boss, but if the people whose names are in it find out that you let it slip through your grubby paws, they won't be too happy with either of you two ass-clowns, now would they? No sir. I don't think I'd want to be in your shoes."

I tried not to sound scared out of my wits and call his bluff, but I could hear my voice shake a bit. This covert operation stuff isn't so easy!

"You're starting to get on my last nerve kid. Hand it over, or I'm going to start at your kneecaps and work my way up until I get what I want," he sneered.

A bolt of lightning suddenly lit up the sky which caused me to flinch. For a second, I thought for sure he had pulled the trigger. The storm outside was blowing harder, and no traffic had been by the diner since I got here. The rain was coming down in sheets and was deafening inside the small building as it beat down and the wind swept it against the windows. Every time the thunder rumbled over, the entire building would shake. It was unnerving. I had to admit, he was right about no one hearing a gunshot. I almost laughed out loud at my predicament as it seemed so cliché'.

Schofield gestured with his gun again. I could see the anger on his face in between the lightning flashes.

"What's the deal, kid? Where's the ledger? Don't make me have to shoot you," he said sternly.

"I want a guarantee that you will let me go once you have it back. Look, Mister, I know they nabbed you this morning on murder one charges, and somehow you bonded out just as fast. The way I figure it, you must have friends in high places, but I'm also willing to bet that those same friends don't have a clue that you ever had such a thing with their names in it. And if they ever found out that you no longer possess it…" I let that hang in the air a moment to let it sink in.

"That's none of your concern kid," he replied.

"You're right it's not my concern at all. It's no skin off my nose, but it could be yours. We both know that if word gets out that you don't have that ledger, you're a dead man. If it fell into the hands of the cops, or somehow went viral on the internet, I don't think there would be a place in this world where you could hide that they wouldn't find you."

"I'm starting to think I should just shoot you anyway and take my chances."

"I don't believe you want to do that Matthew." A woman's voice drifted out of the cover of darkness from the kitchen. "A dead body would simply… complicate matters," she said.

Schofield quickly spun around, momentarily giving me a reprieve. After a brief pause, he must've recognized the new visitor to our little pow-wow.

"Hello, Michelle. What brings you down here? Slumming? I suppose that's nothing new for you," he said with obvious contempt.

She must've slipped in through the back door just moments after me because she wasn't wet from the rain. She was also holding a gun, but at least hers was aimed at him. I didn't mind as long as it wasn't pointed at me.

"Tsk tsk, my dear Matthew. That doesn't seem too - friendly," she said with a slight hint of amusement.

"Friendly would imply I liked you in the first place."

"We may not be friends, but here we are nonetheless, partners of sorts," Michelle Richards laughed.

"I don't know what you're talking about," Schofield said heatedly. "We're not partners by any stretch of your twisted imagination. I'm willing to bet that you're the one that planted the gun in my car."

"Now Matthew, it sounds like you have all sorts of problems. I overheard your conversation with the kid here. Arrested for murder, soon to be indicted for bribery, extortion, fraud, blackmail, and I'm sure the list goes on and on," the lady said with sarcasm dripping off her every word, but she still had a somewhat sultry and melodic voice. "But, for your information, I'm not quite the antagonist you make me out to be."

"I don't believe you. Why should I? I should just shoot the both of you," he said heatedly while gesturing wildly with his gun.

"How would that do either of us any good?" she asked rhetorically.

"It will make me feel better." He sneered.

The lady strolled over to stand in front of the attorney. Her heels clicked on the hard floor with each deliberate step. Even in the darkness, she radiated a stealthy sexiness about her that seemed more like the sleekness of a cobra ready to strike than the beautiful psychopath she obviously was. When she stood near him, she lowered her gun, slowly reached out to put her hand on his gun hand and pushed it down away from her. "We both know that it was you that killed the commissioner anyway. You killed him because he wouldn't play ball, but that's no concern of mine. I only want one thing," she said.

"I had nothing to do with his death. I met with him, sure, but I damn sure didn't kill him!"

"Whatever, Mathew, it doesn't matter. I want control of CGI, and I don't care how it happens," she said.

"You want the company?" Schofield laughed. "If it were up to me, I'd give it to you."

"Why do you say that?"

Schofield laughed just as the booming thunder shook the windows and lightning flashed like a strobe, cascading shadows of street lights on the buildings down the street. The diner was illuminated for a brief second, and I could see her staring at him with a smirk on her face and a gun in her hand. I had no doubt she was ruthless enough to use it if she had to.

"Just why do you find that so funny?" she glowered.

"CGI is living on borrowed time," Schofield replied. "Your dear brother has the company so far in debt that the only thing holding it up is that ledger."

"What are you talking about?" She straightened her posture, suddenly more interested in his answers.

"I'm talking about leverage. For years, Lucas has used borrowed money, massive unsustainable debt to finance one failed project after another. Coupled with production inefficiencies, negative cash flow, and just plain bad management, CGI is hemorrhaging money to the tune of millions if not billions, not to mention the overseas accounts that he's been funneling cash into that I'm not supposed to know about."

"Ah, now I'm starting to see just why it's so important to you. It *is* the only thing holding it all together." She paused. "I suppose you plan on leveraging it the same way you did your investors cash except you're planning on using it as blackmail to save your hides. That's a dangerous game you're playing."

"Not to save *our* hides, but to save *mine*!"

"Ah, now I'm beginning to understand. You're planning on throwing Lucas under the bus," she laughed. "That's just perfect. We truly should be working together now don't you think?

40

Lexi hurried down the sidewalk and quickly slipped into the back seat of the parked sedan. She closed the door just as the rain began hammering down on the city. Lightning splintered the night revealing the faces of the two men sitting in the front seat.

"Glad you could grace us with your presence, Miss Osborne," Frank said. His tone laced with more than a little sarcasm.

"I'm sorry Detective, but I had a good reason."

"I'm sure you did. Now, tell us what's going on. I guess you heard from Valentine?"

Lexi leaned forward with her arms on the backs of the front two seats to face the detectives. "Exactly, and he's in trouble. I met him at the library. That's where I ran off to. They grabbed him on his way to work, and they beat him to a pulp. It was horrible."

"He's lucky to still be alive. The fact he is tells me he has something they want," Frank said looking from Lexi over to his partner.

Mike chimed in, "So what's the deal now, why are we out here at this hour?"

"Because we're going to help you solve this case and make an arrest tonight Detective," Lexi said austerely. "But, I want your promise that when this is over, I get the scoop. I've been working on this case ever since I first heard about it and I want this story."

"I can't make any promises about that, but I can tell you I don't think any other reporter has the inside dope on all this mess. Now, out with it - who are we arresting and where?"

Lexi sat back in the seat with a heavy sigh of relief and great satisfaction before replying. "Lucas Camden and Mathew Schofield."

41

I knew just as soon as they both turned to look at me that I had better think of something quick. This wasn't working out quite the way I had planned, but I did figure on me having to remain somewhat…flexible. I wasn't quite sure that flexibility could bend far enough when circumstances did a complete 180. I understood why that ledger was so important to Schofield now. Over the years, they'd paid off high ranking city officials, politicians and anyone else that needed persuading to make things happen. If these two joined up together, that didn't bode well for me. I could see Michelle's face as she mulled over what the attorney said and I didn't like what I was seeing.

"You're not involved in any of this right now, Michelle, so it would be in your best interest if you simply walked away," Schofield said.

I could see her giving thought to the attorney's suggestion even in the dimly lit room.

"Oh, jeez lady, you're dumber than you look if you think he's going to let you walk out of here knowing everything you do. I don't believe he plans on letting either of us live through this," I managed to say.

"Shut up Valentine before I shoot you myself," she said. She turned her gun toward me.

"So why did you kill the commissioner?" she asked the lawyer.

"I didn't kill anyone. That had to be all Lucas. He insisted the commissioner had to be eliminated. Apparently, Wood found out about CGI being over-leveraged, he didn't know to what extent, but once he knew issues were surrounding the financing, he threatened to withdraw his recommendation to allow the sale of the land. That land is worth potentially hundreds of millions. There's no way Lucas would let that happen. That's what my meeting was about that I had with him just before he was killed. I tried to sweeten the deal for him, but he just had to be stubborn and refused to budge, so Lucas dealt with the problem before he could officially back out."

"Do you expect me to believe that he shot him right out in the open?"

"Please, even your brother wouldn't have the nerve to do something like that. When I couldn't persuade Wood to stick to the deal, Lucas used a professional to kill him. It's logged in the ledger. I knew about it, of course, but I had no part in it."

"Interesting," Michelle said. "Makes that ledger even that much more valuable to me. Okay, so what happens now?" Her gun was still raised and pointed in our general direction, which I didn't care for.

Schofield turned back to me and said, "First, I get the ledger, that's my insurance."

Great, now they turned their attention back to me. After Schofield's admission, I knew he wasn't going to let me out of this thing alive. My only hope now was that Lexi would be able to pull her part off.

"So, your plan is to get the ledger then kill the kid?" Michelle asked. "What about your little issue with your arrest? Don't you think you're under a microscope?"

"Hey wait a minute, nobody needs to kill the kid," I said. As far as I was concerned, neither one of these two needed to get their hands on that ledger.

"I'm certain of it, but it won't matter if I have that ledger. It has enough information in it to keep me out of prison even if I were to take out city hall in broad daylight."

"Even more reason not to kill me!"

"Look here Valentine, I'm all out of patience. If you don't hand it over now, I'm starting with your kneecaps!" Schofield growled. He stepped toward me and aimed his pistol at my knee.

"Wait a minute. I don't have it here with me. I stashed it in an old, abandoned warehouse on my way over here. I can take you to it."

"Seriously? In this storm?" Schofield said. "You're an idiot."

"It is what it is, buttercup, take it or leave it, that's the best I can do for you," I managed to swagger out.

I knew it was a longshot, but there was no way I was bringing it with me until I had assurances that I'd survive this little ordeal. Well…I suppose at this point there were no guarantees, but I was gambling on other factors to come into play.

"Okay, kid, but you better keep in mind that any funny stuff will get you killed!" Schofield said.

"How about it, Matthew, work together?" Michelle asked.

"Sure, why not."

"Good, I'm coming with you," Michelle said.

"Suit yourself." Schofield pulled his cell phone out of his pocket and made a quick call. "Pull the car up front."

A few seconds later I saw his goon, Big Ugly himself, drive up and Schofield ushered us out the front door. The rain was coming down in sheets, and the thunder and lightning boomed overhead. The storm raged in full symphony. This wasn't the best idea I'd ever had, but it was the only play I could come up with at the time. The attorney opened the door and motioned for me to get in the back seat. He slid in beside me with his gun pushed into my ribs.

The Richards lady climbed in front with Big Ugly who was behind the wheel. He turned around and smiled at me. I hated that guy.

The streets were empty at this hour, and it didn't take but a few minutes to get to the old, abandoned warehouse where I had stashed the ledger.

"There's a door in the back that's busted. We can get in there," I said.

"Pull around back and park close to it Sean," Schofield told his driver.

I preferred to call him Big Ugly, or jackass. Either one worked for me. He did as he was told and drove around back and parked. When the car stopped, Schofield nudged me in the ribs with the gun. I didn't want to get out into the storm, but I sure as heck didn't want to spend any more time sitting in this car with these maniacs either. I knew just as soon as he got his grubby paws on that ledger, he'd kill me just as sure as the day is long. My mind whirled, trying to figure out my next play and just hoping things worked out in my favor.

"Let's go Valentine, and you better not try anything stupid," he said.

I opened the door and stepped out into the pouring rain just as he instructed. Big Ugly parked close to the building, but there were too many old bricks and busted boards lying around to get close to the door. I heard Schofield tell him to wait in the car when he climbed out behind me.

"I've no desire to let you two out of my sight," Michelle said.

She climbed out and unfolded an umbrella which was quickly snatched out of her hands by the wind. I heard her shriek as the wind carried it away, but I didn't have time to give a hoot. I was getting drenched, and it wasn't like a hot shower, this rain was cold and miserable.

Schofield shrugged and shouted over the cacophony of the storm. "Whatever. Let's go, kid,"

I have to say, at this point, I was glad to be outside even though the storm was practically drowning me. If I was miserable, I knew these two ass clowns were just as miserable if not more so.

I took off jogging toward the door, and Schofield stayed right with me, but Richards seemed to struggle to keep up with those high heels she wore. When I ducked into the building, I immediately smelled smoke. Apparently, my two chaperones did as well.

"What's that smell?" Michelle asked.

"Smoke. It's coming from over there in the corner; just a couple of homeless bums," Schofield replied.

I saw it too. Smoke and glowing red embers rose in the soft, orange glow of the fire from behind a makeshift pony wall that acted as a wind block. A couple of scruffy looking bums wearing stocking caps were huddled under blankets next to it. They weren't here earlier when I stashed the ledger, but I can't say that I blame 'em, I wouldn't want to be out there in this blasted storm either. I'd be hunkered down somewhere too if I weren't caught up in this mess.

"Go on Valentine, lead the way," Schofield prodded.

I turned and headed toward the old staircase at the end of the building. I could see my way well enough because of the lightning outside. It was almost like a disco strobe. Schofield had his cell phone out with his flashlight on too. When I reached the bottom of the stairs, I turned and glanced behind me.

"Keep moving," Schofield growled.

"Please do, I'd rather be somewhere warm and dry," Richards said.

I looked over at her when she spoke, which was a mistake on my part as I nearly pissed myself. The rain had made her makeup run, and she looked like a circus clown with a bad paint job, and her hair was dripping wet like a long-haired poodle. She no longer looked like the strong, defiant woman in charge. She more resembled a drowning rat. She held her gun out in front of her though she trembled from the cold rain. She reminded me of the worst looking Joker in the Batman movies.

I turned back to the stairs and slowly made my way up. It only took a few minutes, and we were standing on the third floor of the old warehouse. There were several offices along the front overlooking the huge bay below. When the lightning lit the place up, I could see everything in the warehouse as we walked by the windows including the small fire in the trash can near the corner. The bums were gone. They must have seen us come in and bounced quickly when they saw the guns.

"As I understand it, once I give you the ledger, you're going to let me leave, just walk right out and not bother me anymore, right?" I asked.

"Sure kid, no reason to complicate things any more than I have to," he sneered. "I just want the ledger."

Yeah, I believed him too, about as much as I believed in the tooth fairy! I could feel my knees trembling, but I knew it wasn't from being cold and wet. I've been in plenty of tight situations before, but this was completely different than anything else. I mean, I knew neither of these two idiots had a care for me, I was just a clog in their sink. Once I was gone, they wouldn't give me another thought. I'm sure they've done worse than offing some nobody, short-order cook.

The office I led them to was big and had lots of old junk lying around. I had stashed the ledger in a busted up wooden crate and buried it under a bunch of old wooden chairs in the corner.

"Well, where is it?" Schofield asked.

"Don't take all night, it's cold, and I'm soaking wet. I don't wish to be out here any longer than necessary," Michelle said.

"It's under all this junk in an old crate," I said. "I gotta move all this stuff off."

I began shifting the broken chairs and old pallets off the pile. My heart raced a hundred miles an hour, and I thought I would pass out any second. My legs shook so badly I could hardly stand on my own. I kept thinking my plan had already backfired on me and no help would be coming. I was in this thing alone now. Lexi must not have been able to convince the detectives to come after all.

The attorney reached down and grabbed an old chair and threw it off the pile with his empty hand. He still held the gun in the other, but at least it wasn't aimed directly at me. The Richards lady waited in silence as we worked to get to the bottom. When we finally got the last broken pieces off the crate with the ledger, I stood up and looked at the attorney.

"It's in there, can I go now?" I asked.

"Just as soon as I know for sure. Open it up." He glared at me and kept his gun aimed at me.

My legs felt like jelly, and my hands were trembling like a wino with the shakes. I bent down to pick it up, and to my surprise, I could lift the small wooden crate and stand back up to face him without collapsing. I carefully watched his face and slowly opened the lid of the box to reveal the ledger he so desperately sought.

***

The storm raged on. Thunder boomed and crackled rattling the windows as veins of pure white energy splintered down lighting up the warehouse into brilliant and blinding incandescence. I glanced out at the exact moment, which was a mistake on my part because the bright flash all but blinded me. When I turned back and allowed my eyes to readjust to the luminescent building, I saw the attorney leering at me.

"You mentioned copies going out on the internet. You must've taken photos. Where are they?"

"They're on the cell phone in the box."

He glanced inside the box and saw the cell phone. He seemed satisfied. "Nice. Stupid of you, but convenient for me."

"Wait a minute, just tell me something first? I know you stole the ledger from your boss and trashed his office to make it look like a break in. You must be planning on using it as leverage to get out the jam you're in for your part in killing the commissioner. It also seems rather obvious just as to *why* you plan on throwing your boss under the bus, but what I'd like to know is, how do you think you're going to get away with it and how the lady here fits into it? You can't afford any loose ends. Even with the ledger, I just don't believe that you'll be able to skate free."

Another voice drifted in from the darkness. "That is a good question, Mathew! Just how do you see my lovely sister fitting into all of this?" Lucas Camden asked as he walked in out of the darkness.

***

Camden stood smiling, jamming a gun in the back of the attorney he had known for many years.

"Lucas, it's not what you think," the attorney stuttered as he held his hands up.

"I'll take that," Camden snarled while retrieving the gun out of his lawyer's hand.

"Hello, Lucas. I suppose it's safe to assume you also received a mysterious phone call? My guess is it came from none other than our Mr. Valentine here," Michelle said with a laugh as she skewered me with a tense glare.

"Now, it's your turn sis," Camden said. "Drop it!"

"Sure, Luke, but I don't think you would shoot your own family, not your own flesh and blood," Michelle mused. She smiled at him, but it wasn't filled with fondness.

"I think you would be wrong to believe that, Michelle. Nothing would give me more pleasure, so if I were you, I'd not push the matter," Camden said.

"Lucas, wait a minute, I can explain this. It was the kid that broke into your office and stole the ledger. I suspected it was him all along and I've been working on getting it back," Schofield pleaded.

"Sure you were. I knew it was you all along. Besides, you're the only one with access," Camden said. He edged over to me and reached into the crate and removed the ledger.

"It's this little book right here that's going to see me safely in the clear, unfortunately for you and my dear sister." He laughed. "Now, both of you face down on the ground."

"You won't get away with it, Lucas. If I go down, I'm taking you with me!" Schofield threatened.

"That's where you're wrong, Mathew. You're never going to get the chance to tell your side of any story. You're going to kill your girlfriend and then yourself. Murder-suicide with well-placed incriminating documents in your jacket will give the cops everything they need to close this case. I'll skate free, and no one will give it a second thought as I play the part of a grieving brother."

Michelle Richards and Mathew Schofield lay face down on the floor of the old warehouse. I took a chance to open my trap.

"I did as you asked, Mr. Camden. Are we good?"

"Sure kid, beat it."

Just as I turned away, we heard shouting from the doorway and what sounded like a herd of mastodons racing up the stairs. Bright lights pierced the darkness of all the crooks and crannies of the warehouse office where we stood.

The police SWAT team that accompanied the detectives stormed into the room with Detective O'Conner in the lead. Their weapons were trained on Camden, and as they advanced, they shouted for everyone to get down on the floor with hands out. Lucas Camden saw what he was up against, dropped his gun, threw his hands up and carefully knelt down on the floor.

"Interlace your fingers behind your head," Frank shouted. "You're under arrest."

"For what? I didn't do anything," Camden demanded.

"Kidnapping for one thing," O'Conner stated. "Take him downtown for booking fellas, and get these two on their feet to keep him company."

I breathed a huge sigh of relief when I heard the detective's voice. Honestly, I was a little amazed that through all of this, I hadn't pissed myself.

"You okay, kid?" Frank asked. "You look like hell."

"Yeah, I'm all right, looks worse than it is. Never thought I'd be happy to see you again," I answered.

"Not sure how to take that," the detective replied.

"Sorry, didn't mean it like that."

His partner and several uniformed cops shuffled off downstairs with Schofield and the dark-haired femme fatale.

"It's okay. I know what you meant, but you do have a lot of explaining to do. Interfering with a police investigation and all. You're just lucky that we got here when we did. It's a good thing your girlfriend was able to reach out to us tonight, or you may have ended up in the river."

"My girlfriend – you mean Lexi. She's not my girlfriend. We're just friends. Where is she? Is she okay?" Suddenly I heard heels on the steps and turned to see Lexi hurrying toward us.

"Leo! Thank goodness you're alive," she shouted, throwing her arms around my neck. "Don't ever do anything that stupid again. You could've been killed."

"Tell me about it," I replied. "I didn't think I would be making it out of this thing alive."

I hugged her back, tightly. Maybe I was just glad to be alive, but I didn't want to let go. Being there at that moment in time, holding on to her felt good, it felt like…

"Hate to break up such an endearing moment as this is, but I need to get you two down to the station. This isn't over. We're going to have reporters all over the place in minutes. You and I need to talk. There are still a lot of questions to be answered, and I have a feeling that this ledger is going to open up a huge can of worms," Detective O'Conner said.

There went my one moment of elation. Can't a guy catch a break in this town? I was reluctant to let go of Lexi, but just as I did, there was a split-second of eye contact. I wasn't exactly sure of what it meant, but it was still nice.

"About that ledger," I began,

"Hey, what gives? It's blank?" Frank exclaimed.

"I can't give what I don't have," I muttered.

"What happened to it?" the detective demanded.

I shrugged, "No idea. When I went back to my apartment to get it, it was missing. All I could do is get a new one from the store. I had to take the chance that you would be here in time before they knew it was a fake. Someone must've followed me and snatched it from where I had it hidden."

Several officers were milling about waiting on orders from the detective. It made me more than a bit queasy knowing just how close I had come to catching a ride on the last train out of here, a fishing trip to the bottom of the river where I was to be the bait.

Lexi and I walked down the stairs with the detective which was harder than I imagined. My legs were still wobbly from being wet and cold, but the adrenaline was still pumping through my veins and would be the case for quite some time. The storm outside was now a steady rainfall as the thunder and lightning had moved out of the area. The detective didn't say much on the way down. Not until we got in the car anyway.

"Tell me something, kid," the detective began as he put the car in drive and pulled away from the curb. "We have enough charges on these three to put them away for a long time, but we're still no closer to finding the killer. Are you sure you don't know what happened to the ledger?"

"Not a clue, but I think I can help you out anyway, Detective. It was Camden and Schofield – well, not exactly. They *ordered* the hit anyway," I explained. "I don't think we will ever know who the real trigger-man was, but I'm one-hundred percent certain that it was both Camden and Schofield that was behind it."

"How so?" the detective asked.

I hit the playback icon on a hidden cell phone I had taped to my chest. I had counted on Schofield to find the first one. When the detective heard the confessions of all three of the suspects he smiled. "Good job kid! You may live through this thing yet!"

42

Twenty minutes later the detective separated Lexi and me. He ushered her off to another room. After several long minutes of Q and A, I was given a pencil and left alone in an interrogation room. The detective tried to tell me it was an empty office, I'm sure to make me feel more comfortable, but I knew better. They don't make offices with large windows that you can't see out of in the middle of the building. I'm not complaining, mind you because at least the door wasn't locked and it was quiet. He left me alone with clear instructions - write down everything I knew about the case including the part where Schofield kidnapped me. Two hours later he came to check on me.

"How's it going, Valentine? Sorry, I wasn't back earlier, I was giving the captain a quick briefing."

"Finishing up now, just going back over it to make sure I have everything. I mean, I can remember everything perfectly clear from all the way back to when this whole thing started, but my hand kinda cramps up on me, ya know?"

"Are you sure you don't know where the ledger is?"

"Sorry, no idea,"

He gave me a quizzical look but didn't push me further.

"Let me see here," he said as he picked up the pad to read over my statement. After a few minutes of reading and a few, Hmmm's and Oh's littered in between his reading, he tossed the pad back onto the table and smiled at me. "You have quite a remarkable memory, this will do fine."

"Yes sir, I guess I've always been that way. I can remember things fairly easy."

"Funny what greed can do to a man, not funny haha, just – funny," he stated rather whimsically. "Go figure, two men that worked together for years, they had everything, money, cars, houses, a jet..." he trailed off.

"Yeah, makes you wonder about people," I mumbled. "I guess it's true what they say?"

"Yeah? What's that," he asked.

"A house divided against itself cannot stand."

The silence lingered a moment.

"I've got a few more papers for you to sign and then I can cut you loose. I'll be back in a few. Sit tight," he said before hurrying out the door.

No sooner had the detective walked out of the room when the door pushed open again. I nearly fainted when I saw who it was.

"Hello, Leonard. I'm so glad you're okay," my new visitor said as she stepped into the room and closed the door behind her.

"Briana?" I said surprised. "How'd you..." She stopped me with a finger over her lips.

"I wanted to stop by and check on you," she purred, "and to make sure you remember our deal?"

"Of course, I remember. Not a word about you, you can count on me," I replied.

"Good boy. Now listen to me. What you did was brave, but stupid. Just because those two idiots have been caught, doesn't mean that this is over. This is just beginning. You need to be cautious and always keep an eye out, got it?"

I trusted she knew a lot more than I did about this and I knew I had better listen to her advice.

"Yes ma'am, I have no intention of…"

"I've got to go now, but remember, not a word of this to anyone, ever."

"But what about if I have to testify in court?" I asked.

"That's not going to happen, trust me."

For a woman that routinely says to trust no one, she sure throws that out a lot.

Briana stood and exited the room without as much as a glance back in my direction.

Ten minutes later, the detective walked in with papers in hand. I signed my best John Hancock, but I doubt anyone could read it as shaky as my hands were. "Can I go now?"

"Sure thing, I'll have one of the uni's give you and your girlfriend a ride home. Sit tight, and I'll round someone up," the detective said.

"She's not my…" I started to correct him, about her not being my girlfriend and all, but decided better of it and let it drop; it doesn't matter at this point. "She's still here?" I asked. I guess I was a little surprised she waited on me this whole time. When the detective split us up to get statements, I figured they let her go long ago.

"She's been waiting for you the whole time. I'll send her in."

When Lexi walked into the room I expected her to be tired and ready to collapse from the long night, but she was surprisingly energetic, though not in a good way.

"I can't believe you waited this whole time, I thought for sure you would be home in bed asleep by now," I said.

"No chance! We're in this together, right?" she asked as she gave me a quick hug and looked me up and down.

"Of course, but you didn't need to…"

"Just stop arguing and let me look at you. It looks like everything is superficial, but we should take you to a doctor to be checked out anyway."

"I'm fine. Just going to be sore for a few days, but I'll survive," I said with a quirky smile. She gave me a look that I took as unsatisfactory, but she wasn't going to argue. "You don't look happy. What gives?" I asked.

"I just got off the phone with my editor. I wrote the piece on the murder of Commissioner Wood, sent it in, and she refuses to allow me to write it. She said for me to provide the information to a senior staffer. All of my work on this case and now I won't even get the credit for the story!" she exclaimed.

"I'm sorry, that sucks."

Detective O'Conner, accompanied by a uniformed patrol officer, came walking down the hallway. "This is Officer Gates. He will drive you home. Try to get some rest, and if you need me, you have my number. I'll be in touch."

When we walked out of the police station, the wind was blowing at a good clip, but at least it wasn't raining any longer. I noticed a long black limousine on the opposite side of the street pull away from the curb. Even though I couldn't see inside, I knew it was Briana Fitzgerald. I'd never been more curious about the woman than at that moment, and I was confident that wasn't the last I'd see of her. I knew better than to drop her name, and I certainly didn't put it in the statement. Honestly, I didn't see a reason to.

43

"Leonard, where's my order?" Greely growled.

"Coming up now boss."

It felt good to be back in my kitchen and on a regular schedule again. It's been a few weeks since that stormy night when I was almost, certainly killed. Camden clammed up tighter than a drum and admitted to nothing, but, unfortunately for him, I had the recording of that entire night. He's going away for a very long time.

And Schofield, well let's just say that once his boss tried to set him up to take the fall for the murder of Wood and then kill him and Michelle in the warehouse in some murder/suicide thing, the cops couldn't keep up with everything he started squawking about. He turned out to be their best freaking witness. Even though they had him dead to rights guilty of kidnapping, assault and battery, and attempted murder among a slew of other charges, he'll probably skate light. I don't think that he will walk though, at least not very far. I'm sure that some of those people whose names were in the ledger will have something to say about that. I would not want to be in his shoes!

Apparently, it was Camden that initially made a deal with Wood for him to sign off on the sale of the land to CGI. When the commissioner found out that CGI had financial concerns, he backed out of the arrangement, but before he officially rescinded it, Camden put out a hit on him.

Michelle Richards was just a disgruntled family member that managed to trip the others up. She admitted to conspiracy charges among a few other minor things. I doubt that she will serve much if any time in jail, but I was never worried about her, just the two ass-clowns from CGI. Once she found out that CGI was overleveraged and drowning in debt that they had no possible way to recover, I don't think her plot to take over the family business tasted as sweet as it once did.

Lexi was mostly right about what happened, but she never got her ghost assassin, and probably never will. I suppose it doesn't matter as long as the cops have someone to pin the murder on, but I still felt bad for her. She got robbed on the story and couldn't get the credit for it, mainly because her editor said something along the lines of it belonging to a senior reporter. At least she was given credit for helping to break the case. Detective O'Conner had seen to that with a meeting with Lexi's boss to thank her for her assistance. Unofficially, of course.

As for me, I've healed up nicely with no scarring on my gorgeous mug. My modeling career is still intact. Greely didn't say much for me missing work as he knew the circumstances. He harrumphed a bit, but that's all I heard about it. The others still made comments now and then, but they knew I didn't want to talk about it, so they mostly let it drop.

The biggest mystery to me is Briana Fitzgerald. Why would she take an interest in me? Who am I to her other than some kid that happened to see her at the wrong place and the wrong time? Her comments about knowing who my parents were - correction, who my father is - is somewhat disturbing. Is she saying that he's still alive? If so, boy, do I have a lot of unanswered questions! I have plenty of time. I may only be a short-order cook around here, but I'm also the chief bottle washer, and I'll figure it out.

Leonard P Valentine

The End

A note from the author

More and more authors are self-publishing every day. With over 4 million titles on popular eBook sites, gaining a presence in the world of readers can be a daunting task for new authors. Thus, reviews generated by readers become an important factor. The thoughtful feedback provided helps to create exposure for authors in such a robust market, and it also helps the author hone their craft.

It is my hope that my stories will instill a sense of wonder, excitement, and eagerness for more when finishing one of my novels. If you enjoyed this book, please consider posting a review. It only takes a moment and is very much appreciated. You have my thanks and gratitude.

Paul G Buckner

About the Author

Paul G Buckner is a Cherokee Nation citizen, musician, an amateur photographer, and an avid outdoorsman.

He attended Northeastern State University where he graduated with a bachelor's degree in Business Management and a Masters of Business Administration. He spent several years developing curriculum and teaching business management principles to Native American nonprofit groups and enjoys volunteering with local community organizations.

Please be sure to follow Paul on his website
www.pgbuckner.com

Other Titles Available by Paul G Buckner

Siege at Hawthorn Lake – Murder on the Mountain

Available at your preferred online retailer

Made in the USA
Columbia, SC
08 September 2018